THE
PRESCOTTS

Stupid
LOVE

TARA WYATT

FREE DOWNLOAD

Download Tara's story Reload for free!

Get started here: https://www.tara-wyatt.com/newsletter

*T*heo Prescott dropped down into one of the leather dining chairs surrounding a large, round table, flashing an apologetic grin at his brothers. Their table sat alone in the empty nightclub owned by his brother Lucian, the stark white tablecloth a sharp contrast to the club's elegantly dark interior. As usual, they were set up in their regular location on the upper level overlooking what would become the dance floor in about three hours.

He slipped his messenger bag off over his head, setting it on the floor at his feet. Shit, even Max was already here, and he was always late for their usual Friday dinner at Lucian's. And that was when he could tear himself away from work long enough to even make it to their weekly tradition of steaks, whiskey, and shooting the shit.

"Sorry. Sorry," said Theo, pulling his chair in. "Client got served at like 4:58."

"Only the worst kind of human would do that on a Friday," said Lucian casually, sliding a tumbler of whiskey towards Theo, who accepted it gratefully.

"No kidding. Her ex seems like a real piece of work, and I know his lawyer. Lies in court, drags things out as long as possible, hides information, advertises himself as a pitbull. He's a total scumbag who lives to make people miserable."

"As opposed to the loving, kind, altruistic divorce lawyer that you are," said Sebastian, batting his eyelashes at him and laughing at his own joke.

Theo took a sip of his drink and raised his hands in defense. "Hey, I try to treat people fairly, okay? I'm not out to ruin anyone's weekend by serving papers at the last minute on a Friday. That's a dick move."

A waitress who worked for the club approached and set down a large basket of warm, fresh bread along with a plate of artisanal olive oil in the center of the table.

"Thank you, love," said Lucian with a charming smile. She smiled back, running her fingers up Lucian's arm before sauntering away, her tight black outfit leaving nothing to the imagination.

"So, Bastian, how's the merger going?" asked Max, who lived to talk about business and almost nothing but. He'd founded his own tech company at twenty-five and happily worked eighty-hour weeks. If you could describe anything Max did as happy, anyway.

Sebastian leaned back in his chair, his fingers curled around his glass. He was the VP of marketing and project management for a large real estate development firm, although you wouldn't know it from his behavior. "It's not. The lawyers—" At this, he shot Theo a derisive look, "—are still arguing over contract terms. We're completely stalled."

"Hey, don't shoot dirty looks at me," said Theo, reaching for a piece of bread and dragging it through the olive oil. "I have nothing to do with corporate law. I took the high road and instead try to prevent millionaires from killing each other and using their children as pawns when they discover that happily ever after isn't actually a real thing."

"A-fucking-men to that," said Sebastian, clinking his glass against Theo's. Theo chuckled, glancing around the table at his brothers. They were only missing one other sibling, their sister Aerin who'd left Manhattan for a fresh start in Dallas after her messy divorce a few years ago. She and Theo were the lawyers in the family, although she'd parlayed her law career into one as a very successful sports agent. She was also the only one currently in any kind of romantic relationship. She'd gotten engaged to her boyfriend, MLB manager Javier Flores, last year, and their wedding was quickly approaching. She was the only one of the Prescott five to have ever gotten married—probably because she was insane—and now she was doing it *again*. Yes, when Aerin and Javi had hit a rough patch, he'd encouraged her to find a way to work through it, but he hadn't been suggesting she hop on the matrimony wagon again. Not by a long shot.

There was a small commotion by the front door, and Lucian turned, glancing over his shoulder. His eyebrows slashed downward and his eyes narrowed. "Excuse me. Just a little business with our friendly neighborhood drug dealers." He pushed up from his chair and, with a quick tug on his suit jacket, hurried down the curving staircase that led to the main level of the club.

"You know, sometimes I think we should probably be scared of him," said Max almost idly, ripping a piece of bread to shreds without actually eating it. Theo was pretty sure Max never actually ate carbs. He was far too rigid and disciplined to indulge in something like bread. The fact that he'd been a chubby kid and had been teased mercilessly for it was probably a contributing factor too. But long gone were the days of Pudgy Prescott. As an adult, he ate healthy, lifted weights almost daily and went for weekend runs through Central Park.

Sebastian shook his head. "Nah. He's one of us. Other people should be scared of him, sure. I mean, if I heard that Lucian Prescott was coming for me, I'd probably shit my pants. But..." He looked around the club and shrugged. "He's had my back more times than I can count."

Theo nodded, but he wasn't as sure as Sebastian. Granted, he was the well-behaved one in the family. He didn't get himself into trouble with loan sharks or the mafia or whatever the hell else Sebastian managed to tangle himself up in.

But they all had their demons. They all had their scars. How could they not, after the way they'd grown up? Sure, they'd had money. But money couldn't replace stability and affection. Money couldn't make up for the way their father had never believed Lucian to be his son, and had treated him like absolute dirt because of it. Money couldn't make up for the way their mother had drank and popped pills and neglected them, if not financially, then emotionally. Money couldn't make up for the way their father had cheated, over and over again, driving their mother insane. Money couldn't make up for the way they'd used the five kids as pawns in their inevitable divorce.

Theo turned, craning his neck to see what was happening downstairs. It had gotten very, very quiet. He couldn't hear what was being said, could only see Lucian talking very intently to a group of young Asian men. He pointed to the door and they all turned and left as quickly as possible, proverbial tails tucked between their legs. Lucian turned, once again adjusting his suit jacket, and came back up the stairs.

"Well. Where were we?" he asked, sitting down and tossing back the rest of his whiskey.

Sebastian grinned. "Theo was late because his client's ex is a dick, the merger is on hold because lawyers are dicks, Max only wants to talk about work because he's a dick, and you...what just happened there?" Lucian raised an eyebrow, but before he could say anything, Sebastian shook his head. "You know what? I don't think I want to know."

Lucian waved it away. "It's nothing. Just some stupid kids who keep trying to sell drugs in my club. It's been dealt with."

Lucian, at forty-three, was the oldest Prescott sibling, followed by their sister, Aerin. For a while, they'd been the only two Prescott children, but then Max, Sebastian and Theo had come along one after the other as their mother had tried in vain to make their father stop cheating by getting pregnant over and over again. Now, Max was thirty-five, Sebastian was thirty-four, and Theo, the baby, was thirty-two. And they were all single—purposely, deliberately single— except for Aerin. Who Theo adored, but still thought was batshit for wanting to get married again.

"I offered to do a prenup for Aerin and Javier," he said suddenly, tapping his fingers restlessly on the table. "She turned me down."

Three sets of eyes landed on him, all of them as disbelieving and incredulous as he felt.

"She what?" asked Max, frowning. "Who the hell would get married without a prenup?"

Theo sighed. "Someone who thinks they're actually in love." At that, they all shook their heads. Poor Aerin. She was the only Prescott who hadn't learned, apparently.

Lucian tilted his head. "Can you make one for her without her knowing?"

Theo laughed. "Uh, no. That's not how contracts work." Lucian opened his mouth to argue, but Theo cut him off. "I'm talking about *legal* contracts."

"Ah. Well, then. That would be your area of expertise, not mine."

Theo shot him a look. "I don't know whether to laugh or have you investigated."

Lucian smiled. "Surprise me."

Max and Sebastian chuckled. Studying his eldest brother, Theo wondered if Lucian was at all curious about his paternity. Theo and his sister Aerin both had dark blond hair and blue eyes, just like their mother, although Aerin's eyes were a darker, almost grayish blue where Theo's were lighter. Max and Bastian looked the most alike, both having their father's dark brown curls and their mother's blue eyes. But then Lucian...his hair was almost black, and his eyes were a deep brown. He had the kind of eyelashes that made it look like he was wearing eyeliner or mascara or whatever. And his facial structure...it was just different. Theo, Bastian, Aerin, and Max all looked like siblings. But Lucian...it was hard to say.

"Aerin's a lawyer. I'm sure she knows how to protect herself," said Max. Just then, the waitress returned with a large, round tray laden with plates. The scent of seared meat filled the air, making Theo's mouth water and his stomach grumble. It had been a busy day, and he hadn't had anything to eat since the protein bar he'd scarfed down around 11:30. He'd had court that morning, followed by a mediation hearing, then a few hours trying to dig out of his inbox, a phone call with a potential client, and then that damn filing that had come in at the end of the day.

Theo nodded. "Yeah, I'm sure it's fine." It didn't feel fine. He worried that his sister—the one who'd loved him and protected him and nurtured him as best she could while they were growing up—was making a huge mistake and would end up shattered again, just like after her first marriage had ended. The one time he'd tried to talk to her about it, she'd just smiled coyly at him, as though she were privy to some universal piece of knowledge he was lacking.

The conversation moved back to business, which was only natural, given that Lucian was an entrepreneur, Max was leading his own tech company, and Sebastian was always happy to shoot the shit about corporate stuff. As they talked, Theo enjoyed his steak, sighing and putting his fork down when he heard his phone buzzing from inside the pocket of his messenger bag.

"Theo Prescott," he answered, picking up his whiskey and wandering away from the noisy conversation at the table.

"Hey, Theo, it's Bradford. Sorry to call you on a Friday night." Bradford Kingston was a family law attorney at a rival firm, and even though he and Theo often found themselves in the role of opposing counsel, they had an easy, collegial relationship.

"No problem. What's up?"

"It's about the Harris-Dearborne prenup. There's no way she's going to sign this thing. I can't in good conscience advise my client to agree to waiving alimony."

And Greg Dearborne, Theo's client, was hell-bent on not paying Alison Harris a cent if they split up. He rubbed a hand over his mouth. "Remind me again what Ms. Harris does for a living?" He knew, but he was taking Bradford somewhere and wanted him along for every step of the argument.

"She's an anesthesiologist."

"Right. Impressive. That's a pretty lucrative field, no?"

"Just tell me what you're thinking, Prescott."

"Listen, Greg's loaded right now. He's got the chain of stores, the software company, tons of investments. But your client's career and earnings potential are a lot more stable than his. The stores could go under. The software company could bust. The investments could tank. He could wake up in six months and have nothing. It's not outside the realm of possibility that she could wind up making more money than him in the future. If she waives alimony, so does he. It protects her, too."

"Hmm."

He smiled. "Talk it over with your client and let me know."

"Will do."

He sat down and dug back into his steak. Five minutes later when his phone chimed, it was a text from Bradford, a single thumbs up emoji. He grinned and finished his whiskey. It was in moments like this that he really loved his job. He'd gone into family law because he'd wanted to protect the children of divorce from going through the same thing he'd had to endure, and he did that on an almost daily basis. But more than that, the high of successfully arguing a case was addictive and one he'd never get tired of. He'd developed a reputation of being able to get his clients whatever it was they wanted, not because he was some kind of ruthless shark—he most definitely wasn't—but because he was very, very good at convincing his clients that they wanted what he'd be able to get them. It didn't hurt that his career also afforded him a very comfortable lifestyle. Recently, there'd been rumors that he was being considered for a junior partnership given how much money he brought in to the firm, but he'd yet to hear anything concrete about it. Still, just the idea filled him with excitement. A junior partnership would mean bigger cases with more high-profile clients and the chance to really make his mark on the firm.

"Anyone staying tonight?" asked Lucian. "I have a VIP booth no one's booked yet that you're welcome to."

Theo shook his head. "Can't. It's Lauren's birthday. I'm meeting up with her and some friends at a karaoke bar later."

"Ah, Lauren," all three of Theo's brothers said in unison, feigned sappy grins on their faces.

"Lovely Lauren," said Lucian.

Max smirked. "Luscious Lauren."

"I can't think of something that starts with L, but she's fucking hot." Sebastian shrugged.

Theo set down his steak knife, a surge of protectiveness charging through him. "If any of you ever," he swiveled his gaze from one brother to the next, "ever, *ever* make a move on Lauren, you're dead meat."

Max chuckled. "That a threat, counselor?"

Theo didn't laugh. "You're damn right it's a threat. Seriously. All three of you—Lauren is off limits."

Lucian held up his hands, a shit-eating grin on his face. "I would never make a move on your woman."

"She's not my woman." And it was true. She wasn't. And she never would be, even if he did want her in every imaginable way. "But she is my closest friend."

Max and Sebastian exchanged a look. "Uh huh. Yep. Just your friend," said Sebastian, popping a bite of asparagus into his mouth. Even though his tone was teasing, the words had a bite to them. Yeah, he and Lauren were friends and had been for a long time now. Yeah, he had feelings for her of the completely non-platonic variety. But he'd ever act on them, because she deserved so much better than anything he could ever give her. She meant so much to him, and he didn't want to risk ruining their friendship.

Besides, it wasn't like she felt anything beyond the platonic for him. So, end of story.

"And how old is Lauren?" asked Lucian.

"Twenty-nine."

"Actually twenty-nine, or really thirty something but in denial twenty-nine?" asked Sebastian.

"Actually twenty-nine."

"Well, do tell her we all wish her the happiest of birthdays," said Lucian dryly. "O fierce protector of Lauren and her virtue."

Theo rolled his eyes. "I don't care if she dates anyone else." Which was a big fat lie. The last time she'd had a semi-serious boyfriend, he'd been jealous as hell.

Lucian stared at him in a way that had Theo wondering if he was about to call him out, but then he shrugged. "Anyone want another whiskey?"

2

*L*auren MacKinnon looked up from her computer at the man standing before her. He had a glint in his eye she both recognized and dreaded, but she forced herself to plaster on a professional smile. "Hi there. Can I help you?"

The man's eyes traveled up and down her body, starting with her hair and ending where her body disappeared behind the hulking reference desk. "Yeah, I've got a question for you." She braced herself, but relaxed a little when the man continued speaking. "I'm looking for this book I checked out a few years ago. Maybe it was longer ago than that, I'm not sure. Anyway, I don't remember the author or the title, but I recall that the cover was red."

"Mmmhmm," she said flatly. Working at the reference desk at the 53rd Street branch of the New York Public Library, she got this kind of question on a regular basis. Sometimes, she hoped that she didn't know the answer just so patrons would learn to manage their expectations a little better. How the hell was she supposed to know what red-covered book this dude read years ago? "Do you remember anything else about it? More detail about the cover, the genre, anything?"

"It was definitely fiction. And it had big, yellow lettering on the front. Hmm, I wonder if it was more of an orange than a red, now that I think about it."

Lauren tucked a strand of hair that had come loose from her bun behind her ear. "Do you remember what genre it was?"

"I think sci-fi," he said, scratching his chin.

Well, crap. She was pretty sure she did know the book he was talking about. "Is it *Ready Player One* by Ernest Cline?"

He snapped his fingers and pointed at her. "Yes! That's the one! Do you have it?"

She did a quick search on the computer. "It's not on the shelves here, but we do have other copies in the system. Can I put it on hold for you?"

"Sure." He fished out his library card, attempting to flirt with her while she scanned his barcode and placed the hold. When she was finished, she handed his card back to him, not responding to any of his overtures.

"You'll get an email when it's in."

He made a big show of checking out her name tag, just above her left breast. "Thank you so much, *Lauren*." He walked away, glancing once over his shoulder at her. She fought the urge to make a face.

"Ugh, what a creep." Lauren turned to see her friend and co-worker Dorinda—Dori for short—standing there, holding an armful of binders. Her black hair was piled high on top of her head, her enormous glasses sliding down her nose. She set them down in a messy heap on the other end of the reference desk and leaned forward, peering at Lauren's name tag from just a few inches away. "Lau-ren. Hmm. What an interesting name. Why don't I buy you a coffee and you can tell me how your parents came up with something so unique?" Dori, a librarian-slash-stand-up-comic and *Saturday Night Live* hopeful—she'd already auditioned twice in the past three years—had a knack for knowing exactly how to make her laugh.

Lauren giggled, the tension from the previous interaction dissipating. "Yes, Lauren is *such* a unique name, so rare in its stunning beauty."

Dori made a face at her. "Hey, at least your name isn't Dorinda Dong, okay? I'd take boring any day. I am literally a fish and a dick."

Lauren smiled at her. "But you're my favorite fish and dick. That counts for something, right?"

"Sure does, my friend," said Dori, squooshing Lauren's cheeks between her palms. "Let me go put away these training binders and then we can get out of here. I'm so glad it's your birthday because I've been wanting to go out for sushi and karaoke for a while. So thanks for designing your birthday celebrations around my cravings. You're a true friend."

Lauren laughed and started logging out of her computer. "I live to please." She was joking, but also not really joking. She *did* live to please. Keeping others happy made her happy. Plus she hated conflict. Just the thought of the word was enough to make her break out into hives. She gathered up her notebook and lanyard and rose from her swivel chair.

"So," said Dori, falling into step beside her as they walked toward the staff workroom. "Will Theo be joining us tonight?" She stretched out the two syllables of Theo's name —*Theeeeeeeeeeoooooooooooohhhhhh*—in a teasing singsong.

"Yep. He's having dinner with his brothers first, but he's meeting us at karaoke later."

Dori froze, mid-step. "Wait. He has *brothers*? You mean to tell me that there is more than one guy with those Prescott genes walking around?"

"He's got three, actually. And they're all kind of a mess, so you'd probably do best to stay clear."

"But Theo's not a mess."

"Mmmm," she said, making an *I'm not so sure about that* sound. "I mean, he's definitely less of a mess than, say, Sebastian, or Lucian." She shrugged. "But he's still kind of a mess."

Dori's eyebrows rose above her glasses. "Really? In what way?"

"Oh, you know," said Lauren, setting her notebook down on her half of the L-shaped desk that she shared with another technical assistant. Several empty Starbucks cups sat in the corner, her little collection of chai lattes delivered by Theo over the past couple of weeks. She hung onto them for far too long because he had a habit of leaving her little doodles on them. Her current fave was a cartoony mosquito with the caption *I Suck*. "Just the crappy childhood creating a dysfunctional view of the adult world kind of way."

"Oh. Yeah, that'll do it."

"Yeah. His parents put him and his brothers through the wringer when they were younger, and now he's super jaded about dating and relationships and all that jazz."

Dori made a sad sound. "Too bad. Dude is fine as hell."

Lauren chuckled, not saying anything, mostly because she couldn't disagree with Dori's assessment of her best friend. Fine as hell pretty much summed it up when it came to Theo. Her stomach did that stupid little flippy thing it had a habit of doing when she thought about him. Not that she had any hopes of anything romantic ever happening between them—she knew that relationships and love were a no-go territory for Theo, and honestly, it was probably for the best that things between them stayed firmly in the "just friends" category. She didn't want to risk her closest friendship for a relationship that inevitably wouldn't work out because of Theo's baggage.

She'd first met him eleven years ago, when she'd been a freshman at NYU and started dating this really cute senior named Josh. Her relationship with Josh had fizzled before Christmas break, but the easy friendship she'd struck up with his roommate Theo had stuck. Despite her almost immediate crush on Theo, but she'd accepted early on that they were better off as friends given his aversion to relationships. Over the years, they'd grown closer and closer, and now, he was her best friend. Numero uno. Like a brother, really.

A brother she wanted to hump, but still. Brother-ish, if you conveniently ignored the sexual attraction.

But ignoring the sexual attraction was easier said than done. God, Theo. That soft, thick blond hair. Those blue eyes. That wide, mischievous smile with those full lips. The neatly groomed scruff that clung to his jaw. And then, there was the rest of him. The muscles. The big hands. The fact that he was six foot four of droolworthy masculine yumminess.

Fine. As. Hell.

Also strictly her friend, and totally off limits romantically. Or sexually. Or in any non-platonic way. Which was fine. Fine. *Fine fine fine.*

"You're thinking about how sexy he is right now, aren't you?" asked Dori, pulling on her denim jacket and then slinging her cross-body bag over her shoulder.

Lauren blushed a little, but shook her head, busying herself with tidying a pile of already tidy papers on her desk. "No, I'm not."

"Uh huh. You're thinking about Theo with his shirt off and in those beat up Levi's he has, just the top button undone, playing treasure trail peek-a-boo. Aren't you?"

Lauren's mouth went dry as she pictured exactly what Dori had described. Her stomach gave an answering dip and swirl at the image. "Well, now I am, thanks to you." She pulled her trench coat on and grabbed both her purse and her guitar case—she'd been busking at lunch, as usual. "Trust me, as sexy as he is, it's never going to happen for a lot of reasons. Theo doesn't date or do relationships. I would never want to risk ruining our friendship. Besides, I'm pretty sure he sees me as more like a sister than a chick he'd like to bone."

Dori shrugged. "If you say so. I'm going to walk home to change. Meet you at the restaurant, okay?"

Lauren nodded. "Yeah, sounds good. I'm going to change too, plus I want to put my guitar away."

"Is Aspen coming?" Dori asked, making a little face as she referred to Lauren's roommate.

"Maybe to karaoke, but not to sushi. She's vegan, remember?"

Dori let out a little laugh and smacked her palm against her forehead. "Right. How could I forget?"

"It'll be me, you, Willa, and Brandon for dinner, and then Theo, Kayla, Aiden, and maybe Aspen all joining us for karaoke." They fell into step as they headed out of the library and out onto West 53rd Street. The mid-September air was cool, but the sun was still warm and felt like heaven on her face. With a wave, she parted ways with Dori and started her

twenty-minute walk home to the tiny apartment on West 46th
she shared with Aspen. She could've taken the F train if she
wanted to shave a few minutes off her commute, but she
didn't mind the walk in the beautiful fall weather. Besides, it
was a pain hauling her guitar on the subway.

There was something almost magical about New York
City in the fall. The changing leaves, the city's unwavering
enthusiasm for all things Halloween, new museum
exhibitions, outdoor movies on a cool night. Even a city as
vast and cold as New York felt cozy in the fall. Having grown
up in Vermont, she sometimes longed for the quiet coziness
of home, but her life was here now. She had her job at the
library, and a solid group of friends. Plus the music scene in
Montpelier was just *slightly* lacking in comparison with New
York City.

She hummed to herself as she walked, working out a new
melody that had popped into her head that morning in the
shower. The music she wrote and performed (and poured her
heart, soul, and time into) was mostly folk-tinged pop—or
maybe it was more like pop-influenced folk—sort of like
Taylor Swift crossed with Joni Mitchell, a dash of Maren
Morris, and a hint of Regina Spektor. She'd been writing and
performing her own music for nearly fifteen years now and
had written well over a hundred songs. She'd played
thousands of gigs both as a solo artist and as part of Fiddle of
Nowhere, the folk-rock cover band she'd been part of for the
past three years.

Thousands of gigs, hundreds of original songs, two
degrees—an arts and science degree in music, followed by a
masters' degree—and exactly zero record contracts. She'd
hoped that by thirty, she'd be at least making a living from
her music. That if she found the right combination of

songwriting and performing, she could cobble something together. But here she was, newly turned twenty-nine, and still working forty-hour weeks at the library to pay the bills. It wasn't that she didn't make any money from music. She did. It just wasn't steady enough to depend on. Some months she made a few thousand dollars. Other months, it was more like a few hundred. And frankly, her landlord didn't care that she could play a flawless rendition of "Flight of the Bumblebee" on her acoustic guitar, or that she could play almost anything by ear on the piano.

She rolled her shoulders and tried to physically shake off the frustration building inside her. Today was her birthday, and she was going to have an awesome night with her friends. She didn't want to start the evening off as Debbie Downer because she officially only had a year left to meet her goal. A lot could happen in a year. A year was so much time.

Right.

She let herself into the five-story apartment building where she lived and jogged up to the second floor. Before she'd even reached her front door, the scent of incense invaded her nostrils and she grimaced slightly. She could hear sitar music and what sounded like voices coming from inside the apartment. Great. Aspen was probably having some lengthy conversation with her spirit guide or guardian angel again. Who knew that guardian angels could be so chatty? Then again, they were dead, so who did they really have to talk to?

Slipping her keys in the lock, she pushed the door open with her shoulder, her guitar case bumping against the worn frame. And right there, in the middle of their tiny living room, was Aspen, naked and covered in oil, riding a man Lauren didn't know. They moved slowly together, breathing and chanting in what sounded like Sanskrit or some other ancient language.

Normally, Lauren would've been shocked to find her roommate naked and having tantric sex with a strange man, but unfortunately, this wasn't the first time Lauren had walked in on something like this. And knowing Aspen, it probably wouldn't be the last.

"You have a bedroom!" she shouted over her shoulder as she moved past them, trying to block her view with her guitar case, holding it like a shield.

Aspen paused in her movements and said serenely, "The energy was all wrong in my bedroom and I thought you'd be mad if we used yours."

Lauren's eyes widened. "Oh. My. God." She practically sprinted to her room, slamming the door behind her. She closed her eyes, trying to push away the image of Aspen and whoever the hell was in her living room. Was there such a thing as brain bleach? Because she could use about a gallon of that right now.

She set her guitar down in the corner, propped carefully up against the exposed brick wall. Below, police sirens wailed as two cruisers fought their way through Hells Kitchen. Sinking down on her bed, she stared out the window at her view of the entrance to a parking garage across the street. Her room was small but comfortable, with enough space for a double bed, her guitar and her keyboard, a nightstand, and a small computer desk. She'd made it cozy with art on the walls, a couple of plants, warm lighting, and throw blankets and pillows. She always treated herself to fresh flowers from the bodega on the corner every Sunday, not only because having something colorful and alive brightened up the room, but also because it wasn't like she had anyone else to buy them for her. Currently, the little vase on her desk was filled with a bunch of half-wilted orange and yellow carnations. She loved peonies best, but carnations were much more budget-friendly.

From out in the living room, a series of long, loud gasping moans vibrated through the thin walls, going on and on and on for what felt like forever.

Lauren sighed. "Oh yeah, I'm definitely living the dream."

3

*T*heo stepped inside the noisy karaoke bar, scanning his gaze across the crowded space for Lauren. As usual, her red hair was the first thing he spotted. It fell just past her shoulders in shiny waves, and he watched as she tucked a strand of it behind her ear as she chatted with their mutual friend Brandon. The simple movement made his fingers tingle, itching to repeat it. So he curled his fingers into his palm, tucking them safely away.

Shimmying his way between the tables, he made his way toward them. "Hey, sorry I'm late," he said, giving Lauren a hug from behind. She jumped up out of her seat and flung her arms around him. Her warm cinnamon-vanilla scent hit him like a punch in the gut and he hugged her just a little bit tighter, taking the affection he could get. The affection he was allowed. He kissed her on the cheek and then stepped back.

God, she was so beautiful. He'd noticed it the first time he'd ever laid eyes on her, back when she'd dated his roommate Josh what felt like a lifetime ago. Everything about her was so...so delicate. The bright green eyes, the small upturned nose, the wide smile. She was tall and lithe, with long limbs and graceful hands. A constellation of freckles ran across the bridge of her nose, and not for the first time, he wondered just how many freckles she had.

His mind bounced back to the summer, when they'd rented a place in the Hamptons with some friends. Lauren had spent most of the weekend in a retro-style black one-piece and not much else. He'd been disappointed that she hadn't packed a bikini. Disappointed and maybe also a tad relieved because the last thing he'd needed was to be concealing a hard-on in his swim trunks.

"It's okay," she said, sitting back down in her chair at their large table. She kicked an empty one toward him and he sat down, shrugging out of his jacket. "We only got here like ten minutes ago anyway." She leaned forward, a conspiratorial gleam in her eye. "Wanna know a secret?"

"Always." He reached into the pocket of his jacket, pulling out her birthday gift and putting it on the table. "Do you want to open this first?"

Her eyes landed on the small box wrapped in light blue paper and she bit her lip, clearly torn. "Okay, I'll just tell you really fast. One: I ate a lot of sushi. Like, a lot. I don't want to see another piece of sashimi for a really long time. Two: I also drank a lot of sake and am a little drunk." She winked at him. "Now you're up to speed."

Around them, the karaoke bar was filling up, the noise of conversation mixing with the ear-splitting rendition of the Spice Girls' "Wannabe" two college-aged girls were screaming out. Their group was at one of the bigger tables and he waved as Aiden, Lauren's bandmate from Fiddle of Nowhere, and Willa, her closest friend from university—

besides him, anyway—came back to their table with a tray laden with drinks.

"Whoa, guys," said Lauren, holding her hands up. "That is a *lot* of booze." Then she pulled the tray toward herself. "How come you didn't get anything for yourselves?" Everyone laughed and Willa made eye contact with Theo, her eyebrow raised. He nodded once. Yeah, he'd look after Lauren tonight. Of course he would.

"Did they have any kombucha?" asked Aspen from the other end of the table.

"Uh, no. Sorry." Aiden shook his head and then looked away and rolled his eyes.

"Okay, now I want to open this," said Lauren, pulling the little box toward herself after she'd selected a glass of wine from the booze tray.

Theo smiled, sitting back in his chair. "Go ahead."

He loved giving Lauren gifts. Because he could, yeah, but also because of how she reacted to them. She was like a little kid on Christmas morning and it was the most adorable thing—

Stop. He cut himself off mid-thought.

She peeled back the wrapping paper, letting it flutter to the floor, and then opened the simple cardboard box.

"EEEEEEEE! Theo! I can't believe you remembered these!" she said, her face glowing. He grinned at her, his chest filling with a warm, gooey feeling, like his insides were melted marshmallow.

"What is it?" asked Willa, peering over.

Lauren fished the three geometrically shaped stacking rings out of the box. "I saw these in a little store like two months ago and I loved them, but I didn't get them because they were too expensive." She smacked him on the arm. "These are too expensive!" But she put them on her right index finger right away. She smiled at him, her green eyes sparkling, her cheeks flushed and he felt an answering tug in his chest. He reached for his beer, deciding the best course of action was to douse it.

Everyone else started passing their gifts to Lauren, but Theo couldn't help smiling at the way she kept looking at the rings and adjusting them on her finger. She got a candle from Aspen—designed to perfectly align her chakras, apparently —a charm bracelet from Dori, a book from Willa, some perfume from Brandon, who worked at Saks, a mug from Kayla, Willa's roommate, and guitar strings from Aiden.

But through it all, she kept looking at the rings. And he liked that she kept looking at them. Liked it way too much for a guy who didn't do relationships because he didn't believe in love or happily ever after.

As soon as the gifts were opened, the announcer called Lauren to the stage to sing her first song of the night. She walked up to the stage with all of the confidence and swagger of a seasoned musician and took the mic with a smile, shimmying her shoulders a little as the opening strains of Prince's "Kiss" started playing. He took a sip of his beer, almost missing the table when he went to set it back down because he couldn't take his eyes off of her.

A very drunk woman sashayed up to their table just then, her eyes locked on Theo. *Fuck.* All he wanted to do was listen to Lauren sing, not fend off a drunk chick.

"You," she said, pointing at him with a finger tipped by an impossibly long and pointy pink nail. "You are literally the most beautiful man I've ever seen," she said, slurring slightly. "Like, handcrafted by angels or something." And then she planted herself in his lap.

Theo heard Lauren's singing falter from on stage and he craned his neck, trying to see her around the woman.

"Sorry, I'm not interested," he said. He'd learned over the years that bluntness was his friend. Especially considering she was *on* him and he wanted her off. Like, now.

"Oh my God, are you hitting on my boyfriend?" came Brandon's shocked voice. "Honey, are you okay? Get off him. Off off off," he said, making an exaggerated shooing motion with his hands.

"Sorry," the woman mumbled, at least having the grace to look chagrined as she stumbled back to wherever she'd come from. Brandon took her spot, sitting down on Theo's lap and winding his arms around his neck.

"Thanks for the save, man," said Theo.

"She was just like, on you. Ew. So inappropriate. You good?" Brandon glanced back in the direction of the woman, wiggling his fingers at her.

"Yeah. How's everything going?"

Brandon slid off of him and into Lauren's empty chair. "Oh, you know. Great. Still broke, still working at Saks, still trying to write the next gay American novel."

Theo cocked an eyebrow at him. "I thought it was *great* American novel."

"I like my version better." He took a sip of his drink and glanced around the bar. "Sigh. Too bad you're not actually my boyfriend."

"What happened with...I wanna say Derek?"

Brandon waved his hand. "Daddy issues."

"That sucks, man. I know you liked him."

Lauren finished her song and made her way back to the table, picking up her wine and taking a big swig. She gestured at Theo's lap. "What was that all about?"

Brandon stood from Lauren's chair and made a face. "Just some shameless hussy making a play for our Theo. Don't worry, she thinks he's with me."

Lauren grinned. "You two would make an adorable couple."

Brandon laughed. "I know, right? You just need to convince him of that."

"I don't think I can convince Theo that he's gay when he's not."

Brandon cupped Theo's face. "Are you sure you're not gay? Like, 100% sure?"

Theo grinned and nodded. "Yeah, Bran. I'm 100% sure. Sorry, dude."

"Fine. Break my heart." He gave Theo a teasing once over. "What a waste. Please tell me you're at least having regular sex with someone."

Lauren's glass froze halfway between her mouth and the table, and Theo could feel her eyes on him. He rubbed a hand over the back of his neck and shook his head. "Nope. I haven't even been on a date in months."

"You don't have to date someone to fuck them."

"Brandon," admonished Lauren. Theo was surprised to see her cheeks were a little pink.

"What? Just saying." Brandon shrugged and popped a deep-fried mushroom from the basket on their table into his mouth. He turned to respond to something Kayla had said and Lauren's hand wrapped around Theo's bicep. Her fingers curled into him in a very appealing way.

"Oh my God, I forgot to tell you what happened earlier," she said, taking another big sip of her wine. She leaned in close, her hair tickling his cheek as she whisper-shouted in his ear. "I walked in on Aspen and some rando having freaking tantric sex in our living room."

He almost choked on his beer. "What? You what?"

"Uh huh. Incense, sitar music, oil, chanting. The whole nine yards."

"But why did they have to do that in the living room? She has a bedroom."

Her fingers curled even tighter into him and he felt a warm little tug in his stomach. "That's what I said! She's nuts."

"Truly," he agreed, glancing down the table at Aspen, who looked like she was trying to do some kind of healing thing on poor Dori.

"Hey!" shouted Lauren suddenly, following his gaze. "No reiki at the bar!"

Aspen pouted but left Dori alone. Dori sent her a grateful smile.

"Do you want to stay at mine tonight?" he asked. It wasn't an unusual question. He had a three-bedroom condo all to himself and Lauren crashed at his place regularly, usually because Aspen was driving her bananas. Plus tonight, his place was a lot closer than hers.

She bit her lip, something flickering in her eyes that he didn't know how to read. "Sure, yeah. That'd be great. Then Aspen can do her sunrise yoga naked like she prefers."

Theo chuckled, wondering how Lauren put up with her, but he didn't feel like it was his place to question their odd friendship.

"Mr. Theodore, I need your help," said Willa, leaning a hip against the table and nursing a gin and tonic.

"Sure, but only if you promise not to call me Theodore ever again. I am not one of the Chipmunks."

"Oh, but Theodore was the cute one! Alvin was a brat and Simon was a nerd, but Theodore was so sweet." When Theo just shook his head, she stuck her tongue out at him and smiled. "Anyway, I was wondering if maybe your brother Max's company is hiring? My last contract just ended and I thought maybe..."

Kayla set her drink down on the table hard. "Oh no. You do *not* want to work for a Prescott, trust me."

"I keep forgetting that Sebastian's your boss," said Lauren, finishing her drink and picking up a new one from the almost empty tray. "No bueno?"

"God, no. Sorry Theo. We love you, but Sebastian's a dick."

Theo blew out a breath, trying not to laugh. "Trust me, I'm not in the least bit shocked to hear that."

"Okay, but I'm asking about working for Max," said Willa cheerfully, waving away Kayla's comment. "I have a masters' degree in software engineering and I want to put it to use."

Kayla made a face. "I bet Max is a dick, too."

Theo tilted his head, considering. "I mean, he's grumpy as hell, which sometimes comes across as being a dick. But he's...less rough around the edges than Sebastian." He looked over at Willa. "I'll ask him if there's anything available at Tapp."

She pressed her hands together. "Thank you. I really appreciate it."

Lauren smiled ruefully and shook her head. "Funny how in a city of eight and a half million people, the world can still be so small."

Dori suddenly appeared, carrying a new tray covered in shots. "Okay, enough chit chat. Lauren is twenty-nine, which is almost thirty, which means it's time to draaaaaank."

Aiden stood and grabbed a shot from the tray, tossing it back. Then he gestured in the general direction that the drunk woman had come from. "I don't know how you do it, man. You've gotta teach me some of your moves."

Theo laughed, but before he could say anything, Lauren cut in. "Please. Theo doesn't have any moves."

He swiveled to look at her. "Oh, yeah?"

She smiled sweetly at him and then booped him on the nose. "Your only move is looking like a long-lost Hemsworth brother."

"Damn. Can't really copy that one," said Aiden, smiling ruefully. Lauren laid a hand on his shoulder.

"Aw, Aiden. You're cute as shit, you're a talented musician, and you're a total sweetheart. I know there's someone out there for you." She squeezed his shoulder and he smiled at her, laying his hand on top of hers. Something hot and prickly stuck in Theo's throat as he watched them and he took a swig of his beer, trying to swallow the sensation down.

Lauren broke away from Aiden and picked up one of the shots. "To the last year of my twenties!" she said, and everyone raised their drinks.

"Happy birthday, Lauren!"

4

"Oh, God," Lauren groaned, hugging the cool porcelain of the toilet in Theo's guest bathroom. "Fucking shots. Fucking Dori. Fucking...oh no." Her stomach heaved, her muscles tightened and her eyes watered as she threw up again. From just behind her, Theo adjusted his gentle grip on her hair, holding it carefully out of her face, while his other hand rubbed soothing circles on her back. She shuddered and reached forward, flushing the toilet. Backing away oh so carefully, she curled up into a ball on the tile floor. The intricate gray and white herringbone pattern made her head swim, so she closed her eyes.

Theo gently tugged on her arm. "Come on, Lo. Let's get you up and get you some water."

"No," she moaned. "I live here now. Just leave me. Save yourself." She waved him away with a lazy swatting motion.

She heard him laugh softly and opened her eyes just in time to see his bare feet move away through the curtain of hair in front of her eyes. She pressed her cheek into the cold tile, taking several deep breaths and wishing her stomach would calm down. Her throat burned, her head was pounding, and her mouth tasted like vomity booze.

"Ugh," she groaned, forcing herself to sit up. She curled her legs into her chest and rested her forehead on her knees. Those last three or four—okay, let's be honest, it was five—shots definitely hadn't been necessary. But she'd been having so much fun, drinking and eating and singing with her friends. She and Theo had done their usual duet of "Islands in the Stream," and she'd sang with both Aiden and Brandon, too. Each drink had gone down easier than the last and by the time she realized that she'd overdone it, it had been too late. They'd left the bar after one and she'd started feeling queasy in the cab back to Theo's.

Theo came back into the bathroom and set a few things down onto the spacious counter. "Come on. Up you get," he said, extending one of those big hands to her. She laid her fingers in his palm, her skin tingling at the contact. She let him help her to her feet, but he didn't let go of her hand. Probably because he didn't trust her not to fall over.

"I brought you a spare toothbrush, some toothpaste, and some clothes to change into if you want. Get comfy and then I've got a bottomless glass of water with your name on it. Oh, and there's Advil in that drawer," he said, pointing to the top middle drawer in the massive vanity.

"'Kay," she managed to croak out. He gave her hand a squeeze and then left her alone in the bathroom, the door closing quietly behind him.

With sluggish movements, she stripped off her black blouse and skintight maroon-colored jeans. Standing in her bra and panties, she splashed come cool water on her face and then took a few deep gulps right from the tap, the water smoothing over the rough burning still lingering in her throat. She patted her face dry with the fluffy hand towel by the sink and then brushed her teeth, eager to get the taste of puke out of her mouth. Once she was finished, she pulled on the clothes Theo had left for her—a pair of black leggings she'd left here not long ago, and his beat up navy blue Columbia Law hoodie. She tugged it on over her head and inhaled deeply, her stomach moving in a much more appealing way at the subtle hint of Theo buried in the worn fabric.

She checked herself in the mirror, wiping away a small mascara smear from beneath her eye, and then made her way into the living room, her fingers curled into the sleeves of the enormous hoodie. "Hey," she said, smiling sheepishly at Theo, who was on the couch, two glasses of water on the coffee table in front of him along with a banana, some saltines, and a little bowl of cashews. He was still wearing the light blue sweater and dark jeans he'd worn to the bar. He had this way of wearing clothes that she envied. Like he'd just tossed on whatever and it looked perfect. Like he'd just stepped out of the pages of a J. Crew ad, no big deal.

"You should try to eat something. It might help settle your stomach."

She plopped down on the couch, still feeling a little shaky despite the fact that she was mostly sober now. Throwing up had a way of killing the party vibe. She surveyed the food warily before picking up a glass of water and a saltine. She nibbled delicately at the edges of it, testing the waters of her still unsettled stomach.

Theo turned on the TV and scrolled through his streaming apps before selecting one and then putting on an episode of *Friends*. She grinned, taking a tentative sip of water.

"We don't have to watch this. I know you hate it."

He leaned back against the couch, one arm slung casually across the back of it. "First of all, it's your birthday, so hell yes we're going to watch your favorite show. Second, I don't hate *Friends*. I just hate Ross. Joey was Rachel's lobster, and that's a hill I'm prepared to die on."

She took another bite of her cracker, brushing away a few crumbs that landed on her/Theo's oversized sweatshirt. "What? You're crazy. Joey was not her lobster. That was a throwaway storyline that started in season eight when the show was starting to run out of steam. Rachel was always meant to be with Ross."

"No, *you're* crazy. Ross and Rachel were horrible together, mostly because he's a toxic, insecure asshole."

She shrugged, watching the episode play. "I mean, I never thought Ross was Prince Charming or anything, but..."

"Ross was the fucking worst. He's whiny. He's pathetic. He's jealous and needy and doesn't give a shit about what Rachel wants. He was incapable of putting her first. Ross," he said, pointing at the TV screen, "is not the kind of guy who buys Rachel flowers on the regular."

She ate some more of her cracker and tucked her legs up under herself. "Okay, okay. I get what you're saying. But that doesn't mean Joey was her lobster."

"But he was. And it's mostly because they were friends first. That's how all the best relationships start."

Lauren froze, her glass of water halfway to her mouth. "What do you mean?" she asked, trying to keep her voice casual, even though her heart had just doubled its tempo. He wasn't talking about them...was he? Did she hope he was talking about them? She honestly wasn't sure. Yeah, she was attracted to him and they had an amazing connection but...was that something she was willing to risk? Neither of them had the best track record when it came to love and relationships.

"Joey knows Rachel better than almost anyone. They cheer each other on and support each other. They see each other's flaws and accept them. Ross felt entitled to Rachel. Joey just wanted her to be happy."

"So you think because they were friends for years and years first, that set them up for success?"

"Yeah. Because he never stopped treating her like you would a friend. He never stopped supporting her, or believing in her, or putting her needs first. He let her move in with baby Emma even though it meant giving up part of his living space, sacrificing his sex life, and living in baby-proofed craziness. He fell in love with her when she was pregnant with another man's baby! And even when they broke up, he was respectful of her feelings. Because he's her friend."

"So if I got knocked up with some other dude's baby, you'd let me move in?"

Something that almost looked like anguish passed over Theo's features, just for a second, before he wiped it away with a smile that didn't quite reach his eyes. He stared at her for another second.

"In a heartbeat, Lo," he finally said, picking up his own glass of water and taking a long sip.

And just like that, she started to cry.

"Shit, I'm sorry, did I—" Theo asked, a look of sheer panic on his face.

She shook her head, wiping away her tears with the cuff of his sweatshirt sleeve. "No, no, you didn't. It's just that..." She bit her trembling lip, her eyes still stinging. She couldn't tell him. It all sounded so pathetic. "It's stupid."

"Give me a dollar," he said, his hand on her shoulder.

"What?" She frowned, wondering if maybe she was still drunker than she'd originally thought.

"Give me a dollar," he repeated. Eyeing him suspiciously, she stood and made her way to the front hall where she'd dropped her purse. She pulled a beat up dollar bill from her wallet and handed it to him, sitting back down. He took it, folded it in half and slipped it into the pocket of his jeans. "Thank you. You have now retained the expert and discreet counsel of Theo Prescott, attorney at law. As part of attorney-client privilege, anything you tell me is completely confidential and will never, ever leave this couch."

She laughed despite the tightness still lingering in her throat. "Wow, your fee is cheaper than I would've expected," she said, gesturing at his gorgeous apartment.

He winked at her. "I work on a sliding scale."

Something inside her chest felt like it was melting, all hot and slippery over her insides, and she didn't know what to do with that. So she pushed it away, wiped at her eyes and sighed.

"I'm going to die alone." Her voice came out a little croaky.

Theo blew out a breath and then pulled her into his chest. "Come here." He wrapped his arms around her and she settled her head on his broad chest, breathing in his reassuring scent, savoring the gentle thump of his heart against her cheek. "What brought this on?"

She shrugged, using the movement as an excuse to wriggle into him a little bit more. God, it felt so good to just let him hold her like that. As though with his warm, solid body sheltering her from the world, everything would be okay. Which was a very dangerous way to think, because while he was lots of things, Theo wasn't boyfriend material—something she thought she'd accepted a long time ago. "I'm twenty-nine, no closer to living my dream than I was five years ago, single AF with zero prospects, and..."

"Shhh," he whispered, pulling her tighter against him. "You're not going to die alone," he said, weaving his fingers into her hair. "Dating is hard, but I know there's a guy out there for you."

She made an indelicate snorting sound.

He sat up a little, holding her away from him so he could meet her eyes. "Lauren, listen to me. You are beautiful, and smart, and kind, and so unbelievably talented. You're incredible. You know that, right?" He cupped her face, trailing his thumb over her cheekbone. "You're funny and driven and I know it's all going to come together for you. And I promise you, you're absolutely not going to die alone, because you've got me and I'm not going anywhere."

"Theo," she whispered, letting herself lean into his touch.

"I mean it," he said, dropping his own voice to a whisper. "You're amazing."

She licked her lips and his eyes dropped to her mouth. Heat pulsed in her stomach, her heart fluttering wildly in her chest. Theo's eyes had darkened, the lids heavy as he still stared at her mouth. He shifted a bit closer. Holy shit, he was thinking of kissing her, wasn't he?

He tilted his head and moved in closer, so close that she could feel his breath on her lips. Her entire body pulsed and tingled with how badly she wanted him to kiss her. With how badly she wanted to explore the underlying but ever-present chemistry between them. She still had just enough alcohol in her system to push away the fear that they'd wreck their friendship and he'd break her heart, all in one fell swoop.

His hand slid into her hair, his breath warm on her lips, and her eyes fluttered closed. A loud pounding on Theo's door made them both jump and he snatched his hand back from her face as though he'd been caught doing something very, very wrong. He turned to face the door, shielding her with his body. Another round of insistent pounding erupted and he pushed up off of the couch.

"Theo, come on man. I know you're home. I need help."

"Fucking Bastian," he grumbled, striding toward the door. He undid the locks and flung it open. "What?" He practically spat the word out, and Lauren pressed her fingertips to her still tingling—and sadly unkissed—lips.

"I need some money."

"Hello to you, too."

"No, listen listen," said Sebastian, stepping inside and kicking the door closed. "Oh hey, Lauren. Happy birthday, yeah? Anyway, I need a thousand bucks." Sebastian's eyes were bright and he seemed particularly amped up.

"Do you have a black eye?" Theo asked, tilting his head and peering at Sebastian.

Sebastian smiled like he'd just won the lottery. "Yeah. Dude. I found it. I found that secret underground fighting ring I've been looking for. I'm a little light right now, and the buy in is a thousand bucks. I can go fight right now!"

"I take it the first one was free?"

"Free and so, so good."

"You like getting punched in the face?" Lauren asked, scrunching her face up.

Sometimes she was totally convinced that she was never, ever going to understand men.

Sebastian didn't answer her, too busy pacing back and forth with his frantic energy. Theo crossed his arms over his chest and shook his head. "No. No fucking way I'm giving you a thousand dollars so you can go get beat up."

"What makes you think I'll lose?"

Theo lifted his hand and flicked Sebastian's emerging black eye.

"Aaaaahhhh, shit man!" Sebastian yelled, bending over with his face in his hands. He stood, ripping his hands away from his face. "That fucking hurt!"

A muscle in Theo's jaw jumped as he stared his older brother down. "Go home. Sober up. And for fuck's sake, find a better way to deal with whatever it is that's going on. Like, I don't know, therapy."

"So you're not giving me the money for Fight Club."

Theo let out a world-weary sigh. "No, Bastian. I'm not giving you money for Fight Club."

"Goddammit," he muttered. "Fine. Fine. Yeah. I'll see you later." He turned and left as abruptly as he'd shown up.

"What on earth was that about?" asked Lauren, rubbing her hands over her face as exhaustion pulled at her.

"That was about Sebastian being a motherfucking mess. Look up self-destructive in the dictionary, and boom."

"There's his picture?"

"There's his *mugshot*."

"But why?"

Theo shrugged, a sad expression on his face. "I wish I knew. He's not exactly the caring and sharing type."

Lauren nodded and licked her lips, entirely unsure what to say next. Which was a really weird feeling, because she always knew what to say to Theo. Always.

He glanced at her and rubbed the back of his neck, his gaze darting around the apartment. "Anyway, I think I'm gonna crash."

Oh. So he was just going to pretend he hadn't been half a second away from kissing her.

"Yeah, that's cool. Coolcoolcool."

He hesitated. "You're okay?"

She picked up the banana and started peeling it. "I'm good. I'm going to hang out here for a while."

"Sure, yeah. Mi casa and all that," he said. He moved toward her, causing her heart to pick up speed again. He reached out his arms like he was going to hug her and then awkwardly patted her on the head. "Uh, good night."

"Night, Theo."

He disappeared into his bedroom and she returned her attention to the TV, their earlier conversation replaying over and over in her brain.

They were friends first. That's how all the best relationships start.

And it was right then—watching *Friends* alone in the dark on the night of her twenty-ninth birthday—that Lauren realized that she wasn't just attracted to Theo. No, she had feelings for him.

"This is bad," she whispered, snuggling deeper into his sweatshirt. The faintest whiff of Theo hit her and her stomach exploded with butterflies that didn't do much to help her barely contained nausea. "This is so, so bad."

5

*T*heo was having the day from hell. And not just because it was a Monday, or because he'd managed to spill almost an entire latte on his brand new Hugo Boss shirt, or because one of the senior partners had reamed him out for a settlement he'd negotiated on behalf of a client—apparently Theo hadn't been greedy enough. Which was the last thing he needed if he was really being considered for a junior partnership at Kingston, Lennox and Finley. It was one of the most prestigious family law firms in Manhattan, and getting this promotion was only step one of many on his ten-year plan.

He could be a shark when he needed to be, but it wasn't the way he liked to operate on a regular basis. He'd gone into family law to help people and protect kids, not be a ruthless and greedy asshole. If he could prevent even one kid from enduring the shit he'd been put through, then he was doing something right. And the higher up he got, the more positive change he could affect.

But back to the day from hell. Lots of things had gone

STUPID LOVE | 41

wrong, but the day was made ten times worse by the fact that he couldn't seem to focus on anything. All he could think about was how he'd almost kissed Lauren on Friday night. What the hell had he been thinking? He'd risked ruining the best relationship of his life. He had to find a way to get his attraction to her under control.

Because no matter how he felt about her, he couldn't be the guy for her. He refused to be the one to break her heart, and he knew he would, too. He'd dated throughout his twenties and had nothing to show for it but a trail of broken hearts. He'd hurt the women he'd been in relationships with because he'd always bailed as soon as things got the tiniest bit real. The idea of getting close to someone—the idea of true intimacy—scared the everloving fuck out of him because he'd seen just how deeply people could hurt you when you let them get close. He'd seen it with his parents, and he saw it in his office on a daily basis.

He refused to add Lauren's name to that list of broken hearts.

"Theo, the courier just dropped this off for you," said his paralegal, Carmen, from the doorway to his office.

"The one you like?" he teased her, moving out from behind his desk and accepting the box from her. It was surprisingly heavy. Carmen was in her early forties and recently divorced. Her husband had cheated on her and left her for a younger woman after fifteen years of marriage, making her a single mom to twin ten-year-old boys. Theo had handled her split, making sure she and the boys were well taken care of. She'd just started dating again, and while he was happy for her, he had a hard time understanding how people could just put themselves out there again after experiencing the worst possible fallout. It was like going skydiving again after jumping out and having your parachute malfunction. Miraculously, she'd survived and she was somehow ready and willing to jump out of a plane again.

Insanity. Pure insanity.

Not that he'd ever tell Carmen that. She was a sweetheart, but also a little scary when she wanted to be.

"Yes, the one with the very cute buns," she said, smiling and fluffing her black curls.

He laughed and put the box down on his desk, slicing the packing tape open with a letter opener. It was shaped like an imperial moustache; Lauren had given it to him years ago.

Lauren. The almost kiss. God, he'd replayed the moment so many times, allowing himself the private luxury of imagining what it would've been like to actually kiss her. It would've started off gentle, sweet and slow as he tasted her for the first time, her soft lips moving against his. A gasp as his tongue slid against hers and then a deepening of the kiss because he needed more of her sweetness. Fingers in her hair, a needy urgency spreading between them as the kiss became hotter, deeper, all of the pent-up lust of the past decade spilling out between them. Her hands at the hem of his shirt, pulling it up, his lips on her neck and—

"Theo? Hello? Where'd you go, honey?" Carmen snapped her manicured fingers in front of his face. He blinked rapidly, the letter opener still clutched tightly in his hand.

"Sorry," he said, swallowing thickly and setting the letter opener down before he did some serious damage with it. "Just a lot on my mind."

"Mmmhmm," said Carmen, giving him a knowing smile. "How was Lauren's birthday on Friday?"

He opened the box, pulling out a ridiculously massive binder. "It was nice. I think she had a good time."

"And what about you? Did you have a good time?" Her big brown eyes zeroed in on him, her tone teasing.

He shrugged. "Sure." And it was true, he had. Right up until he'd almost kissed his best friend and messed everything up.

Carmen crossed her arms, staring him down and shaking her head. "You're lucky you're cute."

"And why's that?" he asked distractedly, thumbing through the binder. Jesus Christ, it was hundreds of pages of allegations against his client. *Fuuuuuuuuuuuuuuuuck.*

"Because you're really dumb sometimes."

He glanced up at Carmen. "What?"

She patted him on the shoulder and smiled sweetly. "You'll figure it out. Eventually."

Shaking his head as Carmen went back to her desk out front, he sank down into his chair. The binder contained exactly 662 pages calling his client, Miranda Simmons, a negligent mother and all-around horrible person. And, Theo could see from the paperwork included with it, opposing counsel had already delivered a copy to the custody evaluator in the case as well.

This split was a particularly nasty one. Miranda Simmons was a successful fashion designer whose husband had left her for another woman. Not only did he want sole custody of their six-year-old daughter, he also wanted insane amounts of both child support and alimony from Miranda.

His phone started ringing, and sure enough, Miranda's name flashed across the screen.

"Miranda, hi," he said, putting the call on speaker phone as he continued flipping through the binder.

"I just heard from the custody evaluator who told me I needed to talk to you ASAP. What's going on?"

He grimaced. "Massimo and his lawyer are playing in the mud. I just got a 600-page binder full of allegations about you."

"*What?!?* Oh, that cretinous, dickless, shit eating fuckwit."

He smirked. "Nicely put."

"I'd say I can't believe this, but it's Massimo, so..." Not to mention that Massimo's lawyer was a total scumbag. "Well, I want to retaliate. Oh, boy, the things I could tell you about him. Forget 600 pages, we can put together 1000 pages of stuff about that sewer rat. He thinks he can get away with calling me a bad mother, well, he's an even worse father!"

Right then, Theo's heart broke a little for six-year-old Mila, caught in the middle. It was so unfair to her. So unfair what all of these failed marriages did to kids. He closed his eyes and pressed his fingers to the bridge of his nose. "Miranda, do you want revenge, or do you want custody? Because I can only get you one of those things."

"What do you mean?"

"I think our best course of action is to take the high road. Let's focus on the fact that Mila's been in your care her entire life. Between traveling for work and the separation, Massimo's hardly been around."

There was a lengthy pause. "But I can't just let him get away with saying whatever the hell it is he's saying." He was relieved to hear that some of the fire had gone out of her voice. Miranda hadn't gotten where she was in her career by letting people walk all over her, but he knew that how they handled this could make or break the case.

"Do you trust me?" It was a question he asked clients often, because if they didn't trust him to do his job, it made doing his job infinitely harder.

"Of course I do," she answered, sounding put out. "I

wouldn't have hired you and paid your ludicrously expensive retainer if I didn't." At the mention of his retainer, his mind went back to Friday night again, when he'd asked Lauren for a dollar. His chest hurt as he remembered how crushed she'd looked when she'd told him her fear of ending up alone. And he'd meant what he'd said—she'd always have him.

Which was why it was for the best that they hadn't kissed. Because if they kissed, it would change things. They'd be headed into territory he didn't know how to navigate without crashing.

"Then trust me now when I tell you that firing back is not the winning strategy. This," he said, zipping his thumb along the edges of the binder's hundreds of pages, "will backfire on him. Judges hate when parents badmouth each other, and this is more than badmouthing—we'd have a good argument for parental alienation of affection should we need to use it. Let's stay focused on the actual issues instead of attacking him. Tit for tat won't get us anywhere, and it definitely won't be good for Mila."

She paused at the mention of her daughter, and he crossed his fingers, hoping that what he'd said had hit home.

"Okay. Okay. You're right. I need to focus on doing what's best for Mila." She sighed. "So what do we do now?"

"We've already submitted everything to the custody evaluator. So now we wait and we don't even acknowledge this binder of stupidity."

They talked for a few more minutes until he was satisfied she wasn't going to do anything impulsive that might ruin their case. As it stood now, Miranda had a very good shot at sole physical and legal custody and he wanted to keep it that way. Living full time with her mother was definitely what would be best for Mila, so that was the outcome Theo was angling for.

"Knock knock," came a familiar voice from his doorway. He tore his eyes away from the binder in front of him, his heart thunking heavily in his chest at the sight of Lauren.

They hadn't talked about the almost kiss at all. He hadn't brought it up and neither had she, and he planned to leave it that way. It was for the best to just pretend it hadn't happened.

"Hey," he said, flashing her a smile. "What's up?"

She lifted her hands, showing off a bag emblazoned with the King Tacos logo. "Hungry? I was in the area and thought you could use a break."

Just then, his stomach let out a loud rumble and they both laughed. "Maybe a little," he admitted. "Come on in." She stepped further into his office and set the takeout bag down on the small table in his office that he pretty much only used for having lunch with Lauren when she stopped by. He counted his lucky stars that there was a music store that she loved just down the street from his firm.

She sat down and opened the bag, filling the air with the scents of spiced beef, melted cheese, and cilantro. He sat down opposite her, inhaling appreciatively before digging in, and they ate in silence for several moments.

"So," she said, pressing her fingers to her mouth to conceal her bite of taco. "I landed a last-minute gig at this bar in Williamsburg tonight. You wanna come?"

He smiled, then picked up a napkin and wiped at his mouth. "Duh. Text me the time and address and I'll be there." He loved watching Lauren perform, especially when she was singing her own songs. He always felt this heady mix of pride and hope and happiness when she was up on stage, doing her thing.

"Okay, cool." She took another bite of her taco, glancing at him furtively. Crap, she wanted to ask him about the almost kiss. And he was an asshole, because he wasn't going to give her an opening. He knew Lauren well enough to know that she hated anything that felt even remotely like conflict or confrontation, so if he didn't bring it up, he was willing to bet she wouldn't either. But then she set her taco down, glanced at the door, which was open only a few inches, and then cleared her throat. "So, um, are we just gonna not talk about it?" Her cheeks blazed red, and he could see what this question was costing her.

He grimaced and rubbed a hand over his mouth. "Talk about what?"

She snorted out an adorable little laugh. Then her cheeks turned an even deeper shade of red and she leaned forward, her voice just barely above a whisper. "The fact that you almost kissed me on Friday night."

He hesitated, feeling this strange tug in his chest. He blew out a breath and pushed his hand through his hair, trying to think. "I'm sorry, Lauren. I don't know...I don't know what I was doing. It was a dumb move, and I'm really sorry. I never meant to make you feel weird or anything. It shouldn't have happened."

She held very still, and then after a moment, she picked up her taco again, taking a massive bite. After she'd swallowed, she said softly, "Okay, then."

He frowned. Did she look...disappointed? No. Definitely not. If anything, she was probably just annoyed with him for being an idiot, which was totally fair.

"I'm really sorry if it made you uncomfortable. That's

obviously the last thing I'd ever want to do," he said cautiously. "And I promise it'll never happen again." His desk phone started ringing. "Shit, I gotta answer that."

"No problem," she said, taking her last bite of food. "I should let you get back to work. See you tonight." Her voice was a bit flat, but Theo didn't really have time to digest it because the mediator he'd been trying to reach for the past week was finally calling him back. As he spoke on the phone, Lauren packed up, tossed the garbage from their lunch, waved and left. When he got off the phone twenty minutes later, he sat back in his chair, swiveling around to look out his window at the East River and the Brooklyn Bridge.

As much as he cared about her, he couldn't date Lauren. It was only inevitable that he'd fuck it up royally, hurt her, and ruin their friendship. He'd completely sworn off serious relationships over two years ago because he'd gotten sick of hurting people, plain and simple. Logically, dating didn't make sense when he couldn't make it work, so he'd stopped pursuing anything beyond the casual. The only reason he dated at all was because he wasn't a monk and sex wasn't something he was willing to give up. So, even if he was attracted to Lauren—check—and even if he had feelings beyond the platonic for her—double check—their friendship mattered more to him than anything else. He had a responsibility to protect her from the damage he knew anything romantic between them would cause.

And so he took what he was feeling, took the lust simmering just below the surface, and imagined squeezing it into a tiny little ball and then throwing it into the East River, where it could never hurt her.

Lauren sat on a little stool backstage, tuning her guitar one last time. She could hear the buzz of the crowd on the other side of the wall, the hum of voices giving her a jolt of nervous adrenaline. She'd been performing for a long time, but she still got butterflies before going out on stage. And she was glad for it, because the butterflies meant she still cared. They meant she was still passionate about this thing that she wanted so badly. This thing that she was scared might become more hobby than career.

"Here," said Willa, handing her a bottle of water as she tucked a strand of her chin-length brown hair behind her ear.

Lauren took it and sipped, letting the cool water slide down her throat. "Thanks." Willa had been coming to Lauren's shows since their college days, often helping with hauling gear and providing support. She was a ray of sunshine in a sometimes grimy world, and Lauren was grateful for her.

"Are you going to play anything new tonight?" she asked, her tone *almost* casual, but not quite.

"Actually, yeah. I have a new song called 'Looking In.'"

Willa nodded and then leveled her gaze at Lauren. "Is it about Theo?"

Lauren's heart jumped up into her throat. She hadn't told anyone about her near kiss with Theo, so how did Willa know that yes, the song was about her feelings for Theo and how she didn't know what to do?

"Um..." She said eloquently, suddenly becoming very interested in one of the strings on her guitar. "What?"

Willa shrugged. "Well, most of your songs are about Theo, aren't they?"

"What?" Lauren repeated, her face hot.

"Come on, Lauren. It's just me. You can be honest."

She set her guitar down and stood, rubbing her suddenly sweaty palms on her jeans. "A few, okay? So what?" She normally wouldn't have been so defensive, but she was still feeling a bit raw after he'd apologized for almost kissing her and assured her that it would never, ever happen again. She kept telling herself that she should feel relieved, but all she felt was rejected.

"You're on in two minutes," said the stage manager/bartender, poking his beanie covered head into the room.

Lauren plastered a smile on her face. "Great, thanks."

"Does he know?" asked Willa, apparently not willing to let this drop.

"Of course not. He'd run screaming in the other direction. In fact..." She took a deep breath, needing to share this with someone. Needing to get what had almost happened out of her brain and into the open. "We almost kissed on Friday night. After my birthday."

Willa's mouth fell open. "What? What happened?"

"We were at his place, on the couch, and I was feeling a bit down because of, you know, my birthday and not really being where I want to be in life, and he was comforting me. Then, all of a sudden, his arms were around me and he was telling me how amazing I am, and we were like *thisclose* to kissing when Bastian ruined everything."

Willa's eyebrows knit together. "How did Bastian ruin everything?"

Lauren waved her hand. "By being the train wreck that is Bastian. Still think you want to work for a Prescott?"

"Well, Max is a totally separate person from Sebastian. Besides, I already have an interview at Tapp on Wednesday, so..." She shrugged. "And we're not talking about me right now, anyway. We're talking about you."

"Right. Anyway, we didn't really talk about it. I brought it up when we had lunch today and he apologized like he'd run over my dog or something. Like, the idea of it was just so awful to him."

Willa's face lit up. "Maybe you need to—"

"Please welcome to the stage Lauren MacKinnon!" Lauren shot Willa a smile before strapping on her guitar and stepping out onto the small, brightly lit stage. Without preamble, her band launched into the first song, the new one she'd written that weekend as she'd tried to work through her feelings about the almost kiss and Theo in general.

It was an upbeat folk-pop song with a pretty standard D-A-G chord progression at its core. The melody was fairly simple, mostly because she'd spent the majority of her time working on the lyrics. Fingers anchored on her guitar strings, she stepped up to the mic and started to sing, wondering if Theo was here.

"I don't know what I'm looking for
Maybe just a reason
That we could be more
That we could change like a season
Sometimes I think we should take that chance
Seems so simple at first glance

But I don't know because I'm on the outside
Know you so well, but you don't let me in
Think I don't see you for who you are
And that's fine, I'll stay right here
Looking in..."

She strummed her guitar and bopped along with the music as they headed toward the second verse. Out of habit, her eyes skimmed the crowd and then her heart slammed into her ribs so hard she almost lost her place in the song. There was Theo, at a table in the corner with Brandon, Dori, and Willa, beaming at her. He had this way of smiling that she loved—it was like he smiled with his entire face. The skin around his eyes crinkled and his eyes gleamed. His cheeks moved up, making room for the wide, often open-mouthed smile. Even his nose got in on the action, wrinkling just the slightest bit. Theo's smile was, hands down, her favorite smile.

He winked at her, and it was a good thing she was such a seasoned musician, because her stomach did this funny flip floppy thing that might've thrown a less experienced performer off. She tore her gaze away from him, her eyes moving around the rest of the crowd. Theo was not boyfriend material. He didn't do relationships, and oh right, he'd rejected her after nearly kissing her. He'd put her back in her friend place. Where she'd be smart to stay.

Pushing all of that away, she poured herself into the performance, singing and playing the guitar, belting out songs she'd written. Songs about falling in love, about heartbreak, about hope, fear, loneliness, bravery. Some were more personal than others, but she was willing to open herself up because part of the beauty of creating and performing music—part of the wonder of it—was the connection it fostered, between her and the listener, or multiple listeners all relating. All seeing themselves reflected back through something she'd written.

About an hour and a half later, she joined her friends at

their table, a little sweaty and breathless after her performance.

"Hey, hey," she said, stepping up beside Theo and hip checking him. She had that post-show buzz going on that made everything seem golden. Life, her relationships, everything. It was like being high, but in a totally non-drug induced way.

"Hey. That was really awesome," he said, smiling at her and plucking one of the empty pint glasses from the stack and pouring her a glass from their pitcher.

"Thanks!" she said. Music was the one area of her life where she wasn't afraid to own her talent, and she accepted his compliment easily.

"Seriously awesome show," said Willa, giving Lauren's shoulder a squeeze. "Remind me again why you don't have a record deal?"

"Because every single demo I've sent out has either gotten ignored or rejected." She'd put out a few albums independently over the years, but it wasn't the same as having the backing of a major record label. "But I do have some exciting news. Thanks to a connection of Aiden's, I have an audition to open for Lynne Townsend."

"Oh, I love her music!" said Willa. "That's awesome!" Lynne Townsend was a country-folk-rock singer whose debut album had burned up the charts and found massive crossover success. Her fans were exactly the kind of listeners Lauren wanted to connect with. If she could just get in front of the right crowds and build a big enough following, she had a feeling good things would happen.

"When's your audition?" asked Brandon, picking at the almost empty plate of nachos on the table.

"Next week. The tour would be all next spring."

"If you need something to wear, come see me at Saks. I'll hook you up."

"Thanks, B. I appreciate that, although I'm not sure Saks is really what the other indie folk singers are wearing these days."

He shrugged. "Oh, true. Well, if you ever want to look like Lady Gaga, let me know."

"Okay, so I have an idea," said Willa, the words practically bursting out of her mouth. She clasped her hands together, her eyes bright. A tiny shiver made its way down Lauren's spine. Willa was dangerous when she got that look on her face. She was an incurable meddler, and Lauren had a feeling she was about to become Willa's meddlee.

"What?" asked Theo, taking a sip of his beer.

"Okay, hear me out. Theo, you're single."

"Yeah..." he said, setting his beer down slowly, his tone wary.

"Right, and Lauren, you're single."

"Uh huh."

"And you guys are best friends."

"Sure," said Lauren, a cold knot forming in her stomach. Wherever this was going was probably very, very bad.

"Okay, so why don't you set each other up?"

Lauren froze with her mouth open for just a second too long. "Set...what do you mean?"

Willa beamed, clearly beyond proud of herself for this idea. "You set Theo up with someone who you think would be good for him, and Theo, you set Lauren up with someone. You guys know each other so well, I can't see how you'd pick bad dates for each other."

Theo was staring at her with a weird expression on his

face. He hesitated, shaking his head. "I don't know. I'm not really looking for a relationship right now."

"No, but Lauren is," said Willa, slipping an arm around Lauren's shoulders. "And who better to set her up than you?"

He glanced at Lauren, uncertainty etched across his handsome face. "Okay, I get what you're saying. But why can't I just set her up? Why do I have to suffer?"

"Ah, you're assuming there will be suffering involved." Willa shrugged. "Maybe your picker's just as broken as Lauren's and you need her help to actually find someone you'd be down to date. Maybe if the two of you both start seeing someone else, you'll be a little less attached at the hip and more open to new relationships."

He hesitated again, toying with his beer glass before nodding. "That's not the worst idea. I mean, obviously I want Lauren to be happy, and if she's going to date someone, maybe I should too."

Lauren had heard the expression "to have your heart sink" before, but she'd never really experienced it as intensely as she did in that moment. It felt like her heart slowly became heavier and heavier before sliding sickly down into the pit of her stomach. Theo regretted almost kissing her. Now he was happy to set her up with someone else. More proof that she needed to get over him because anything romantic was never, ever going to happen between them. Ever. And that was for the best, because they'd end up crashing and burning and only ashes would remain of their friendship.

She cleared her throat, swallowed, and when she still couldn't get her voice to work, took a big swig of her beer. Before she could answer, Willa leaned over and quickly whispered in her ear, "This is your chance to get over him, babe. Trust me on this."

Lauren blinked slowly as she digested Willa's words. Huh. She hadn't looked at it that way. Her immediate reaction had been to focus on what she'd be letting go of as opposed to what she might gain.

"What was that?" asked Theo, one eyebrow cocked.

"I was telling her that you probably know all kinds of cute lawyers. Or, hey! Maybe one of your brothers!" she said, snapping her fingers.

"No, not my brothers," said Theo at the same time as Lauren shook her head vehemently. Sebastian was a mess, Max was an extreme workaholic and a total grump most of the time, and Lucian...well, he was straight up terrifying.

"Okay, fine, not your brothers. But you must know some eligible bachelors. And Lauren, you know some single ladies, right? Come on guys, this is genius!"

Lauren locked eyes with Theo, trying to read his mind, but for once, she didn't have a clue what was going through his brain. She held his gaze in what felt very much like a game of chicken. After a moment, he blinked and looked away, and for some reason, that solidified her choice.

"Okay. I'll do it. Theo?"

He rubbed a hand over the back of his neck and then smiled, but it wasn't one of those whole face smiles. Not even close. "Yeah. Okay. I guess I'm in."

6

*S*weat ran down Theo's face, his chest, and his back and his heart throbbed against his ribs. He could feel his pulse everywhere, and his limbs were heavy. "Oh, God," he moaned, breathless, panting with exertion.

"Stop complaining," said Max from beside him. Totally not sweaty. Totally capable of normal conversation. "We've only been running for three miles. One mile to go. Come on, champ. I thought you were in better shape than this."

Theo stopped on the path, bracing his hands on his knees. He'd thought he was in good shape, too. He hit the gym regularly, lifted weights, even did yoga sometimes. But this...running was just not his thing. "I am in shape. I just don't usually torture myself like this."

"Hey, you're the one who asked if you could come on my run," said Max. He jogged on the spot, seemingly boundless with energy. Theo wanted to punch him.

He squinted at his older brother through the sweat dripping into his eye. "My mistake, apparently."

Max stopped bouncing—thank God—and jammed his

hands on his hips, an assessing look on his face. "Why *did* you want to come?" Other joggers moved around them, giving them dirty looks for stopping right in the middle of Central Park's four-mile loop path.

"I thought some exercise might help," he said, still panting as he tried to catch his breath.

"With what?"

Theo shrugged, struggling with how to put into words what he'd been thinking and how he'd been feeling the past few days. "Life, I guess." He'd hoped that a run would clear his head and give him the chance to organize his thoughts, but instead, his inability to keep up with the brutal pace Max had set was only making him feel worse.

Max tipped his head in the direction of a path that led out of the park and towards the Met. "Let's grab a coffee. I think you might need an ear more than a workout right now."

"Yeah, okay," said Theo, managing to stand upright. "But we're walking there. I'm never running again."

"Fine. I know a place on East 80th."

Theo groaned, because he knew that meant even more walking in the long run. In order to get back to the West Side, he'd have to walk to the 72nd Street subway station to get the Q. But it was his own damn fault for thinking a run through Central Park on a beautiful morning might actually be nice. He should've known better. Max was excellent at chasing anything nice away.

They walked in silence as Theo chugged down his entire bottle of water, letting the Saturday morning crowd buzz around them. It was a gloriously sunny fall morning. The air was cool and crisp, and the leaves on the trees in the park were starting to change, the green giving way to orange and red and gold. Theo loved New York in the fall. Granted, he loved New York all the time—he couldn't imagine ever wanting to live anywhere else—but the fall season that led up to the sparkling rush of the holidays was the best. Everything just felt so alive. So fresh with promise.

The small coffeeshop was adorned with a plain red awning, wedged in between a bodega and a Duane Reade. It didn't look like much, but the coffee smelled divine. Yeah, Max had been right—a coffee was much more sensible than the seemingly unending torture of running. Once they had their drinks—a latte for Theo and a black coffee for Max— they snagged a small table near the back, away from the constant action near the cash register.

"Okay, so what's going on with you?" asked Max, leaning back in his seat, once again leveling that CEO stare at him. "You were quiet last night at dinner and then when you texted me to go jogging this morning, I thought you were joking."

"I don't know if I should be offended by that," said Theo, taking a sip of his latte.

Max snorted. "Interpret that however you want. But seriously. Something's eating at you."

Theo exhaled sharply, toying with the brown paper sleeve on his cup. "So, Lauren's friend Willa had this idea that because Lauren and I are both single and we both know each other really well, we should set each other up."

"Like on blind dates?"

Theo shrugged. "Basically, yeah. I'm supposed to set her up with someone, and she's supposed to set me up with someone."

Max tilted his head, his eyes narrowing. "Interesting. That's really interesting." He pulled his phone from his pocket. "Hang on, I'm getting an idea," he said, his fingers flying across his phone screen as he typed at a furious pace.

"What?"

"A new dating app. What if there were something like Tinder or Bumble, but instead of *you* swiping left or right, you have a friend who swipes for you? They choose, swiping yes or no, and then you get your matches."

Theo's eyebrows rose. "Interesting idea."

"It's like a blind date, but not. This...Yeah, I'm really liking this," he said, still typing away.

"I'm glad my problems are so inspirational to you."

At that, Max's head shot up and he set his phone down on the table. "And the problem is..." he asked, rolling his fingers in a *get on with it* gesture.

That was the million-dollar question, wasn't it?

"I don't...I'm an asshole, okay? I can't date Lauren, but I don't want to set her up with anyone either." Guilt gnawed at him, and he tried to drown it with sugary caffeine.

It didn't work.

Max leaned forward, elbows braced on the table. "Tell me again why you don't want to date her? Because she's beautiful, and sweet, and hilarious and you clearly care about her. I don't get it."

Theo shook his head slowly, staring at his paper coffee cup. "It's not that I don't..." He shook his head again. "I can't."

"Because...?"

"Because it'll wreck everything. It's inevitable. You and I both know how relationships always end up. I'm not going to throw away my best friend just because I'm attracted to her."

"And you have feelings for her."

Theo's eyebrows shot up. "What? I didn't ever tell..."

Max snapped his fingers. "Aha! You *do* have feelings for the lovely Lauren."

"Don't call her that."

"Lauren and Theo sitting in a tree, K-I—"

Theo shot his hand out, swiping up Max's phone. "Finish that rhyme and I delete these notes." His thumb hovered over the screen, poised to strike.

"Okay, okay. Jeez. Touchy. So you don't want to date Lauren because you're just as jaded as the rest of us, but you don't want to set her up with someone else because you do have feelings for her."

"Like I said, I'm an asshole."

"I don't know about that."

But Theo shook his head. He definitely felt like one. He couldn't reasonably expect Lauren to stay single forever. Eventually, she'd meet someone and they'd start dating. They'd get closer, then maybe they'd move in together. Before long, they'd be ring shopping, and—

He dropped his head into his hands as his stomach twisted itself into knots. "I don't know what to do." He couldn't tell Lauren how he felt—not only because he was worried about wrecking their friendship, but because he couldn't be the guy for her. She deserved so much better than a commitment-phobe with an airliner's worth of baggage when it came to relationships. But the thought of losing her to another guy...fuck. It sucked just as much.

"What do you want?" It was a point-blank question, and one Theo didn't have the answer to right now.

"I don't know. I mean, obviously I want Lauren to be happy."

"Well, for God's sake, don't set her up with anyone good,"

said Max, as though it were the most obvious thing in the world.

Theo lifted his head. "Wait, what?"

"You're a mess right now. You don't know what you want, but you definitely don't want to chance her falling for someone before you figure your shit out. So set her up with a dud. It'll buy you some time to figure out what to do." Max shrugged, taking a long sip of his coffee. "For what it's worth, I think the fact you don't want her dating anyone else is pretty telling, brother."

Which was exactly what Theo was afraid of.

"Don't you think setting her up with someone bad on purpose is kinda shitty? To Lauren?" asked Theo, pulling the paper sleeve off of his cup and ripping it into tiny pieces.

"I think not wanting her to date anyone while refusing to fully acknowledge your feelings for her is kinda shitty, too. Face it—you're going to do something kinda shitty here. How can you come out of it unscathed? How can Lauren? Because I think, deep down, if you're honest with yourself, you already know what you want. You're just scared to go after it because all you ever see is failure."

"You should start charging by the hour for this shit," said Theo, Max's words hitting home. Hitting the motherfucking bullseye.

Max just laughed. "So, the way I see it, you have two options. Set her up with a dud to buy yourself some more time, or tell her how you feel."

The idea of telling Lauren how he felt was far too risky. Far too terrifying. So, plan A it was.

For the first time that morning, Theo grinned as inspiration struck. "I think I know just the guy."

"His name sounds very sexy," said Aspen from where she sat perched on Lauren's bed. "Giovanni Damico." She closed her eyes and took a deep breath. "Yes, definitely a name with a high vibration."

Lauren fought back an eyeroll as she slicked on some lip gloss, giving herself a final once over in her bedroom mirror. Aspen was annoying sometimes and took the whole New Agey thing to a new level, but she meant well and wanted only good things for Lauren. She was crunchy as hell but had a heart of gold. So, even if she was annoying sometimes, she was a good friend.

When she wasn't boinking some rando in their living room, that is.

"He's a lawyer at Theo's firm. He honestly didn't tell me much about him, just connected us."

"Where are you meeting him?"

Lauren glanced down at her phone, double checking the instructions. "We're supposed to meet at a coffee bar and then dinner."

"Well, good luck. I'm sure you'd much rather be dating Theo, though."

Lauren froze, her phone slipped halfway into her purse. "What do you mean?"

Aspen smiled. "You should see your aura when he's around. It's the most beautiful reddish pink color."

Lauren plopped down on the bed next to Aspen so she could pull on her gray suede knee high boots. She loved wearing them with the camel-toned sweater dress and floral scarf she'd chosen for the date. "And what does that color mean?" she asked, telling herself that she didn't care. Plus it wasn't like auras were actually *real* or anything.

"Well, the pink tones indicate friendship, but also love. Now, it can sometimes be a platonic love, but you've got this really vibrant red in there too." Aspen leaned in, bringing a whiff of patchouli with her. "And that means you want that man inside you. Like, yesterday."

Lauren's cheeks flamed as her stomach flipped over on itself, her heart starting to throb. Just the idea of Theo inside her...Unf. Her entire body was like a riot of giddy arousal. Which, obviously, was bad. She shouldn't even let herself go there. For the sake of their friendship, she needed to get it together.

"I gotta go. See you!" She pushed off the bed and gathered up her purse, giving herself one final glance in the mirror.

"Wait, before you go...do you want to borrow one of my crystals? I have a rose quartz one that's really great at attracting love."

Lauren paused. First of all, it wasn't like she believed in crystals or any of that woo-woo shit. The most woo thing Lauren ever did was read her horoscope once in a while, and she took that with a grain of salt. Unless Mercury was in retrograde. Even she knew not to mess with that energy. Second...she was pretty sure she didn't want to fall in love with Giovanni, seeing as how that would probably enormously complicate the whole feelings-for-her-best-friend thing she had going on.

Crap. Crappity crap crap crap.

"Oh, um, no thanks." She shot Aspen a smile, who seemed completely unoffended by Lauren's rejection of her offer.

"Good luck!"

She headed out of the apartment and towards the subway station. The coffee shop and restaurant Giovanni had suggested were both in SoHo, which meant she needed to walk to the 42nd Street Station and catch the A train to Canal Street. Jamming in her earbuds, she cued up her playlist and started walking the four blocks to the subway.

Lately when she listened to music, she felt this odd, uncomfortable tug of war going on inside her. She wanted to just listen and enjoy it but couldn't seem to stop herself from analyzing everything about the song—the melody, the lyrics, the arrangement, the production values. She couldn't seem to switch that technical part of her musical brain off these days. And it kinda sucked because sometimes she just wanted to tune out the world and listen to music, the way she used to.

And then, underneath all of that, was an even subtler tug. A judgmental one that asked questions like *how come she has a record deal and I don't? My songs are just as good*. She tried not to go there, not to dwell in negativity, but it was hard sometimes. Really hard. There were days when she wasn't so sure about her music career anymore. The audition to open for Lynne Townsend had gone well, but she hadn't heard anything yet, and she was starting to think she wasn't going to.

She wasn't sure about much these days, really. Her career, her dreams, her feelings for her totally off-limits best friend —all enormous question marks. She'd hoped to be so much more settled by twenty-nine. She'd hoped for more out of life. Maybe that was unreasonable and unrealistic. Maybe she needed to lower her expectations.

Why did she have to want such hard things? A career in a ridiculously competitive industry and a man who was allergic to relationships? Sometimes she thought her life would be so much simpler if she didn't want what often felt like the impossible. What would it be like to just work at the library, hang out with her friends, and date a cute guy? Just the idea of it felt freeing. But also like a complete and utter cop-out. She couldn't change who she was or what she wanted any more than she could rearrange the freckles on her face.

But she nodded as she took the steps down into the subway station, deciding to be as open minded as possible tonight. Maybe she needed to look beyond her tunnel-vision-esque view of what she wanted her life to be.

By the time she got to the coffee bar, she was feeling more positive about her blind date. After all, it wasn't like Theo would set her up with a total loser, right?

The coffee bar was a cute little white brick building between a French bistro and an elegant jewelry store, every single storefront reminding her that this was SoHo, where people had money. The sidewalks were busy, bustling with people, but she noticed a very tall man standing out front, his attention on his phone. As she got closer, she could see that he was wearing an impeccable suit that looked custom-tailored to his somewhat lanky frame. He had thick dark brown hair that he'd slicked back with a little too much product. Just then, he looked up and he pointed at her.

"You must be the infamous Lauren MacKinnon. Theo said you had red hair, but I was expecting, you know, like a fake redhead? And you're a real one. At least, I think you're a real one. Guess we'll find out, huh?" He winked at her and then held his hand up for a high five. She stared at him, trying to compute what he'd just said. "C'mon Red, don't leave me hanging."

"Oh." With an awkward movement, she reached out and touched her hand to his in the world's quietest high five.

Giving it any sound would've made it seem like she was condoning what he'd just said, and she most definitely, absolutely, was not.

Maybe he's just nervous, she thought, trying not to retreat too far into her shell at Giovanni's outward bravado.

"I actually live around here, but I always have my dates meet me here first."

She smiled, hoping she looked a little more relaxed than she felt. "The coffee's that good, huh?"

"Who cares about the coffee? I just don't like giving out my address to strange women in case one of them turns out to be a..." He cupped his hand around his mouth and sang the next word. "...*stalker!*"

"Right. Wouldn't want that." Did she have the wrong guy? This guy seemed like a total douche. And there's no way that Theo would deliberately set her up with a douche. But he'd known her full name and that she had red hair. Oh, right, and he'd mentioned Theo, too. Crap. "Uh, should we go inside and sit down?" she asked, but Giovanni didn't seem to hear her. He was too busy practically drooling over the ass of a woman who'd just walked by.

"*Daaaaaaaaamn,*" he said, shaking his head. "You into women at all, Lauren?"

"Excuse me?"

"Where do you fall on the..." He waved his hands in a small arc. "...rainbow spectrum?"

She narrowed her eyes at him. "You didn't just ask me that."

Giovanni laughed awkwardly and then turned and held the door open for her. The inside of the coffee bar was busy and they had to elbow their way to the front, where Giovanni ordered an Americano and Lauren ordered a chai latte. Once they had their drinks, they snagged a small table near the front.

Still determined to make the best of this and not jump to conclusions, she attempted conversation again. "So, Giovanni..."

He smiled at her, leaning back in his seat. "I'm all yours."

"Did, um, did Theo say why he thought we'd be a good match?" He hadn't told her anything at all, a fact that was starting to set off alarm bells in her brain.

"Well, for starters..." He swept his hand down over his body. "There's this." He cocked an eyebrow at her. "Any further questions?"

She practically snorted chai latte through her nose. This guy couldn't be for real.

He flashed her a smile, clearly misinterpreting her snort. How was this guy a lawyer at Theo's high-priced firm? He was a total clown.

"So, Lauren...you know, that's kind of a boring name. Can I fix it for you? Let me fix it. You look more like a...Lola. Boom. Name upgraded."

She blinked at him. "Uh...please don't call me Lola."

But he didn't hear her, because his phone rang and he actually answered. "What up, big V? No, no, I'm not busy. Just hanging out with this smokin' hot redhead. Lola. Yeah. Yeah. Nice." And then, just when she thought he'd already scaled to the peak of Mount Douchemore, he pulled the phone away from his ear and tipped his chin at her. "Sorry, gotta take this. But then we can bounce, bounce, bounce, bounce, bounce," he said, rapping the words in a staccato rhythm.

Lauren took a sip of her latte and then fished her phone out of her purse, sending a single text message.

Theodore William Prescott, I am going to KILL you.

7

*T*heo swung open his front door, bracing himself for whatever awaited him on the other side.

"*What*," said Lauren, stepping inside and whirling to face him, "and I cannot emphasize this enough, *the fuck*?"

He closed the door, following her into his apartment. He'd seen her text message from earlier, but in all honesty, he'd been too chicken to reply. At first, he'd thought setting her up with Giovanni was harmless. Maybe a bit of a jerk move, sure, but ultimately harmless.

But then, knowing that Lauren was out with him and then seeing her text message, he'd felt like an asshole.

"I take it your date was a bust?" he asked, rubbing the back of his neck, feigning innocence.

"I'm going to take off this boot and beat you with it. Theo! I can't believe that's who you chose for me. What the hell, dude?"

"Okay, I'm sorry. Listen. I can explain, okay?"

She stared at him, her arms crossed over her chest, but she nodded. "Okay."

"You want something to drink?"

"You have any more of that cider?" she asked. She sat down on the couch and started unzipping one of her knee-high boots. Theo stared as inch after inch of creamy, pale skin came into view, the zipper sliding lower and lower. He shook his head and cleared his throat.

"Uh, yeah, I still have some." He went to the fridge and retrieved two bottles of her favorite pear cider and headed back into the living room. She'd ditched both boots and was now sitting on the couch with her feet tucked up under her. His heart smashed against his ribs at the sight of her, curled up and at home on his sofa, like she was right where she belonged.

God, he was so fucked, wasn't he? He had feelings for her, feelings that he couldn't act on, feelings he didn't know how to process, feelings he wished would just fuck right off.

He took a breath and then sat down beside her, handing her one of the bottles.

She took a sip and then leveled her gaze at him, pinning him in place with those gorgeous green eyes. "Okay. Start explaining."

"Let me just start by saying that I'm sorry, okay? I know Giovanni's a dick."

She smacked his arm. "So then why did you set me up with him?"

He shrugged, once again playing at innocence. Normally, he was honest with Lauren, but he couldn't be honest with her right now. Not about this. "I don't know a lot of available guys who aren't my brothers. It was the best I could do on short notice and I didn't want you to think I wasn't taking this whole Project Set Each Other Up thing seriously."

Her eyes narrowed. "I think you're lying."

Panic shot through him, and he raked a hand through his hair. *Lawyer mode activate! Activate!* "Lying? What makes you think I'm lying?" He took a sip of his cider to force himself to stop talking. From all of his time in court, he knew that often the best defense was to just shut the hell up.

"Because you have liar face right now."

"Liar face? And just what does liar face look like?"

She pointed at him, wiggling her index finger in a circle. "Like that. Theo, God. I've known you for a decade. I can tell when you're lying."

He closed his eyes, pressed his fingers to the bridge of his nose and then sighed. Maybe a half-truth would do. Maybe. "Okay. Okay. Don't be mad."

She arched an eyebrow at him. "That's a reassuring start."

"I set you up with Giovanni knowing you'd hate him."

"But why would you do that? I don't understand."

"Because I'm a selfish asshole." When she didn't say anything, he kept talking. "I was worried that if I set you up with someone you like then...then things would change."

"Change how?"

He shrugged. "What if you started seeing someone who isn't cool with you having a dude for a best friend? And even if he was, we probably wouldn't hang out nearly as much. You'd never crash here. You'd just be...things would be different." He took another sip of his cider, trying to chase away the burning feeling in his throat.

Her expression softened. "Theo, me starting to date someone wouldn't change our friendship."

"No? What about when you dated Andrew? I barely saw you for the entire eleven months you guys were together. And then there was Robbie, that was a six-month disappearance. And let's not forget the entire year you were with Tyler. When you're in a serious relationship, it does change things. Past behavior predicts future behavior." The words all came out in a rush.

"Okay, okay. Maybe I've lost myself a little in the past, and I'm sorry if I made you feel abandoned. That was never my intention, and when I start seeing someone again, I'll try to do better with that. But, um, you know, my goal isn't to stay single forever. Remember, the whole scared to die alone thing?"

"I know. I know. And I want you to be happy. I just...I wasn't ready to face it yet, so I, yeah, I picked someone shitty for your date."

"Boy, did you."

"That bad?"

She took a sip of her drink and grabbed the throw blanket slung over the back of the couch, arranging it around herself. The fact that she was settling in was a good sign that she wasn't pissed at him anymore. Or, at least, not super pissed.

"Let me see. We met at a coffee bar where he proceeded to tell me that my name was boring and he was going to call me Lola, basically asked me if I was up for a threesome, said I might be a stalker, implied he'd get to find out if the carpet matches the drapes, oh, and he answered his phone and said he wasn't busy. All within the first ten minutes."

"Holy shit. I knew the guy was a tool, but I didn't think he'd be such a fucking douche. I'm so sorry, Lo."

"Oh, it gets better. So we went to dinner after at this Italian place. Because, you know, I'm a nice person and I want people to think I'm nice, so I didn't just ditch him after that even though I totally should've. I took a piece of bread from the breadbasket and he made a dig about laying off carbs, then hit on the waitress in front of me."

"Wow. Just...wow. I don't even know what to say." But he couldn't stop the chuckle from erupting, even though he tried to stifle it with a sip of cider.

"But wait, there's more!" she said, doing her best infomercial voice-over impression. "When the bill came, he slid it my way, saying some bullshit about feminism and equality. So I paid and I was ready to leave—"

"You actually paid?"

"I did. You owe me a hundred and ten bucks."

"I'll Venmo it to you right now." It was the least he could do after deliberately setting her up with Giovanni. He pulled out his phone to send her the money.

"Thank you. Anyway, he insisted on walking me to the subway—like, the only nice thing he did all night—and a cab drove by and splashed him a little. Theo, this guy lost it. He ended up getting into an argument with the cabbie. They were yelling at each other on the corner of Canal and Broadway, and I just headed for the subway, ready to be done with him."

He let out a laugh, then pressed his fist against his mouth, trying to stifle it. "I'm sorry. It's definitely not funny."

She smirked at him, the corner of her mouth twisting up. "No, it's definitely not funny."

"He called you Lola." Theo snickered, trying to hold back his laughter. Trying and on the verge of failing.

"He asked me if I was into women!" She giggled, just a little.

"He thought you'd be so into him that you'd turn into a stalker." He chuckled, pressing his lips together.

Lauren's eyes met his, and she bit her lip. She was able to hold back for about a second and a half before the laughter came spilling out of her, melodic and light. "I can't believe you set me up with that guy!" she said, laughing into her hands, her shoulders shaking. "I should be so mad at you."

He glanced at her, giving her very deliberate puppy dog eyes. "But you're not?"

The rest of her laughter died out and her shoulders slumped as she shook her head. "No. I was pissed, but I'm not anymore. I...I get it." Relief rushed through him. Relief and something else, something he wasn't quite sure what to do with. She twisted her fingers together, looking down at her lap. "I mean, I'm not sure how I'd feel if you started dating someone. It's been a while since you've had a girlfriend, and things..." She bit her lip and shook her head, as though struggling to physically contain whatever it was she was going to say. "Anyway, I get it."

He leaned back, his arm sprawled over the back of the couch. The tightness in his chest had eased with their laughter and he felt like they were back on an even keel. "So does that mean I'm off the hook?"

Her eyebrows rose so high they almost reached her hairline. "Oh, *hell* no. I'm setting you up, and you are *so* going."

He took a sip of his cider, dread settling in the pit of his stomach. "That's what I was afraid of."

Theo opened the glass door of the Integrity Souls meditation center and stepped inside, already plotting all of the ways he was going to get revenge on Lauren. He wasn't going to buy her a chai latte for a month, for starters. He'd come up with other methods of payback, too. Even though he knew he should just accept this date and whatever was about to happen as punishment for making her endure an evening with Giovanni, he was still feeling prickly about it.

"Theo?" A petite blonde woman with the left side of her head shaved approached him, her hands clasped together in prayer at her heart. "Are you Theo?"

He nodded and forced himself to smile. "Yeah. You must be Bliss."

Lauren had set him up with Aspen's younger sister. Honestly, it was a pretty great move on her part if she wanted to make him miserable because she knew he couldn't stand any of this crunchy spiritual shit. She'd swung and knocked one out of the park when it came to payback.

He held out his hand for a handshake, but she bowed, keeping her hands pressed together. "Namaste."

He didn't bow, just let his hand drop to his side. "Uh, yeah. Namaste, I guess."

"Okay, everyone, grab your partner and find a comfortable spot," said a woman from the front of the room. She was dressed in a long caftan embroidered with colorful beads and a pair of leopard print leggings. Her feet were bare, and Theo noticed that each toenail was painted a different color.

Bliss had suggested meeting here for a class of some kind, and Theo had agreed, thinking a class sounded harmless enough. They'd sit through it, maybe get a coffee after, and done, date over. They probably wouldn't even have to talk that much, depending on what type of class it was.

Bliss took his hand and led him across the hardwood floor to a corner of the small room. Pillows and yoga mats were scattered everywhere, and a floor-to-ceiling mirror covered the wall at the teacher's back, reflecting the small space back on itself.

"This will be such a great way to get to know each other," she said easily, sitting down on one of the mats. She gestured for Theo to sit down across from her. He thought he'd dressed casually, but now he felt out of place in his light gray sweater, jeans, and brown boots. Everyone else was in yoga gear and bare feet.

"Uh...should I take my boots off?"

"If you wish," said Bliss with a little shrug. "However you're comfortable." He shrugged and unlaced them, slipping them off and setting them to the side of his mat.

From the front of the class, the teacher rang a bell. "Everyone, please take a seat," she said, zeroing in on Theo, who was the only one still standing. Awkwardly, he sank to the ground, sitting facing Bliss. The teacher dimmed the studio's lights and turned on some gentle, pulsing music.

"Welcome to Tantric Couples' Meditation for Beginners," she said in a soothing voice as something that felt a hell of a lot like panic shot through Theo. Tantric? Wasn't that, like, sexual? "Today, I'm going to guide you through the basics of the art of Tantra to help you better connect with your partner." The panic intensified, feeling like fire ants crawling up and down his spine. He didn't want to connect with Bliss. Not because there was something wrong with her. He didn't think there was, although he'd only just met her five minutes ago. They didn't seem to have much in common, but that wasn't what had him on the verge of a minor freak out.

No, that was entirely related to the fact that she wasn't Lauren.

"Please make sure your phones are turned off," she continued. "We don't want any distractions during our journey this evening. Now, to begin, face your partner and find a comfortable seated position. We're going to begin with some synchronized breathing. Keeping still and without touching—don't worry, there'll be plenty of that later on—look each other in the eye and focus on your breath."

Not wanting to be a jerk, Theo settled himself, met Bliss's eyes, and started to breathe. It was just a meditation class. He could get through this. He could endure this as his penance for setting Lauren up with Giovanni.

"Good. After a moment, your breathing should start to naturally synchronize. Don't force anything, simply relax into the breath while maintaining eye contact."

Holding her gaze, he continued to breathe. He was surprised at how nice it felt, and he started to actually relax for the first time in a while. He held Bliss's gaze, but even though he as looking at her, he was imagining Lauren's green eyes. The eyes he wished he were staring into right now, not only because they were beautiful, but because they were eyes who saw him as he was and made him feel safe and accepted and cared for, no matter what. Even when he did douchey things, like set her up with an asshole because he couldn't get his head sorted out.

An image flashed vividly across his mind: Lauren naked, spread out on his bed, staring up at him with those gorgeous green eyes as he moved inside her. He could almost feel it—her hard nipples against his chest, her fingers in his hair, her legs around his thrusting hips. Soft moans and strangled cries filling his ears as her wet heat engulfed him, pulling him deeper inside, finally, finally...Blood rushed to his dick, making it strain against his jeans. He shifted subtly, trying to hide what was happening inside his pants.

God, he was the worst, wasn't he? He was here on a date with another woman—because he was too fucking chicken to be honest with the only woman he cared about—getting hard thinking about Lauren. Lauren who he wouldn't let himself date because he knew he'd screw it all up, and then he'd lose her. The thought of a Lauren-less life was a cold, dark one. He couldn't let that happen.

"Be as present as you can with your partner," said the teacher, ripping Theo back to the classroom and out of his thoughts. "If your mind wanders off, gently guide your attention back to the breath and your partner's eyes. Relax. Let it come naturally."

Right now, with all of his warring thoughts about Lauren swirling through his mind, relaxed was pretty damn far from how Theo felt. But he forced himself to stay still and do his best to be in the moment.

Just then, a thought occurred to him. Had Lauren set him up with Bliss as a punishment, or had she done it for the same reasons he'd set her up with Giovanni?

Whoa.

What if...?

His insides felt like he'd been struck with lightning, all hot and glowing and fully charged with energy.

"Tantra is all about being conscious and loving with your partner in the present moment," said the teacher, once again interrupting his train of thought. "Now that we've connected mentally, we're going to spend the next five minutes connecting verbally with our partners. Share what's on your minds, remembering that this is a judgement free zone. Be fearless! Listen attentively and share boldly."

Theo shot Bliss a hesitant smile. "Would you like to go first?"

She tipped her head to one side. "Sure. I'll tell you a bit about myself, and then you can do the same. I'm a Pisces and I own my own shop here in Chelsea. It's called Earth's

Garden, and we sell all kinds of things, from crystals and tarot cards to books and incense. I started it about three years ago and we're doing well." She tapped her finger on her lips. "What else? I'm single, obviously, and I grew up in a spiritual community with my sister and our parents. I'm looking for someone open-minded, loving, caring and in touch with his spiritual side. My dream is to open more stores under the Earth's Garden umbrella. I'd also like to travel more. Last year, I went on a tour of Irish forests led by druids. I'm a raw vegan and living as natural a lifestyle as possible is very important to me." She let out a little giggle. "I sound like I'm writing an online dating profile! Oh! And I have a Scottish Fold cat named Gaia. Okay, I've talked enough. Tell me about you."

He cleared his throat. "Uh, well...my birthday is January 31st, so I think that makes me an Aquarius," he said, flashing her a smile, "and I'm also a family law attorney. I've been practicing for about five years now. Um..." He trailed off, trying to think of something else to say. "I'm also single, obviously, and Lauren—Aspen's roommate—and I have been friends for like ten years now. I have three brothers and a sister who I'm close with, but I don't really get along that well with my parents."

"And what are you looking for in a partner?"

He hesitated. "Uh, well...I don't really date much, to be honest, so I guess I haven't given it much thought."

"Why don't you date much?"

It was a simple enough question, but not one he felt like unpacking here and now with someone who was practically a stranger. "Uh, just busy, I guess."

She narrowed her eyes slightly, as though she didn't believe him, but the teacher began talking again. "We're now going to move into a new meditation position. Everyone, please stand."

Reluctantly, Theo pushed to his feet. Thankfully, the conversation had killed his hard-on. More and more, this whole date was just feeling like a bad idea. Like he was doing something wrong by being out with another woman.

"Make eye contact with your partner," continued the teacher. "And then step closer together." He took the smallest possible step forward. A prickling sense of discomfort crept along his skin. "Place your right hand on your hearts." He did, feeling the soft thump of his heart against his palm. The skin there tingled, vibrating with how badly he wished the woman standing in front of him were Lauren. How badly he wanted to reach out and touch her heart. Feel its beat underneath his palm. "Now we're going to perform something called the tantric cosmic handshake. Take your left hand and place it over the penis or vagina of your partner."

"Whoa," he said, raising his hands in front of him, immediately stepping back, although he was relieved to note that Bliss hadn't reached for him. "Yeah, that's not happening."

Bliss pressed her fingers to her lips, letting out a little giggle. "I didn't realize it was going to get so intimate so quickly. Do you want to go?"

He reached down and picked up one of his boots, shoving his foot in it, having to hop in place to keep his balance. "Definitely. No offense. I just...we just met, and..." He didn't know why he felt the need to explain himself. After all, she was the one who'd chosen the class as their date. With one boot on, he grabbed for the other one, jamming his foot into it. His balance wavered and he hopped to the right, trying to steady himself. He'd almost steadied himself when he hopped sideways just a little too far and crashed into the large gong in the corner of the classroom, a loud clashing sound erupting from it. He managed to right both it and himself before any major harm was done. Every single set of eyeballs in the room was glued to him, most of them glaring with impatience.

"C'mon," Bliss said, heading for the door. Around them, couples stood with their hands on each other's' fun bits, frozen like awkward, erotic statues. Once they were out on the sidewalk, he released the breath he'd been holding. His skin still prickled, the humiliation at crashing into that stupid fucking gong still fresh. He pushed a hand through his hair, relieved to be outside. "My store's just around the corner," she said, apparently completely unfazed by the class or Theo's awkward display. "Want to check it out?"

"Uh, sure," he said, glancing back at the meditation center, wondering what the hell else was going to happen in there tonight. He shuddered to even think about it. His fingers itched to pull his phone out of his pocket so he could call Lauren and tell her all about it. And he would, but later. He'd already been enough of an ass tonight. The least he could do was keep his phone in his pocket and not pull a Giovanni.

Bliss's store was on West 25th, one of many little shops in a row. She fished a set of keys out of her enormous mesh bag and then pushed the door open, a set of chimes tinkling overhead. The store was dark, having closed for the day at 6 pm, and it smelled of cinnamon and incense. The inside was small but every single possible space was used, displaying shelves of candles, oils, and incense. Another row of shelves held loose leaf tea and mugs, and another at the back was lined with books. Theo's eyes roamed over the displays of crystals, tarot cards, dried herbs, Native American dreamcatchers, and little fairy statues.

"This is really impressive," he said, stepping further into the store. She flicked on a lamp behind the glass counter lining the far wall.

"Thank you," she said with a little shrug. "I love helping other people connect to the spiritual world. In fact..." She leveled her gaze at him. "Would you let me read your cards?"

Theo frowned. "Um, I don't think..."

"Oh, come on. It'll be fun. Let me do a reading, and then you can go home."

Guilt gnawed at him, and he opened his mouth, but Bliss cut him off with a raised hand and a smile. "We're clearly not a match of any kind, Theo. It's okay. I'm not into you, either. Like, at all."

He felt both relieved and mildly offended. "Oh."

"Let me read your cards. I have a feeling that you're working through something right now, and the cards might be able to provide some guidance."

He shrugged. "What the hell. Sure."

"Go select a deck that speaks to you," she said, pointing in the direction of a shelf lined with decks of various designs. He strode over to the shelf, feeling like a complete idiot, and glanced at the rows of cards. There were decks that featured sea creatures, fairies, the planets, angels, flowers, and cats. He ended up selecting a fairly simple one with medieval style illustrations. Bliss nodded her approval when he handed it over to her. "A classic Rider-Waite deck. Very nice." She took the cards out of the box and started shuffling them with her eyes closed. Then, with precise, deliberate movements, she laid the cards out in an intricate spread. She flipped the first card over.

"This card represents your current situation. This is the six of cups, and it's reversed. That means that you're living in the past. You're holding yourself hostage to what was instead of opening yourself up to what could be." She flipped over the next card. "This next card is your action or task card. The nine of wands. Interesting."

Theo found himself leaning forward, peering at the cards, interested despite the fact that he knew this was all baloney. "What does that mean?"

"The nine of wands shows an injured man, clutching a wand. He's hurt. Weary and tired. He's endured battle and survived, but there are scars. To find what you truly seek, this wound must be overcome. You have to find a way to heal in order to attain your heart's desire." Bliss didn't say anything more, just moved to the next card. "This will show us your strengths. The nine of pentacles." She glanced up at him. "You're very self-sufficient. You're financially comfortable and lack nothing. You have a strong work ethic. You're not scared to hustle or put your nose to the grindstone. So let's see how that will help you with this upcoming challenge..." She flipped the next card. "The High Priestess, reversed." She frowned, peering at the card. "Your challenge is that you're disconnected from your heart's desire. You're keeping a secret, and it's eating you alive, Theo. In this particular case, I think your strength might be a weakness, because you won't let anyone else in." She shook her head, almost looking sad. "The final card will show us your ideal outcome."

He held his breath as she flipped the card. His heart pounded in his chest, and he couldn't believe how invested he was in this silly game. But right here, right now, it didn't feel silly. Not with the way each and every card was hitting home.

She flipped the card and Bliss smiled. "I had a feeling this is what we'd be seeing. The Lovers."

"What does it mean?"

"Your ideal outcome is love. Romantic love. Choosing love." She trailed her fingers over the exposed cards. "You live in the past. You have scars because of things that have happened, and you let those scars define you. You work hard and feel that that should be enough to make you happy, but it's not. You know there's something missing from your life. Something you're scared to admit you want because of those past wounds." She looked up and laid a hand over his. "You have to dig deep, find your courage, and choose love in order to be happy. Truly, fully happy." She tilted her head and studied him.

He pulled his hand away, feeling raw and exposed. Shoving his hands in his pockets, he paced away from the counter and the cards that couldn't possibly have shown her all of that.

"I hope I've given you something to think about," Bliss said simply, beginning to gather up the cards and carefully put them back in the box.

"Thanks so much for the reading, and I'm sorry the class didn't work out," he said, heading for the door. "It was nice to meet you."

"Your heart is bigger than your fear!" she called out, her voice mingling with the chimes as he pushed his way out the door.

The evening air was brisk, October now gripping Manhattan in its chilly arms. But even though it was cold and he was over twenty blocks from home, Theo started to walk, needing to burn off the restless energy zapping through him.

The cards didn't mean anything. They were totally random and open to interpretation. It was just a game. A silly, stupid game that wasn't real. It couldn't be real, because if it was, it meant that he really was in love with Lauren. It meant the thing he'd been struggling against for a while now was real.

"Fuck," he whispered, ducking his head against the wind and walking faster, shouldering his way between people on the busy sidewalk at the corner of 8th Ave and 27th. He had to fix this. He had to find a way to get rid of these feelings for Lauren. Because if he loved her, and he told her, and she didn't feel the same, then things would forever be changed between them.

Even scarier was the thought that he'd tell her and she *would* feel the same. Then they'd start dating and he'd eventually freak out and screw it up and lose his best friend in the process.

Neither of those were good options, which left him with figuring out how not to love her.

And he didn't know. He just didn't fucking know.

---

8

*L*auren stood in the middle of Theo's living room. Bright, autumn sunshine streamed in through the windows, making everything look as though it were glowing. Dust motes floated in the air, swirling gently. Theo stood only a few feet away from her, studying her intently, a crooked smile on his face.

"Tell me what you want," he said, his voice low, almost raw. He rubbed a hand over his mouth, his thumb lingering on his lips as his eyes devoured her.

She took a step toward him, closing the distance between them and took one of his hands—so big, so strong, so perfect—and placed it just above the apex of her thighs. Then she arched up on to her tiptoes and whispered in his ear.

"I want you inside me."

He made a strangled sound, almost like a growl, and then filled his palms with her ass and lifted her. Suddenly, they were in his bedroom, on his bed, Theo coming down on top of her. He lifted himself up onto his elbows and traced her lips with his thumb, groaning when she flicked her tongue out to tease him.

"Don't you want me to kiss you first?" he asked, fixated on her mouth.

"I want whatever you'll give me, Theo. However you'll give it to me."

"Christ," he whispered, then dipped his head and captured her mouth in a deep, slow kiss. Time felt like it was slipping away and jumping forward at the same time. Where had her shirt gone? She'd had it on just a minute ago, but now she was in her bra and Theo's hands were on her breasts, toying with her hard nipples through the thin fabric. She wrapped her legs around his waist, grinding against him, throbbing for him. Wanting this—whatever this was—so badly it hurt. She'd never ached for someone before, but now it was the only thing she could feel, this ache. This wanting and needing that was never satisfied, never enough.

He pushed her bra aside and took one of her nipples into his mouth, sending her back bowing off of the bed, and—

Wake me up! Before you go-go...

Lauren groaned and pressed her face into her pillow as her phone's alarm started going off. Her entire core felt like it was melting, and she shifted her hips restlessly against the mattress. That was the third sex dream about Theo this week. She'd always had the occasional one about him, but now they were coming fast and furious as her attraction and feelings— and subsequent frustrations—grew. Because he was who he was. She had to keep reminding herself of that to try to stop herself from sinking deeper into her feelings for her.

But first, she'd let herself linger in her fantasy just a little bit longer. She rolled over, pulled her nightstand drawer open and dug her hand around inside. Curling her fingers around the familiar soft silicone of her vibrator, she flipped onto her back and turned it on, hoping her duvet was thick enough to muffle the buzzing sound. Not that Aspen would care. But still. Lauren cared.

She closed her eyes and slipped back into the dream, letting dirty images of Theo fill her mind. His hands on her breasts. His mouth on her nipples. His fingers inside her, this thumb on her clit. His face buried between her legs. His cock in her mouth, his hips jerking as she sucked him. Theo inside her, moving and moaning, her nails raking down his back as he fucked her into oblivion.

Her hips jerked off of the mattress as she worked herself into a frenzy with the vibrator, dialing up the speed. "Yes, yes, yes, oh fuck, *Theo*," she panted, totally caught up in her fantasy.

Several minutes later, when she was flushed and shaking and a tiny bit of sweat had gathered between her breasts, she was ready to face her day, which was going to include the man she'd just made herself come fantasizing about. She pushed back the covers, still gripping her vibrator. But it looked...weird. She didn't have her contacts in, so she reached for her glasses.

Oh God. She'd broken her vibrator. The rabbit portion of it was dangling from the body, looking sad and limp.

"Son of a bitch," she whispered as she studied it, half mad, half impressed with herself. She'd used it so much that she'd literally worn it out. Then, because her brain was the *worst*, she wondered if the real Theo had better stamina. "I am officially the most pathetic woman in all of Manhattan," she said, grumbling to herself as she pushed herself up out of bed. She tossed the broken vibrator into the trash by her bedroom door and then headed for the shower. She was meeting Theo, Willa, Kayla, Brandon, Dori and Theo's brother Sebastian for brunch in an hour and a half.

By the time she made it to Gallery Lounge, their usual brunch spot on West 47th, she was only ten minutes late, partly because she'd spent fifteen minutes shopping online and ordering a new—and hopefully sturdier—vibrator. Given the increasing frequency of her sex dreams about Theo, she had a feeling she'd need it.

"There she is!" called out Brandon, waving her over to their table. Lauren loved coming here; it was absolutely beautiful. The ceiling was made of glass and swagged with sheer white fabric, giving the entire space an airy feel. The furniture was made of wicker and rattan, all done in subtle shades of cream and gray. Leafy green plants and macrame-style pendant lights completed the décor, making it feel both bright and cozy. As they were every other Sunday, her friends were ensconced at a table in the back left corner. She waved and then sank down into an empty seat between Theo and Kayla. He was wearing a plain light gray T-shirt and a pair of dark green pants that hugged his muscular thighs. Her eyes lingered on the brown belt at his waist, and her mind ever so helpfully supplied the image of that belt hanging open as he slowly undid the zipper of his pants, and...

"Hello? Earth to Lauren? Are you lost in space?" asked Dori from a couple of seats down. When Lauren frowned, Dori pointed at the server standing just over Lauren's shoulder, coffee pot in hand.

"You want some coffee?" she asked in a bored tone.

"Yes, please," said Lauren, fumbling to turn over her plain white mug, currently sitting upside down on its matching saucer. She almost sent it flying but managed to right it at the last second.

Theo leaned in close, bringing his mouthwatering scent with him. "You okay?" he asked. "You seem a little on edge this morning."

She nodded, stirring milk and sugar into her coffee with such vigor that she sloshed some over the sides. "Yeah, I'm good. Everything's fine."

"Okay. You know if something's up, you can talk to me, right?"

She nodded again. Of course she knew that. And of course she couldn't tell him what was going through her mind almost non-stop lately. Of course of course of course. She noticed there was still another empty chair at the table and was about to say something when Theo's hand landed on her knee beneath the table. Everything inside her went very, very still as warmth radiated outward from where he touched her. He glanced over at her, shooting her a quick smile that was equal parts adorable and sexy as hell. His thumb traced a lazy circle over her kneecap, sending butterflies erupting in her stomach. It wasn't unusual for Theo to touch her, but something about this felt...different. New. Definitely sexier. She bit her lip and sat back a little in her chair. His big hand splayed outward, his fingers covering the territory from her knee to halfway up her inner thigh. Her skin felt like it was going to burn through her jeans. A pulse had started up in her clit, an insistent throbbing she had to fight to ignore. The urge to move her hips was almost too strong. As conversation from their table swirled around her, she glanced over at him. Her stomach bottomed out at the raw heat shining out at her from Theo's gorgeous blue eyes. She'd never seen him look at her like that before.

It was hot. It was really hot, and not helping her mission

to move on from her crush on him one iota. She inhaled a shaky breath, curling her fingers into her palms.

"I thought Sebastian was coming, too," she said, her voice coming out with an awkward squeak. Theo's hand stayed exactly where it was, his fingers moving ever so slowly back and forth, tormenting her beneath the tablecloth where no one else could see.

"Yeah, I don't think so," he said, taking a sip of his coffee, sounding completely casual. Completely relaxed. As though he touched her like this all the time. As though his fingers weren't mere inches away from where she ached for him. "He's still at my place, sleeping off last night's shenanigans."

Lauren saw Kayla's jaw clench. "*What*? What shenanigans?"

Theo hesitated. "Uh...I think he was out with friends." He scratched at his cheek, which Lauren knew was a sure sign he'd just spilled the beans on something he shouldn't have.

Kayla frowned, her expression murderous. "He was supposed to be working, helping our team put the final touches on the Life Science Inc. pitch. He said there was a family emergency. Figures. Fucking Bastian."

Theo's eyes widened. "Oh. Uh, whoops," he said, rubbing his free hand over the back of his neck.

Just then, the waitress returned to take their order, saving Theo from any further grilling from Kayla.

"Lauren, you never told us how your audition went," said Brandon, thankfully steering the conversation into less tense waters once the waitress had left. "For Lynne Townsend?"

Despite the thrill of having Theo's hand on her thigh, a heaviness settled over her limbs. "Oh, yeah. The audition went fine, but they ended up going with someone with a 'younger vibe,'" she said, making air quotes around the word and wrinkling her nose. She knew that the industry was competitive and that the odds of landing the job had been slim to start with, but the rejection still stung, especially given that the rejection had nothing to do with her music and everything to do with her age. She could control the quality of her performances, but her age? Not so much.

"What?" Theo asked, his strong fingers tightening on her thigh in a way that made her want to whimper, but in a good way. A very good way.

She shrugged, leaning forward to reach for her coffee and taking a sip. "That's the industry. They're looking for a nineteen-year-old, not someone who's almost thirty." Even as she tried to rationalize it and not take it personally, it still hurt. A lot. "Guess I'm just going to work at the library forever."

"Yay?" said Dori tentatively. "You're my work wife. You can't leave."

She shot Dori a smile. "Don't worry, it doesn't look like I'm going anywhere anytime soon." Although she was smiling, disappointment curled through her, so profound that she actually felt like she was sinking.

Clearly, everything she was doing here and now to chase her dream and make it a reality—playing local gigs, auditioning for bigger gigs, circulating demos, putting her stuff online—wasn't working. What was that saying about insanity? Doing the same thing over and over again and expecting different results? Maybe it was time to change her approach. She wasn't willing to give up on her dream, but she also didn't know what to do differently.

Once they'd ordered their food, Willa clasped her hands together and turned her attention to Theo and Lauren. "So? How'd your dates go? Any love connections?"

His fingers curled into her thigh again, giving her that melty rush she couldn't get enough of. He was probably just trying to be friendly, reassuring, comforting. He'd probably be embarrassed as hell if he had any idea how much this was turning her on.

Get. A. Grip.

She glanced over at Theo and saw the humor dancing in his eyes. At the same time, they both started to laugh.

"Is this good laughter, or bad laughter?" asked Willa, her lips pursed.

"You wanna go first?" asked Theo, holding his hand out in an "after you" gesture.

"Theo set me up with his co-worker Giovanni," started Lauren, wondering just how much to share with the group.

"Oooh, sounds sexy," said Kayla, stirring a bit more milk into her coffee.

"Agreed," said Brandon. "Details, please."

Lauren smiled. "He was good looking, yeah. He was also a colossal douche. He checked out another woman in front of me, asked me if I was bisexual, told me I should change my name to Lola, and made me pay for dinner. I'm sure there's more, but I've blocked it out at this point." She pretended to shudder.

"Theo! Why would you set her up with a total loser?" asked Willa, reaching across the table and throwing a sugar packet at him.

He shrugged, looking chagrined as he swatted the packet away. "I have bad taste in men?"

"Ugh," grunted Willa, rolling her eyes. "And how was your date?"

He jerked his thumb in Lauren's direction. "She set me up with Bliss, Aspen's sister, mostly as payback for Giovanni, I think. We, um, we went to a tantric meditation class and when I wasn't down with a stranger grabbing my junk in a room full of other strangers, we bailed. She did read my tarot cards though, which I have to admit, was kinda cool."

"What did your cards say?" asked Dori, leaning forward on her elbows. "Anything interesting?"

Suddenly, he took his hand away from Lauren's thigh, leaving cool air swirling over her as the heat of his touch dissipated. The melty feeling inside her dissipated, too.

"Nothing interesting. You know, just New Age mumbo jumbo." She glanced at him, pressing her lips into a thin line. He had liar face. She could always tell when he was lying because he had this funny way of holding his mouth when he did, like he was trying not to smile but also trying not to frown. Why didn't he want to share what Bliss's reading had said?

Two servers arrived at their table with trays covered in plates. Silence settled over the group as everyone dug in to their food. But the silence was short lived because Willa had never been one to let something go.

She speared a piece of melon onto the end of her fork, shaking her head sadly. "How is it that two people who know each other so well chose so poorly for each other? I don't get it."

"Hey, I told you that I'm not really looking for a relationship," said Theo a little defensively.

"And like he said, he has bad taste in men," said Lauren, ready to let the subject go. But Willa clearly had other plans. She set her fork down and reached for the bottle of sriracha, squirting more onto her eggs.

"Okay, so then let *me* set you up. A blind double date. What do you say?" Before Theo could open his mouth to argue, Willa pointed her fork at him. "You did say you wanted to help Lauren find someone. And maybe if you started dating someone, you both could detach just a little from this co-dependent relationship."

"We are *not* co-dependent," said Lauren, picking up a piece of bacon and taking a healthy bite.

Willa rolled her eyes. "Please. You are and it's only gotten worse since you've both been single for the past while. You consult each other about every tiny decision, you practically live at Theo's on weekends, you text or phone almost constantly...you just seem to arrange your lives around each other, and if you were in a romantic relationship that would be one thing, but you're not, so it's maybe time to seek a little independence before you basically become half of the *Golden Girls*."

Lauren smirked at Theo. "You'd make a good Dorothy."

"I don't know, you always struck me as more of a Commander Riker from *Star Trek: The Next Generation*," said Dori. "You know, manly and smart, hardworking and loyal. Do you play the saxophone?"

"I think he's more like Johnny Rose from *Schitt's Creek*," said Brandon. "You've got money, you dress well, you love the city, and you kind of have a teeny-weeny stick up your ass about schedules and plans and being organized."

Theo leaned forward, a wide-mouthed smile on his face. "What? I do not. Lo, tell them I do not have a stick up my ass."

"I'm not getting involved in this. I don't want to reinforce the idea that we're co-dependent," she said, sticking her tongue out at Willa. "I like this game. Do me! What TV character am I?"

"You're Pam from *The Office*," said Dori. "Like, hands

down. You're creative and love anything artsy, you're a sweetheart and you're a good friend."

Kayla tipped her head. "I don't know. Sticking with Dori's *Star Trek* theme, I think you're more like Deanna Troi. You're very perceptive, but like Dori said, you're also kind and loyal."

"No, no. You're both wrong. Lauren is Dorothy from *The Wizard of Oz*," said Brandon. "Hear me out. You're a girly girl, you're musical, you're kind and...don't hate me, okay, but you kind of have this wide-eyed innocence. It's very charming."

"I'm not that innocent," she said, taking another bite of her bacon.

"Okay, Britney, whatever you say," said Brandon with a shrug.

Before Lauren could defend herself, Willa jumped back in. "So, yes? I'm setting you up on a blind double date? I know some pretty great people who just happen to be single."

"Well, I—" started Lauren, as Theo said at the same time, "I don't think—"

But Willa clapped her hands once, a huge smile on her face. "Awesome. It's settled. I'm going to find the *perfect* matches for you both."

9

*T*he following weekend, Theo held the door for Lauren as they stepped inside the swanky Italian restaurant in Midtown. After their two disastrous blind dates, Theo had insisted on picking the location this time. One tantric meditation class was already one too many, as far as he was concerned. He'd been dreading this night all week. He didn't want to play this game anymore. Granted, he wasn't any closer to figuring out what it was he actually wanted, either.

Wait, no. That wasn't true. He pretty much knew what he wanted. The part he was having trouble with was making peace with the fact that he couldn't have it. Not if he cared about Lauren—which he did, obviously—and not if he wanted to protect her from getting hurt—which, again, he did. Obviously. And it wasn't as though she harbored any kind of latent feelings for him. If she did, wouldn't she have brought up their almost kiss again? Flirted with him? Made some kind of move? Said something about the fact that he'd had his hand halfway up her thigh at brunch? He'd done it to try to get some kind of reaction from her, some tiny clue that maybe, just maybe...but, no. And it wouldn't have mattered anyway. He'd just used that thinking as an excuse to touch her. To pretend he had some kind of claim on her.

Then again, she knew his feelings about relationships, so maybe she wouldn't say anything, and she had set him up on that disaster of a date with Bliss, so...

"I can hear you thinking," she whispered in his ear, tugging him inside the restaurant. "I know you're not interested in meeting anyone, but I am, so come on." She gave another less-than-subtle tug on his coat and dragged him toward the maître d' stand. She shrugged out of her own black coat, revealing a skintight navy blue dress with the thinnest straps he'd ever seen. It dipped low in the front and even lower in the back, showcasing her smooth pale skin dotted with freckles. He sucked in a sharp breath, her cinnamon-vanilla scent hitting him, hard. He licked his lips and clenched his fists in his pockets, trying to get a grip on himself.

"Right this way," said the maître d', leading them into the main dining area. "The other two members of your party are already here."

He let Lauren walk ahead of him, which gave him ample opportunity to stare at her ass in that tight dress. She had what he was willing to bet was the world's cutest ass. Round and tight with just the right amount of jiggle. His palms tingled as he imagined filling them with it, squeezing, pulling her closer before he—

"Here we are," said the maître d', pulling out Lauren's chair for her. "Enjoy your meal."

"Hi," smiled a guy Theo had to admit was handsome from the other side of the table. "I'm Eli. You must be Lauren? And Theo?" He had blond hair, a movie star smile, and dimples. Crap. Lauren was a sucker for dimples.

"Nice to meet you," Theo said, shaking Eli's hand. "I'm Theo," he said, introducing himself to his own date. She was stunning, too. Long, dark brown hair fell to her slender waist. She had brown eyes framed with thick lashes, high cheekbones and a wide mouth, all paired with the body of a fitness model.

"Jenna," she said, shaking his hand and smiling warmly. "Nice to meet you, too."

"So, how do you two know Willa?" asked Lauren, settling back in her seat, her eyes locked on Eli.

"I'm her veterinarian. Or, I guess I should say, her cat's veterinarian. I'm pretty sure Willa doesn't need any flea and tick medication." Lauren laughed, just a little too loudly, which Theo knew meant she liked Eli.

Which meant that Theo instantly disliked him.

"And I know Willa through work," said his date, drawing his attention back to her. "I work in finance, and we both used to work at a big tech company. But she's working at your brother's company now, right?" she asked, pointing at Theo.

He nodded. "Yeah, she just started. So you work in finance? What do you do, exactly?"

The conversation went on from there as they all exchanged details about their jobs, where they'd gone to school, favorite parts of the city. Boring getting-to-know-you stuff that Theo was having a hard time paying attention to because even though his eyes were on Jenna, the rest of him was keenly aware of Lauren. The way she was leaning forward on the table, making her cleavage even sexier. The way she was hanging on Eli's every word, smiling and laughing and flirting. The way Eli seemed just as into her if his body language was any indication.

"So, Eli, I have to ask," said Lauren, tracing the tip of her finger around the rim of her half-empty wine glass, "how are you single? I don't mean to sound rude, but, like...how?" She gestured at him. "You're like the total package."

He grinned, flashing those dimples again. "I'm glad you think so. And to answer your question, I'm not sure. I guess maybe I just haven't met the right person yet." He reached across the table and gave Lauren's hand a squeeze.

"Or maybe it's because you smell like cat pee," muttered Theo under his breath before taking a healthy sip of his wine.

Eli turned to him, still smiling. "What was that?"

"Nothing, just thinking out loud."

Jenna turned her attention to Theo. "I guess I could ask you the same question. I mean, like Lauren said about Eli, you seem like the total package. How are you single?"

Lauren snickered into her wine glass.

"Something to say?" he asked lightly.

She pressed her lips together and shook her head. "No, no. As your closest friend for the past decade, I definitely don't have any insight into why you might be single." She glanced at Jenna. "But, you're right, he's the total package. As long as you're cool with that package including a paralyzing fear of commitment and a history of dysfunction."

Theo's eyebrows slammed down. "Hey. Hang on a second."

Lauren shrugged. "Just thought Jenna might want to know the truth."

Eli and Jenna glanced uncertainly at each other.

"And what about your truth, Lauren?"

"And what would that be?"

"That you're single because you have horrible taste in men."

"That's not true at all. I *want* to find someone to spend my life with, unlike you, and I realize that to do that, I have to put myself out there. Sure, that means I date some duds."

He scoffed. "Some? Try all. You could do so much better than the guys you date. How many men have given you flowers over the past few years?"

She tossed her napkin down on the table. "Just because I'm single doesn't mean there's something wrong with me."

"I'm not saying there's something wrong with you." Oh, God, what the hell was wrong with him? Why couldn't he stop talking?

"Then what are you saying?"

"I don't get it, Lo. You're beautiful and smart and talented and could have any man you wanted. So why are you single? I mean, if you're going to bring up my issues, maybe—"

"Screw you, Theo." She pushed up out of her chair and stalked toward the back of the restaurant.

"Shit." He pushed a hand through his hair and stood. He didn't even excuse himself or say a word to Eli and Jenna, who were watching everything with their mouths slightly agape, eyebrows raised. He felt bad for acting like an ass, but he felt worse for upsetting Lauren. It was totally outside of the norm for them to fight, but clearly tensions were high tonight.

God, he was such a fucking asshole, wasn't he? Projecting all of his issues and baggage and everything onto her. Making her feel like there was something wrong with her when there was something wrong with him.

He rounded the corner and spotted her leaning against the wall in the quiet hallway. She glanced up, her fiery hair swirling around her bare shoulders. Fuck, she was so beautiful. So beautiful it almost hurt to look at her.

"Lauren, I'm sorry," he said. "I shouldn't have said—"

"You're an idiot," she shot back, hurt flashing in her pretty green eyes. "You're such a goddamned idiot."

"I know. I know." He rubbed a hand over the back of his neck.

She let out a sad little chuckle. "No, Theo. That's just it. You don't know. You have no freaking clue."

He took a step closer, feeling as though he were going to vibrate out of his skin with how badly he wanted to reach out and touch her. "Then tell me."

She tilted her chin up, meeting his eyes. "I'm single because I want *you*, you dummy."

Electricity charged through his veins, her words lighting him up from the inside. "Fuck," he whispered. It was the only word he could think of that encapsulated everything going through his brain—the excitement, the relief, the fear, the knowledge that he was about to forever change things between them. He knew he should probably hit pause, take time to think it over and process what she'd just said, but he couldn't. Her words had shredded his restraint, completely and thoroughly.

His palm landed on the wall beside her head, his other hand sliding around her waist. "You want me?"

She bit her lip and looked up at him, her eyes practically molten with heat. "You have no idea how much."

The last of his control disappeared and he lowered his head, closing his mouth over hers. She gasped against his mouth, but then opened for him almost instantly, her hands moving restlessly up and down his chest, as though she wanted to touch him everywhere at once. Her sweet taste flooded him, obliterating everything else around him. The noise of the restaurant, the smell of the food, the hallway where they stood—it all disappeared, everything falling away as he kissed her, her soft lips moving against his hungrily, eagerly. He slid his tongue against hers, wanting more of her mouth, his blood hot to the point of scorching.

He lifted his hand from the wall and cupped her face, wanting her closer. Needing more of her. He tightened his arm around her waist, sealing her against him as he explored her mouth with his tongue. He'd imagined kissing her countless times, but now that he was actually kissing her, this woman that he'd wanted to kiss for the better part of ten years, he knew that his imagination was a piss poor substitute for the real thing.

The pace of the kiss grew frenzied, heat and urgency spreading between them. It was as though he'd opened the floodgates on his lust for her, for this woman who was only supposed to be a friend, and now that he'd opened them, he couldn't close them. He couldn't rein it all back in. It was too late.

She wove her hands into his hair, and while the pace of the kiss slowed, the intensity didn't. He took everything she was offering with long, hot sweeps of his tongue against hers, savoring the soft sounds she was making. God, he felt so fucking alive, kissing Lauren in this hallway. Like he'd been on life support and the only thing that had saved him was her mouth under his.

She broke the kiss, panting like she'd just run a marathon, but he wasn't done with her yet. Not by a longshot. He buried his face in her sweet smelling neck, nipping lightly at the juncture where her neck met her shoulder before kissing and sucking it better, soothing away his bite.

"Oh, God, Theo," she whispered, her hips moving against him. He sucked on a spot just below her ear and she made an undignified but totally sexy "unf" sound. Hooking his free hand under her thigh, he lifted her leg and wrapped it around his waist. She stilled as his hard, throbbing cock made contact with her pussy, only the fabric of her panties shielding her.

He tugged on her earlobe with his teeth, and then whispered, "I can feel how hot you are. If I touched you, my fingers would be soaked, wouldn't they?"

"Holy shit, Theo," she said on a shuddery sigh, her head thudding back against the wall. "I can feel your cock *right there* and this is supposed to be weird, isn't it? And it's not." She cupped his face, pulling him away from her neck. "Tell me this isn't weird for you."

He rocked his hips, dragging a soft moan out of her, and then trailed his knuckles down the front of her breast, teasing her nipple through the fabric. She made a sexy whimpering sound that had sparks flashing in his vision.

"This feels too good to be weird." And then he kissed her again, taking her mouth with long, deep sweeps of his tongue. "Come home with me," he said between kisses.

"So I can sleep in your guest room?" she asked with feigned innocence, her fingers toying with his belt buckle in a way that had him ready to rip her dress off and take her right there in the hallway.

"So I can spread you out naked on my bed and savor this. So I can spend the night inside you," he said, just before he crushed his mouth to hers again. In some distant part of his brain, he knew this was probably a really, really bad idea, but kissing her had slashed his brake lines. Stopping felt like an impossibility at this point. They'd gone from zero to sixty in less than ten minutes and it didn't feel anything but right. So fucking right.

Footsteps echoed, and they broke apart. A man headed for the men's room, and Theo carefully set her leg down and shielded her from view with his body, buying her a second to adjust her disheveled dress. The last thing he wanted was for some stranger to get a view of Lauren that he had no right to. Something fierce and protective gripped him, and he angled his shoulders in a way that kept her out of sight.

The intrusion had him coming back down to earth. Here and now was not the place for any of this, and they definitely need to talk about whatever *this* was.

Tomorrow. Once he'd made her come five or six times and could think straight again. It was hard to sort his thoughts out when all of the blood in his body was concentrated in his aching dick. In some distant, still-functioning part of his brain, he knew that falling into bed with Lauren was probably the wrong thing to do, but he was too far gone to care.

"Come on, let's get out of here," he said, taking her hand and tugging her away from the wall once the man had disappeared into the restroom.

She bit her lip, hesitation written all over her face. "Theo, what if this is a horrible idea? Like, a colossally bad, awful idea?" She stepped closer to him, running her free hand up his chest, tracing the contours of his pecs through his shirt. She let out a soft moan and then moved her hand higher, her fingertips scraping over his stubble, tracing over his lips. He nipped at her fingers as they passed, then teased one with his tongue. "Oh, God," she whispered, shaking her head. "Maybe we should stop."

He nodded slowly, trying to process her words. He cupped her face, tracing his thumb across her cheekbone. "Do you want to stop?"

She closed her eyes and inhaled a shaky breath. "That's what I'm worried about. That I don't."

Somehow, he'd backed her into the wall again, taking them right back to where they'd started. "What do you want to do, then? If you don't want to stop?" Unable to help himself, he dipped his head and kissed a path from her ear to her shoulder. God, her skin was so fucking soft. So goddamned perfect.

A tiny part of him had always known it would be like this with her. Needy and perfect and as easy as breathing. It was why he'd never let himself go there with her, because he'd already been in over his head before he'd ever kissed her. And now?

He was going to drown, and he couldn't bring himself to fucking care.

Her head fell back against the wall, tilting away from him to give him better access to her neck. "Everything. Anything."

He chuckled and raised his head. Pink slashes cut across her cheeks. "Lauren, open your eyes. Look at me." When she did, he felt his heart kick against his ribs, adrenaline and fresh arousal charging through him when her blown pupils swung his way. "It's me. You can trust me. You can say anything to me. You don't need to be embarrassed or shy. Although this blushing," he said, running the backs of his fingers over her warm cheek, "is pretty fucking cute."

She closed her eyes again. "I've thought about it at least a hundred different ways."

He trailed his fingers over the curve of her breast. "Tell me your favorite one."

She turned her head and kissed him, her mouth hot and urgent against his. She nipped at his lower lip, then pulled back. "I just want you everywhere. I don't really care about the circumstances or the location or anything. I want your fingers inside me. I want your mouth on me. I want you in my mouth. I want you, buried inside me. I want to be full of you, Theo. Covered in you and full of you and just...just yours."

Holy. Fucking. Shit. That was, hands down, the hottest thing a woman had ever said to him in his entire life. Need tightened every muscle in his body, and he had to restrain himself from doing something that would likely catch both of them a public indecency charge. So instead, he kissed her again. How had he gone this long without kissing her? How? Now that he had her mouth under his, he couldn't help but wonder if he'd wasted the past ten years not kissing this woman.

Another person passed them in the hallway, this time a woman who cleared her throat pointedly before disappearing into the ladies' room. He broke the kiss, pressing his forehead to hers.

"I guess we better go bail on this date, right?" he asked, once again tugging her away from the wall. His mind was already racing with everything he wanted to do with her once they were alone.

"Right. The date." She looked up at him, a slightly horrified expression on her face. "Oh God, we're horrible people, aren't we?"

"Just because this happened doesn't make us horrible people. A single action does not define a person."

Her lips twisted in a wry smile. "Compelling argument, counselor."

He winked. "It's why I get paid the big bucks."

She swallowed and nodded, then wove her fingers through his. "Okay. Let's go face the music and then get out of here." She gave his hand a squeeze before dropping it, squaring her shoulders and heading back toward their table, Theo following close behind.

"Everything okay?" asked Eli as they approached, a look of kind concern on his face.

"Um, actually, I'm not feeling great, so I think Theo's just going to take me home," said Lauren, frowning and resting a hand over her stomach.

"Uh huh," said Jenna, rising from the table and gathering up her purse. "That shade of lipstick looks much better on Lauren than on you." She pointed at Theo's mouth with a sneer and then stormed off toward the door, heels clicking and hair swishing behind her.

"Shit," he said, rubbing his fingers over his mouth. These were the kinds of details his normally meticulous brain was dropping the ball on thanks to lack of blood flow. Frankly, it was a miracle he could still feel his extremities.

"Oh," said Eli, his gaze bouncing between the two of them. "Oh. Um. Right. Well."

Theo took out his wallet and threw down enough money to cover their table's bill. It didn't really assuage the guilt he felt, but he didn't know what else to do.

"I'm sorry," said Lauren. "I just...I'm sorry."

Eli smiled, but Theo could see the jealousy in his eyes. He had the sudden instinct to slide his arm around Lauren's waist, and for once, he didn't fight it. She melted into him easily, as though tucked against him were exactly where she belonged. He probably had no right to be so possessive, so territorial—and God knew Lauren would flay him alive if she knew about the very caveman-esque thoughts he was currently entertaining—given that they still had a lot of things to talk about and sort through.

He led her out the front door and counted it as a freaking miracle when the first cab he hailed slowed and pulled over. The sex-he-probably-shouldn't-have-with-his-best-friend-but-was-totally-going-to gods were on his side tonight, apparently. With her fingers interlaced with his, he urged her toward the cab. His entire body felt like a bowstring, taut and vibrating with tension. He held the door open for her and she slid inside, Theo sliding in after her. He practically barked his address at the driver before reaching for Lauren.

"Come here." His voice came out rough around the edges, lust pounding through his system. He pulled her against him and she came easily, her body molding against his. His hand landed on her thigh, his fingers splayed over the bare skin where the skirt of her dress had ridden up. She shivered and licked her lips. Her eyes were luminous in the dark of the cab, her cheeks flushed. A pink tinge spread from her collarbones and down to her cleavage. Christ, it was hot seeing her turned on like this.

"We're really doing this?" Her voice was barely a whisper, almost snatched away by the pop music playing through the cab's speakers. He cupped her face, tracing his thumb over her bottom lip, need and lust and adrenaline tightening his gut into a twisted knot.

"It's entirely up to you." Lights strobed across her face as the cab made its way up 6th Avenue and past Bryant Park. "If you want to hit the brakes, we will." He dipped his head, trailing his lips over her neck and earning another sexy shiver from her. "But if you want me, I'm yours. All of me. However you want."

"Oh, God," she whispered just before turning her head and capturing his mouth with hers, the kiss softer and sweeter than the ones they'd exchanged in the restaurant. "I do want you. So much." The kiss deepened as the cab wove its way through traffic, making her sway into him, the press of her breasts against his chest the sweetest torment.

He let his fingers drift higher up her thigh, disappearing under her skirt. He teased the seam where her thighs met, the heat coming from between her legs almost scorching him. Her hips jerked toward him and she stifled a gasp. Her fingers crawled down his chest, over his belt buckle and into his lap. She traced the ridge of his cock with a featherlight touch, and just the sight of her hand with her long, delicate fingers exploring him was enough to make him breathe a little harder. She bit her lip and glanced down, her fingers working over him, outlining him. Then, she traced her fingers down to his root, then all the way back up to his weeping tip in one fluid movement. She frowned slightly and then did it again, this time curling her fingers around him.

"I'm touching your dick, Theo. Your, um, very big dick." She stroked him again, her eyes going a little wide. "Jesus."

"I guess you could say I'm proportional," he said, grinning at her.

She made a humming noise in the back of her throat. "That might be an understatement." She kept touching him, her teasing strokes driving him insane. Heat streaked down his spine, tightening his balls, making him ache and throb. He couldn't remember the last time he'd been this hard. This turned on. This ready to tear a woman's clothes off.

The cab rolled to a stop in front of his building, and after he paid the fare, he pulled Lauren out and onto the sidewalk. A part of him expected her to hesitate, but instead, she wove her fingers through his and practically dragged him into the lobby of his building.

This was really happening.

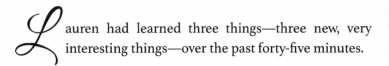

10

*L*auren had learned three things—three new, very interesting things—over the past forty-five minutes.

1. She was braver than she gave herself credit for.
2. She really, truly didn't like olives, no matter how many times she forced herself to try them.
3. Theodore Prescott could *kiss*. Make her toes curl and her stomach twist and her pussy clench with need kiss.

And he was big. Like, really big. Like, make her wet just thinking about it big.

Okay, so she'd learned four things. Four new, very interesting things.

The door to Theo's apartment closed behind them, sealing them away from the world. Alone, together, the entire night stretching before them. A tremble coursed through her, her heart hammering away in her throat. She kept trying to gather her thoughts, but she was too overwhelmed to be coherent, even to herself. Her clit was still pulsing from the cab ride and the teasing, exploratory touches. Her entire body was on fire with wanting him. Needing him.

They locked eyes and a heartbeat passed between them before they came together, a whirling tangle of limbs and mouths. He flung his coat to the floor and then pushed hers down her shoulders, letting it drop at her feet as he devoured her mouth, his lips and tongue hungry and demanding against hers. Then, he lifted her, his hands like a brand on her ass as she wound her legs around his waist, writhing against him. He started walking her toward his bedroom as he kissed her like a drowning man gulping down air.

In his darkened bedroom, she could see the city spread out before them, all gleaming lights and rushing traffic, giving the room a dim glow. Theo tumbled her down onto his king-sized bed and then sat halfway up, his big hand curled around the headboard and his knees bracketing her hips as he gazed down at her, his eyes luminous.

He trailed a hand down her jaw, over her throat and then between her breasts, making her wonder if he could feel just how hard her heart was beating. "Tell me how you want it," he said, his fingers playing with the strap of her dress. God, she felt like she was standing in front of a buffet and she hadn't eaten in days. She sucked in a shaky breath, her entire body feeling electrically charged. He pulled her dress down a little bit further, making her breasts spill free. He closed his massive hand over one and squeezed, his palm rough against her hard nipple. She gasped and arched her back into his touch, her head rolling back and forth. He left his hand where it was, his fingers scraping back and forth over her nipple, teasing and tormenting her. Liquid heat pooled between her thighs.

"I don't know. I just want you inside me. That's all I want. It's all I can think about right now." She skated her fingers up under his black sweater, savoring the dips and ridges of his abs. She gave the fabric an upward tug. "I want this off."

He smiled at her, a wolfish grin full of heat and promise. He let go of the headboard, sat all the way up and then tugged the sweater up over his head.

She'd seen him shirtless before. At the beach, when he'd helped her paint her room last summer, when she'd slept over at his place and he'd padded out of his room all sleep rumpled in nothing but a pair of boxers...But seeing and touching were two very different things. Her fingertips tingled as they slid over his skin, and her pussy clenched, empty and aching, as she traced his muscles. He was lean and strong, his bare chest one of the most gorgeous things she'd ever seen. He was pure masculine perfection. He held still, watching her as she explored him in a way she'd never been allowed to before.

"You're so sexy." Her voice was a hoarse whisper. "Look at you." She moved her hands upward, smoothing over the contours of his pecs, scraping her nails over his nipples. Then, she dragged her hands down to his pants, slipping his belt free of the buckle. Theo's breath was a sharp rasp as she undid the button and the fly, spreading the front of his pants wide. His long, thick cock was visible beneath his boxer briefs and she scraped her nails lightly down his length. His hips jumped and he let out a hiss.

"Fuck, Lo." Hearing his nickname for her ground out all rough and sandpapery as she touched him was beyond sexy.

It made her feel powerful knowing that she was undoing him as much as he was undoing her, and she decided that what she wanted right now was to chase that power. Stroking him through the thin layer of fabric, she blinked up at him.

"I want you in my mouth."

She pushed his pants and boxer briefs down over his hips and then slid several inches down the bed, until his cock was *right there,* less than an inch from her lips. Theo's hand had gone back to the headboard, and he gazed down at her, his eyes shining with lust and need as he knelt above her. She parted her lips and licked the drop of liquid glistening on the thick head of his cock, savoring the first taste of him on her tongue.

The headboard gave an ominous creak, and she could see that the muscles in his chest and arms were taut. She smiled and dragged her lips over the velvety hot length of him, inhaling, pulling his scent into her lungs. Her mouth watered a little, and she traced the ridge of a vein up the length of him with the tip of her tongue. Kissing him and teasing him with little flicks of her tongue, she smiled up at him. The headboard creaked again.

"You want so badly to fuck my mouth like this, don't you?" she asked, giving him another slow, teasing lick. "But you're holding back."

He made a strangled sound that was half groan, half plea. "Shit, I don't...unf..." The headboard creaked again. "I'm trying to be a gentleman, here."

"Do it, Theo. I want it, too. Fuck my mouth. Fill me up, just like I want."

"Oh, Christ," he panted out and then rose up a bit higher on his knees and thrust his hips forward, forcing her to take him deep into her mouth. His musky taste flooded her, overwhelming her, and she moaned around his cock, happily taking what he was giving her. He withdrew and then thrust back in, so deep her eyes watered.

"Your mouth feels so fucking good, sweetheart. Holy shit, I've imagined this so many times, and it's just...*fuck*," he groaned, moving his hips a little faster as she sucked him, swirling her tongue around him. Wetness flooded her at letting Theo use her like this. It was dirty and hot but also safe because she trusted him more than she trusted almost anyone.

His confession that he'd fantasized about her made her heart slam against her ribs, her entire body a riot of giddiness and arousal. She moaned around his cock and bobbed her head faster, finding a rhythm with him as he worked his cock in and out of her mouth, the weight of him deliciously hot and heavy on her tongue.

Before she was finished with him, he pulled out of her mouth with an anguished groan, his cock glistening and rock hard. Feminine satisfaction curled through her that she'd pushed him to the brink so quickly.

"I can't wait another second to find out how you taste," he rumbled out, climbing off of her and immediately settling himself between her legs, his broad shoulders nestled against the backs of her thighs. His hands—so big, so warm, so perfect—skimmed up her legs, taking her dress with it until it was bunched around her waist. He dipped his head, nuzzling her with this nose as he inhaled deeply.

"Fuck, Lo," he ground out. "I can smell how wet you are for me."

"Uh huh," she whimpered, shifting her hips. All of the air went out of her when he kissed her pussy through her panties, his lips and tongue dragging the fabric against her swollen flesh. God, the things this man could do with his mouth. Her fantasies paled in comparison. Every single one of them. He inhaled again, his teeth tugging at the fabric of her panties. She clenched in anticipation, butterflies dizzy with lust flying in circles in her stomach. His fingers curled into the fabric of her panties at her hip, pulling it taut. He kissed her through the fabric again and made a low, growling sound that had her toes curling.

"You particularly attached to these?" he asked, his grip on her panties tightening. She heard a few stitches tear.

She shook her head, unable to get her mouth to form words.

"Good." He tightened his grip, pulling the fabric tight across her pussy. She moaned, the friction delicious against her clit. He let out another sexy growl and a ripping sound filled the air as he tore her panties off. And then his mouth was on her, kissing her deeply and thoroughly, making her hips buck and shake. She managed to push herself up on her elbows, and holy hell, the sight of Theo between her splayed legs, his mouth working over her pussy, was the hottest, sexiest, most erotic thing she'd ever seen. She wove her fingers into his hair and undulated her hips, grinding against his talented mouth.

"Taste good?" Her voice was so husky that she barely recognized it.

He pulled back, sucking at one of her outer lips. He grinned, and she could see herself on his face. "Tastes like my new favorite thing to eat." Then he dipped his head and swirled his tongue around her clit before sucking it into his mouth. She practically screamed his name as she fell back on the bed, everything inside her burning and throbbing. He banded an arm across her jerking hips, holding her in place as he continued his onslaught while he circled her drenched entrance with one of his fingers. He teased her with shallow strokes and light touches as he lapped at her, sucking and kissing until she felt so swollen and achy that she almost couldn't take it anymore.

He added a second finger and slid them both deep inside her. She clenched around him as he licked her and she let go, stars bursting behind her tightly shut eyes as she rode his hand and mouth. Hot pressure coiled low in her stomach and then burst across her body as she went off like a firework. Throb after throb pulsed through her, making her shake and moan, the orgasm shuddering through her for what felt like a very long time.

"You look so fucking beautiful when you come," he said, trailing kisses over her still shaking thighs. She loved getting to see this side of him, this carnal, sexual, dirty side that he'd kept very neatly tucked away. She was already in love with him—with the best friend part of him. Could she have both sides of him? Could she have the guy who brought her lattes and held her hair back when she puked and watched *Friends* on the couch with her *and* who had a gloriously dirty mouth and a huge cock and who could make her come so hard she saw stars?

With the way Theo was staring at her, his heart in his eyes, it felt like maybe she could.

He got up and pushed his pants down over his hips, stepping out of them and then pulling open a drawer on his bedside table, fishing out a condom. As he did that, she squirmed out of her wrinkled dress, tossing it to the floor. Even though she'd just come, she felt crazy with needing him, so she reached out her hand and tugged him toward the bed. He sat down with his back against the headboard and she swung her leg over his hips, settling herself on his lap. She wound her arms around his neck and kissed a path up his jaw, rocking her hips against him. When her still throbbing pussy slid against his shaft, they both moaned. He palmed her ass, pulling her closer.

"Get this condom on me, sweetheart. I need to be inside you," he whispered, trailing kisses down her throat and across her collarbone. With slightly shaking hands, she took the condom from him, tore open the wrapper and rolled it down his length. She wanted to tease him, to draw it out, but she was just as impatient as he was.

"Good girl," he said, his voice raw as he gripped her ass and urged her up, the head of his cock sliding against her slick center. They let out a loud moan in unison, their voices tangling together. She tilted her hips, taking him just the tiniest bit inside, and they moaned again. Heat blistered her from the inside out, and she couldn't wait any longer. Holding his eyes, she sank down onto his cock, taking all of him in one slow slide. She gasped at the molten feeling pulsing through her as she stretched to take him. Once he was fully inside, her body throbbing, she went still, soaking in the moment. He didn't move either, just stroked a hand up and down her spine, his gaze fixed on where they were joined.

"Fucking hell, sweetheart." His voice came out rough, scraping over her like sandpaper. "Your pussy is heaven, Lo. I can't wait to feel you come all over my cock."

She moved her hips up, the friction of him inside her both sweet and intense, and then came back down, somehow taking him even a little bit deeper. "You feel so good, Theo. Oh, God," she said, her voice breathy, almost unrecognizable.

He pulled her against his chest and kissed her, holding

her tight as she slowly rocked her hips. Everything inside her tightened as they moved together, making it hard to breathe, or think, or do anything but feel.

"You fill me up so good," she whispered, burying her face in his neck as they started to move faster. Suddenly, he gripped her thighs and tumbled her backward so that he was on top of her. Lauren swore she felt her heart actually skip a beat in that moment. With Theo gazing down at her, looking so painfully sexy, his thick cock buried inside her, it was all she could do to stop herself from letting out a little sob of happiness. She wound her legs around his waist, wanting him even closer, even deeper. He skimmed a hand up her body, capturing one of her hands as he went. He pinned her hand above her head and wove his fingers with hers.

He flexed his hips, his jaw tight. "I want to fuck you hard and rough, make you feel me as you take all this cock." He gazed down at her, a question in his eyes.

She scraped the nails of her free hand down his back, making him shudder. "I love this side of you. It's so freaking hot. I had no idea..." She shook her head, swallowing her words as he flexed his cock inside her, stretching her even more. He was the biggest guy she'd ever been with—by a lot —and she was already addicted. The feeling of being stuffed full of Theo was pure perfection. Full of him and surrounded by him. Safe and cherished, with her entire body throbbing with pleasure. "Do it. Fuck me, Theo. Fill me and stretch me and take me. It's all for you."

He let out a groan mixed with a growl and thrust his hips against her, the base of his cock rubbing against her still-swollen clit. Letting go of her hand, he pushed up to his knees. Then he gripped her hips and started to fuck her. Like, really fuck her. Hard and fast and dirty and sweaty. The stuff of steamy novels and erotic movies. His grip on her hips was rough, almost punishing, and a completely unevolved part of her thrilled at the thought that she'd probably have fingertip bruises.

Sex bruises. From sex with *Theo*. For some reason, just thinking his name made everything that much hotter. Theo was inside her. Theo had made her come with his mouth and his fingers.

Theo.

With his name echoing through her mind, she started to come again, sudden, harsh throbs pulsing through her, scorching her with heat and pleasure. She moaned, long and loud, as her body pulled at him, wanting him deeper. Wanting everything he had to give her.

Her orgasm seemed to shred the last of his control, and he thrust into her with two, three more brutally hard thrusts and then came. The groan he let out sounded like it was torn from somewhere deep in his chest. It was, hands down, the sexiest sound she'd ever heard him make. She felt each pulse of his cock inside her and she squeezed him back, drawing it out as much as possible.

"Holy shit," he panted out, pulling his hands away and shoving one through his hair. "I...fuck, I think you're gonna have bruises. I'm sorry, sweetheart."

Her heart gave a little shiver. She loved hearing him call her sweetheart in that raspy, sated just-had-great-sex voice.

"Don't be. I'm not. That was hot as hell."

With a rueful grin, he slid out of her and disappeared into the bathroom, reappearing seconds later with a towel. Once they'd cleaned up, he climbed back onto the bed and pulled her into his arms.

"Come here, gorgeous." Her heart gave another happy

little shiver as she settled her head on his chest, listening to the thump of his heart. She knew that they needed to talk about this—what it changed, what it meant, what they wanted—but for now, she was perfectly content to bask in the afterglow of the best sex she'd ever had.

11

*L*auren rolled over and buried her face in the pillow, inhaling the scent of Theo and sex deep into her lungs. She wasn't sure how much she'd slept. She felt tired, yet also buzzing and awake. After the first round, she'd dozed off in Theo's arms, then woke up to use the bathroom and when she'd come back, they'd had a slow and sleepy round two. Lying down behind her with his chest at her back, he'd pushed inside her, inch by inch, slowly working himself in. Then he'd hooked her leg over his hips, spreading her open for him. He'd stroked in and out while massaging her clit with his strong fingers and before long, she'd come, throbbing against his hand and around his cock. She'd thought she couldn't take anymore, but then he'd pulled out and settled himself between her legs, eating her swollen pussy with deep, slow sweeps of his tongue until she'd come not just once, but twice more. Then he'd pushed back inside her, taking her with long, slow strokes and deep, lingering kisses.

She'd come five times last night. It was no wonder she'd fallen into a boneless oblivion.

Also, she'd now learned five new things. Thing five: Theo Prescott was *amazing* in bed.

She opened her eyes and reached for him at the same time, but his side of the bed was empty. Pushing up on to her elbow, she glanced toward the master bath, but the door was open and the room was silent. Maybe he'd gone out to get breakfast. He wasn't much of a cook, and he knew how much she loved a good bagel.

But then she heard what sounded like a groan from the living room, and it wasn't the kind of groan she'd heard from him multiple times last night. This one sounded off in a way that had worry spearing through her, chasing away the last of her sleepiness. She swung her legs over the side of the bed, found a rumpled T-shirt of Theo's to pull on over her head, and made her way into the living room.

He stood in front of the floor-to-ceiling windows shirtless, wearing a pair of low-slung gray sweatpants. He had one hand braced against the glass, the other pressed to his stomach.

"Theo? You okay?" She padded towards him, concern pulling at her.

He shook his head. "I...yeah. Yeah. I'm sure it's nothing." But then he hissed out a sharp gasp. His eyes screwed shut and he seemed to force himself to take a breath. She stepped closer and her concern deepened when she saw how pale he was. Beads of sweat dotted his hairline. "Probably just something I ate."

She frowned, not convinced that whatever was going on with him was simple indigestion. "I mean, wouldn't you have felt sick sooner if it was from dinner?"

He shrugged and then grimaced. "*Shit.*"

She reached out for him. "Come here, sit down. What's wrong?" She guided him onto the couch, frowning again when she touched his skin. He felt hot, but not in the way he'd felt hot last night. His skin wasn't just warm—it was too hot. Unnaturally hot.

He leaned forward, his arms braced on his knees, his face twisted in pain. "I woke up like half an hour ago. I wanted to go out and surprise you with bagels and coffee." He tried to smile but he couldn't seem to force his lips out of their grimace. "But as soon as I walked out here, I had this stabbing pain right here," he said, pointing just to the right of his belly button. "I thought maybe it was indigestion, so I tried to walk it off and that only seemed to make it worse." He sucked in another sharp breath. Lauren lifted her hand and pressed her palm to his forehead.

"You're burning up. Does it hurt if I touch you here?" She gently pressed her fingers against his lower right abdomen. He let out a yelp and practically leaped off the couch.

"Fuck. Sorry, sorry. Yeah, that hurts."

"I think you might have appendicitis. I remember when my sister had it in high school and it was just like this. Fever, pain in her lower right side that came on suddenly."

He tried to laugh but it sounded forced. "What? No. I don't have appendicitis. It's just something I ate. Or maybe a bug. It's definitely not something that..." He trailed off, somehow going even whiter. "Oh no." He got up and hobbled to the bathroom, barely making it in time to stick his head in the toilet and be sick. He moaned and she sank down onto her knees beside him, stroking a hand up and down his back. Her mind flashed back to the night of her birthday and the way he'd taken care of her. The way he'd almost kissed her.

Thinking back, that night felt like the beginning of the change in their relationship.

"I'm gonna grab you some water, okay?" All she wanted to do was to take care of him and make sure he was okay.

He nodded and groaned and then threw up again. When she returned with a bottle of water from his fridge a minute later, she found him sitting with his back against the glass shower door, his wrists on his knees. He took the water with a small smile.

"Sorry."

She sank down beside him. "Don't be sorry. It was me puking in here not that long ago, remember?" He shot her a half smile and then grimaced again, biting back a groan. "Anyway, I think we should go to the hospital."

He scoffed. "We don't need to go to the hospital. I'm fine."

"Oh, yeah? You just gonna walk this off, tough guy?"

He started to push to his feet. "Yep. Prescotts don't go to the hospital." Then he went completely white, threw up again, and laid down on the bathroom floor.

She just shook her head, fighting the urge to roll her eyes, deciding that annoyed was a more productive emotion than worried at that moment. "Stay here. I'm going to get dressed and bring you a shirt. And then we're going to the emergency room, and I don't care what your last name is." She stood and started to make her way back to his bedroom.

"Lo, I think you're overreacting. I don't need to go to the hospital." He started to stand, grunted and then quickly sat back down again. He pressed a hand to his abdomen. "Goddammit. Okay. Okay. Shit." He let out another groan, his eyes screwed tightly shut. Lauren raced back into the bedroom, her irritation with his stubbornness fading as worry and panic rose back to the surface. She found Theo a long-sleeved Henley from one of his dresser drawers and then started to pull on her dress from last night. She felt absolutely ridiculous in a slinky cocktail dress that was slightly rumpled from spending the night on Theo's bedroom floor, but it would have to do for now. She grabbed one of his dress shirts and slipped it on over top of the dress, knotting the ends at her waist in an effort to cover up a little more and look at least somewhat presentable. Well, as presentable as a girl could be wearing last night's dress, a man's dress shirt and no underwear because said man had ripped them off.

As he gingerly pulled on the shirt she'd handed him, she slipped her shoes on, gathered up her purse and phone and then helped Theo into his own shoes. He was now walking slightly hunched over, so she looped his arm over her shoulders for support, guiding them towards the elevator.

Once they reached the lobby, she called out and asked the doorman to hail them a cab. He nodded and hurried outside while she and Theo shuffled their way across the shiny floor of his building's lobby. By the time she got him settled in the cab that the doorman had frantically waved down, he was shaking, his knuckles white. She pried his clenched fist open as they lurched down 9th Ave and wove her fingers through his.

"It's going to be okay. I know it really hurts, but you're gonna be fine. When Emily had hers out, she felt so much better after."

He nodded, his lips pressed into a grim line. "You're gonna stay, right?" His fingers tightened around hers, and her heart throbbed in her chest.

"I'm not going anywhere." And she meant it in every

single possible way she could, because last night had changed everything. At least, it had for her.

An hour and a half after they'd arrived at Mount Sinai, it was confirmed: Theo's appendix needed to be removed. Now. They'd whisked him off to surgery almost immediately, leaving Lauren to sit in the beige and blue waiting room. A muted TV was tuned to HGTV, and the air smelled like coffee and antiseptic. Even though she knew he'd be totally fine, she couldn't seem to dispel the anxiety running through her.

And she wasn't even entirely sure about the source of her anxiety. Did she feel restless and tense because he was having surgery, or because they hadn't gotten the chance to actually talk about anything? Once they'd arrived at the hospital, she'd helped him fill out the admission and insurance paperwork and then they'd taken him for a CT scan. While they'd waited for the results, he'd been in so much pain that she'd been entirely focused on trying to entertain and distract him. She'd done her Kermit the Frog impression, she'd told lame jokes, and she'd made up crazy stories about the people on some home renovation show (they needed to renovate because they were having sextuplets, and they were going to name them Fred, Ed, Ned, Ted, Jed and Dilbert). She would've done cartwheels naked down the hallway if it would've done anything to take his mind off the pain.

Just then, she saw Dori, holding a plastic bag and a tray containing two coffees and a tube of what looked like cookie dough. Figuring that she might as well take care of her clothing situation while Theo was in surgery, she'd called Aspen, but she'd forgotten that she was out of town at some kind of shamanic retreat this weekend. So she'd called Dori, who had graciously agreed to lend her some clothes. She pushed her glasses up her nose with the back of her wrist and tipped her head in Lauren's direction when she spotted her in the waiting room.

"Thank you so much," she said, standing and taking the bag from Dori. "I owe you one."

"You can repay me by explaining why you're in a come fuck me dress at nine in the morning. On a Saturday." She bounced her eyebrows suggestively, then handed Lauren one of the coffees.

"Okay. Just let me get changed first. I'll be right back." She took the bag and sealed herself away in the nearest restroom, grateful as she pulled on the gray yoga pants, beige wrap sweater, socks and sneakers that Dori had provided. The sneakers were a bit tight, probably a half size too small, but they would do. Everything else fit, mostly. And at least she was a lot more covered and comfortable than she'd been in her little dress.

With her cocktail dress stashed in the bag, she sat back down beside Dori, took a sip of her coffee, and then decided to just dive in.

"So...I had sex with Theo."

Dori made a hilarious expression of mock surprise. "*No!* I hadn't put that together at all." She stared at Lauren expectantly. "And? How was it?"

She sighed and slumped back against her chair, her stomach doing a funny fluttering thing as she remembered the previous night. "It was amazing. *He* was amazing. We had sex twice, and I stayed over. Then, this morning, his appendix almost burst, and—"

"From the sex?" Dori cut in, an incredulous look on her face. "Because, uh, I don't think that's supposed to happen."

"It wasn't from the sex. At least, I don't think so."

"I mean, and I'm just guessing here, but given that you guys have wanted to do each other for like, *ever*, there was probably a lot of pent up sexual energy." She curled her fingers into claws and swiped the air, making a little roaring sound. "You probably ripped each other's clothes off."

Lauren felt her cheeks go warm and her stomach bottom out. "Uh, yeah. It was the best sex I've ever had. He's ruined me." She shook her head, staring off into the distance as she replayed last night again. "It was so freaking hot seeing this other side of him. He was still Theo, but like, a dirty talking, take charge, give you five orgasms in one night Theo."

Dori's eyes went wide. "You had *five* orgasms?" she asked, just a little too loudly. An elderly lady looked up from her knitting and frowned at them.

"Shhh! We don't need to broadcast that to the entirety of Lincoln Square, okay?"

Dori took a sip of her coffee. "Okay, okay. Jeez." She paused, a contemplative look on her face. "So what does this mean for you guys?"

Lauren shrugged, taking a sip of her own coffee. "I'm not really sure. We didn't get the chance to talk about it. Last night we were, um, busy, and then this morning he was in so much pain that I was just focused on helping him."

Dori set her coffee down and reached for the tube of cookie dough, producing two plastic spoons from her coat pocket. After she'd pried it open, she handed one spoon to Lauren before digging in. "What do you want it to mean?" she asked through a mouthful of sugary goodness.

Lauren scooped up a small bite, her stomach feeling a

little unsettled from the excitement of the past twelve hours. "I mean, I want to date him. I want to be a couple and see where this goes, because..." She trailed off, shaking her head. "Last night felt like the start of something real. Something good. And I know all about his family, and his jadedness and all of that, but last night felt...it felt like that stuff wasn't important. Because it was me and him and that was what mattered. Yeah, we were like, super horny for each other, but it was more than just getting off. At least it was for me. And I think it was for him, but obviously we do have to talk about it." She glanced over at Dori, who was listening attentively. "Can I ask your advice?"

Dori gestured at the tube of cookie dough. "I'm eating cookie dough before noon. Clearly you've come to the right place, grasshopper."

Lauren laughed. "How should I bring it up? I don't want him to freak out and—"

"Be Theo about the whole thing?"

She pointed her cookie dough laden spoon at Dori. "Yeah. That."

"Well, you could ask him how he feels about you while he's all doped up. That shit's like truth serum." When Lauren's eyes went wide, Dori smiled. "Kidding! But I do think you should ask him how he feels about you. And even if it's not the answer you want, I think you should still tell him how you feel. It might get a little messy, but you owe it to yourself to be honest with him about your feelings and what you want. Wait until he's feeling a bit better and then just dive in. There's no perfect time for a potentially scary conversation. Sometimes you just gotta do it. Not the kind of doing it that you guys did last night, although I'm guessing there will be plenty of that in your future, too."

She sighed and shoved a big spoonful of cookie dough into her mouth.

"Hey, what's wrong? You okay?"

"Oh, sure. Just thinking about my imaginary boyfriend." She shook her head. "You know, I kind of want to get a cat, but I don't want it to eat my eyeballs when I inevitably die alone."

She looped her arm around Dori's shoulders. "Maybe a dog would be better."

Just then, a Black woman in surgical scrubs approached. "Are you here with Theodore Prescott?" Lauren's lips twitched at hearing his full name and knowing how much he hated it. She stood, swiping her palms over her thighs.

"I am, yeah."

The woman smiled. "I'm Dr. Robbins, and I performed Mr. Prescott's surgery. You can rest easy because everything went perfectly. It was a textbook case of appendicitis, and luckily, we caught it before it had the chance to rupture. He's in recovery now and someone will bring him to his room shortly."

"Is he going to stay overnight?"

The doctor nodded. "Yes, most likely, but he should be able to go home tomorrow. The surgery was done laparoscopically, so he'll be back to normal in a week or so. Are you his girlfriend?"

Lauren hesitated before nodding slightly, not entirely sure she was telling the truth.

The doctor seemed unfazed by Lauren's hesitation. "Make sure he doesn't overdo it, especially for the first couple of days. No heavy lifting, no driving for at least a week. Showers are fine, just be gentle with the incision when drying off. The nurse will send you home with more information. Oh, and sexual activity is okay if he's feeling up to it, but nothing strenuous for five days," she added with a knowing wink before turning and walking quickly away.

"Oh man, five days. You gonna be okay, friend?" asked Dori, laying her hand on Lauren's shoulder. Lauren laughed and shook her head, her cheeks warm.

"Are you gonna be okay? Do you want me to come over later?" she asked, worried that Dori was lonelier than she was letting on.

"No, it's okay. Go be with your man. I'm going to go home and eat my feelings. It's cheaper than therapy and it comes with dip."

"Okay. But I'm only a text away if you need anything. Thanks again for the clothes and the healthy breakfast. Oh, um, Dori?"

"Yeah?"

"Can we keep this between us for now? I'm not ready for the rest of the group to know. I mean, I'm not even sure if there is anything to know, and I just don't want—"

Dori cut her off by pressing her finger to Lauren's lips. "I won't say a word about your secret lovah."

"Thank you," she mumbled against Dori's finger. Then she hugged her goodbye and went to go find Theo's room.

When she did, she wasn't quite prepared for the sight of him, dozing in a hospital bed, hooked up to an IV. His color was much better than when they'd first arrived, although the white hospital gown with little gray diamonds on it wasn't doing him any favors, even with the way the fabric stretched across his broad shoulders.

She set her purse down on the little table by the door and took a second to get her bearings. The room was a standard private room, with a single hospital bed, a narrow window with a view of the Manhattan skyline poking up into a cloudy October sky, and a couple chairs for visitors. A flatscreen TV hung on the far wall beside what looked like a closet and the entrance to a private bathroom.

She pulled up one of the chairs beside his bed, watching his chest rise and fall with slow, steady breaths. When she took his hand, weaving her fingers through his much larger ones, he stirred a little, his head moving on the pillow, his eyes still closed.

"You know whasssa really good song?" he asked in a raspy voice. And then he started softly singing "I Wanna Dance with Somebody" in a high-pitched falsetto, the lyrics slurring together. She bit her lip—hard—to keep from laughing. Poor guy was still stoned out of his gourd. She let him sing, high and off-key, getting at least half the words wrong. When he was finished, she gave his hand a gentle squeeze.

"Hey. How you feeling?"

"You wanna know something?" he asked, his eyes still closed, his voice faraway and dreamy. "It's a secret, you can't tell anyone."

Dori's comment about pain meds being like truth serum echoed through her brain. "Um, sure. What's your secret?"

"I had sex with my best friend last night." An adorable smile pulled up the corner of his mouth. "Twice."

She bit her lip, holding back a smile. "Oh, yeah?"

"Uh huh." He sighed, his head moving back and forth slightly on the pillow. "I just..." His voice trailed off and for a second, she thought maybe he'd dozed off, but then he started speaking again, his eyes still closed, his voice still sleepy sounding. "I think I'm in love with her."

At that admission, Lauren's heart leaped into her throat, adrenaline surging through her body and making it feel nearly impossible to sit still. But she managed not to move, not wanting to break the spell. Wanting to hear what else drugged up Theo had to say—about her, about them, about anything. She forced herself to take a deep breath, her heart still pounding away, her pulse so loud in her ears she was surprised she was able to hear anything over it.

"No, I don't think it. I know it. I'm in love with this girl."

Her eyes widened and her heart danced in her chest. Everything she'd hoped for over the past day came rushing to the front of her mind, feeling more and more real. More and more like an actual possibility. She swallowed against the sudden thickness in her throat, emotions charging through her at his admission.

"But I could never love her, you know? Like really love her. I'm too fucked up—I don't even know what loving someone the way she deserves would look like. And she knows that. I know she does."

Oh.

As gently as possible, Lauren untangled her fingers from Theo's and laid his hand on the bed. Emotions slammed through her, one after the other, the most prevalent being crushing disappointment. It felt like a stone giant had her in its arms and was slowly squeezing her tighter and tighter until she couldn't catch her breath anymore. She took a deep breath and wiped her palms on her thighs, trying to think. Trying to process. But it was hard to do anything but feel with disappointment warring for space and attention alongside frustration, anger, panic, and embarrassment. Each one tugged at her, pulling her from one emotion to the next until she felt dizzy.

So she sat by Theo's bed in silence, until finally, after what felt like hours, she knew what to do.

He'd fallen asleep long ago, and she finally stood, careful not to scrape the chair legs over the tiled floor. Then, she bent and kissed his forehead.

"I'm in love with you too, you dummy. And even though you gave up on yourself a long time ago, I'm not giving up on us." After everything they'd shared last night, after hearing his admission that he was in love with her, she had to believe that they could make this work, despite his baggage.

12

*T*heo had never been so happy to see his couch. After spending nearly twenty-four hours in the hospital, he'd been discharged and sent home to recover. He was in some discomfort, but it was nothing compared to how he'd been feeling when he'd woken up the morning after...the morning after Lauren.

Fuck. They needed to talk about this. He still hadn't figured out what to say. He knew they couldn't go back to the way things had been, but he also didn't know if he was ready to jump into a relationship with both feet. They'd had amazing sex, and he wanted her even more than he had before now that he knew how good it was between them, but he was terrified that if they kept it up, she'd get her hopes up and expect something he knew he couldn't give her. In all of this, the only thing he was certain about was that however this conversation went, he was probably going to hurt her in some way, which was why he'd avoided bringing it up. Every time he tried to untangle his thoughts, he just seemed to snarl the knot even more.

He wanted her. He cared about her. Fuck, he was probably in love with her. But he couldn't be the guy she deserved.

He watched as she disappeared into his bedroom with the little overnight bag holding his clothes, then reappeared with a pillow and the duvet from his bed. Without a word, she grabbed the remote and handed it to him, then sat on the far end of the couch with the pillow in her lap. He laid down carefully, and then she arranged the duvet around them. Her fingers found their way into his hair, massaging his scalp. He almost hummed with pleasure, his eyes flickering shut for a moment.

How had they gone so long without this? The easy intimacy, the physical connection that made him feel even closer to her? Was there a way they could still have this without...God, he was an asshole. Everything he was thinking right now was the very definition of having his cake and eating it too. He wanted Lauren by his side and in his bed. He didn't want her to date anyone else. But he knew he should find the best way to let her down gently because he couldn't do this with her. He hadn't grown up with any positive relationship role models, and he'd gradually accepted the fact that he didn't know *how* to be in a relationship. And with Lauren...he was already freaking out about losing her now— what if they dated and then when it inevitably ended, he lost her forever?

Fuck. Fuck. Fuck.

"*The Office* or *Community*?" he asked, turning carefully so that instead of facing the TV, he was looking up at her. His heart did this funny sputtering kicking thing in his chest, like an engine turning over and then backfiring before shifting into a higher gear. His stupid, stupid heart, who was currently in second place for "Theo Prescott's Stupidest Organ" right after his dick.

She smiled down at him, her fingers still sifting through his hair. "Or, I don't know. We could talk about the fact that we had sex."

He swallowed thickly, aware that the moment of reckoning had arrived. And he still had no idea what to say. None whatsoever. So, he took his time sitting up, pretending to be in more discomfort than he was just to buy himself a few precious seconds. Precious seconds that didn't help. How did you tell your best friend that you cared deeply about her and wanted to keep having incredible sex with her, but didn't want to commit to her because commitment would only lead to failure, and failure would mean no more Lauren in his life?

How?

She studied him, her bottom lip caught between her teeth. Waiting. Probably full of hope and happiness that he was about to crush. He hesitated, his gaze darting between her eyes and her mouth, and the urge to kiss her was almost overwhelming. The need to taste her one last time before he ruined everything by asking for something he had no right to ask for.

Finally, after what he knew was too long, she shook her head and held up her hands. "Okay, so before you freak out— because I can hear you internally freaking out from here—I have an idea. And I want you to hear me out before reacting, okay? Just let me get it all out."

He nodded, both relieved and worried that he didn't have to say anything yet. "Okay."

She licked her lips and nodded, as though psyching herself up to jump off of a cliff. "So, um, obviously the other night meant a lot to me. I've wanted that for a long time now, and I don't regret that it happened." She paused and took his hand. "It was amazing, Theo. At least, it was amazing for me."

Unable to help himself, he lifted her hand and brought it to his mouth, kissing her knuckles. "It was amazing for me too, Lo." He didn't want her thinking he was hitting the brakes because she was bad in bed, because she most definitely was not. "You were incredible." She blushed a little, and the sight of her pink cheeks made him want to pull her into his arms. But he stayed where he was, savoring the feel of her small fingers woven through his.

"Okay, so it's safe to say that we both really wanted it, right?"

"I wanted it just as much as you did, yeah. When you told me you wanted me..." He shook his head, his blood heating a little at the memory. "I couldn't hold back."

"And I didn't want you to hold back."

He opened his mouth to try to find the words to tell her that as amazing as it had been, it probably shouldn't have happened, but before he could even make a sound, she lifted her free hand.

"I'm not done yet."

He snapped his mouth shut, his chest a tangled mess of knots.

"We both wanted it, and it was amazing. But I also know that one night of sex isn't a promise. It's not a commitment. It's something that happened, but it's one thing in the face of ten years of friendship."

He let out the breath he'd been holding as cautious relief started to trickle through him. "Right. Yeah."

She smiled at him, her thumb tracing over the backs of his knuckles. "So here's what I'm thinking. Let's stay friends. I'm not asking you to date me or make me any promises because I know that's not your jam. But I'd also be lying if I said I didn't want back in your bed." She scooted closer and then leaned forward, her breath tickling his skin as she whispered in his ear, "I can't stop thinking about how good you feel inside me."

Arousal and need jolted through him, and acting purely on instinct, he turned his head and kissed her. She let out a soft whimpering sound before parting her lips and letting him in. He lifted his free hand and laid it on her neck, his thumb moving restlessly over her jaw. He couldn't deny that kissing her felt so incredibly right. So perfect and amazing and like he was going to jump out of his skin with how much he wanted her.

The kiss was slow and leisurely, heat building in his gut at the sensation of Lauren's tongue unhurriedly caressing his. She wound her arms around his neck and deepened the kiss. He let out a soft groan and tangled his hand in her hair, pinning her in place as he gave and took. Blood surged to his cock, and his incision started to ache. But that ache was nothing compared to the one right in the center of his chest. The one fueled by the knowledge that this wasn't something he could keep.

Reluctantly, he broke the kiss, his heart catching at the way Lauren leaned forward, chasing his mouth with hers.

"So what *are* you thinking, Lo?" he asked, his voice coming out as a low rasp. He wound a strand of her hair around his finger. He wanted her too much to stop touching her.

"I'm thinking that you don't need to make me any promises, Theo. I'm thinking that we keep doing this..." She traced her fingers over his lips, then crawled them down his chest. "And just see where it goes. No labels. No pressure. We're still just Theo and Lauren. But now with orgasms."

Hope speared through him, so bright and sharp it almost hurt. "Wait, what?"

She blinked at him. "Theo, I know you. I've been one of your closest friends for a decade. I know how your brain works and most of the time, I have a pretty good idea of what you're thinking. And for the past day, you've been trying to figure out how to tell me that you can't commit. So I'm telling you that you don't need to. We don't need to label this, or whatever. We can just take our time and explore. You need time, and I can give that to you."

"I don't know what to say." He shook his head, hope warring with doubt, making his stomach tight. "There has to be a catch."

And yet, the way Lauren laid it out, she made it sound so simple. No labels. No pressure. No expectations. Just two friends casually exploring a sexual relationship. It seemed too good to be true, but he wanted what she was offering so badly that he wasn't going to question it, even though a part of him knew he should.

She shook her head, her cheeks still pink. "There's no catch. I want to see where this goes, and I want to give you what you need."

He frowned, taking her hand again. "And what if it doesn't go where you want?" An icy lump sat in his stomach as he said the words. Because even if they did this, and even if it was great, what if he was never able to give her what she wanted? He realized right then and there that it wasn't that he didn't want to be in a relationship with her. He just didn't know how to be in one and not royally fuck it up. He didn't know how to prevent the inevitable.

She squeezed his hand. "You're my best friend. If we call the sex part off, we call it off. We'll be okay. We have ten years of history to lean on, right?"

He felt his mouth start to stretch into a smile. "Right." He wanted so badly to fully believe it could be that simple. So, so badly. But the doubts were still there, loud and insistent, and in an effort to drown them out, he leaned forward and kissed her. She melted into him almost instantly, satisfaction curling through him. He lifted his hands and cupped her face, and having Lauren pressed against him, her mouth sweet and warm beneath his, felt so right—so fucking perfect—that doubts or not, he knew he couldn't hit the brakes.

A part of him was still waiting for the other shoe to drop, but the rest of him was totally on board with Theo and Lauren: Now with Orgasms.

And he had to admit, the fact that he could just make out with her here on his couch felt pretty freaking amazing. Like something he'd been desperately missing and hadn't even known it.

She broke away, her breath coming in harsh little pants. "The doctor said no strenuous activity for five days. So, I guess four more days to go."

His hand still on her face, he traced her cheekbone with his thumb. "I know. I just want to kiss you." And it was true. He'd wanted to kiss her for so long that now that he could—and could do it without worrying about leading her on—he couldn't get enough. He pressed his forehead to hers. "Thank you. For understanding. For giving me some space to...to process it all."

She smiled and kissed him once, a slow, lingering kiss. "I just want to give you what you need." She kissed him again, and as her tongue slid against his, he moaned and pulled her closer. She hadn't meant it in a dirty way, but her words had all kinds of deliciously filthy images flashing through Theo's overheated brain. Getting her naked and eating her gorgeous, pink pussy until she begged him to stop, right here on his couch. Dragging her into the shower and taking her against the wall. Lauren on her knees, her lips wrapped around his cock as he slowly fucked her pretty mouth. Teasing her clit with his fingers until she exploded on his hand. Waking her up with his face between her legs.

And then there were the full-blown fantasies. Like fucking her someplace semi-public, where the threat of getting caught was a little real. Like binding her wrists and blindfolding her while he tasted her everywhere, taking his time. Like taking her to a fancy hotel room and spending an entire weekend naked. They were fantasies he'd been harboring for a long time now—for *years*—and the fact that he could entertain them guilt-free was almost like an adrenaline rush.

His dick was now rock hard, throbbing and begging for attention. Fuck, could they really do this? Could they make this work? Explore the sexual chemistry between them without the messiness and complication of a relationship?

He guided her hand to his cock, his hips shifting a little as she teased him over top of his sweatpants. His abdomen started to throb and he ground his teeth, knowing that they were going to have to cool down.

"You turn me on so much, sweetheart. You feel how hard you make me?"

"I don't know how I'm going to last four days," she whispered, then tugged on his earlobe with her teeth. "All I want to do right now is suck you until you come." She gave his throbbing dick a squeeze and he could've sworn he saw stars. God, it was so good between the two of them. He'd always suspected it might be, but suspecting it and experiencing it were two very, very different things.

There was no way in hell he was going to last four more days without getting inside Lo. No. Freaking. Way.

But for now, his incision and the muscles in his abdomen were starting to ache in a way that he knew meant fun time was over. For now. He reluctantly pulled her talented hand from his lap and kissed her fingers. "Soon. We'll add it to the list."

She leaned back and arched an eyebrow at him. "The list?"

He grinned. "The list of things I've always wanted to do with you."

Her face lit up, her cheeks going a deeper shade of pink. "Oh! I have a list, too."

"You do?" He leaned in and started kissing her neck, unable to help himself. God, he was in so much trouble with Lauren, wasn't he? He'd never felt like this before with anyone—like he was going to fucking starve if he couldn't have her, over and over again. Like he wanted to spend hours and hours talking and laughing and hanging out, and then spend hours and hours giving each other intense orgasms. It was an incredibly dangerous combination, but they'd agreed they could handle it.

And they could. He knew they could. He had to believe they could.

He trailed his lips over the soft skin of her neck. "And what's on your list?"

She tilted her head back and made a soft purring noise that had him wanting to tear her clothes off. "I want to have sex in every single room of your apartment. On every surface. On the floor. Against the wall. Everywhere."

He mentally filed that one away for T-minus ninety-six hours from now. "And what else?" He sucked the spot just below her ear that he'd quickly learned she liked.

She whimpered, letting out a shaky breath. "I want you to tie me up and do whatever you want with me. I want to watch you get yourself off. I want you to—"

Just then, a knock at Theo's door had Lauren bounding up off the couch and he let out a groan, adjusting himself beneath the duvet as she crossed to the entryway. She rose up onto her tiptoes and peered through the peephole, then opened the door. Theo groaned when he saw three sets of broad shoulders appear in the doorway. Sebastian, Max, and Lucian all stepped inside, and Lauren shot him an apologetic smile as she closed the door. Thankfully for the situation in his sweatpants, the sight of his brothers was an immediate mood killer.

"Sorry, I thought they should know," she said with a little shrug.

"Lauren, lovely to see you, as always," said Lucian smoothly, leaning in and giving her a peck on the cheek. "How is our patient?"

She grinned. "Oh, I think he'll live."

"You feeling okay?" asked Sebastian, plunking himself down on the couch beside Theo.

"Yeah, I'm fine, just a little sore. Why do you keep showing up at my place with black eyes?" he asked, narrowing his eyes at his brother.

Sebastian ignored the question, picked up the remote and turned the TV to the Giants game. They were currently losing

26-16 against the Steelers in the third quarter. "Fuck. I have $500 on this game."

"Of course you do," said Lucian drily, shaking his head. "I hope you didn't place that bet with Fat Joey."

Again, Sebastian ignored the question.

"Fat Joey? What kind of name is Fat Joey?" asked Lauren.

"An accurate one. His name is Joseph, and he's obese. He also happens to be a bookie with a very short fuse." Lucian shrugged. "And now I have a feeling I'll be seeing him very soon." He sighed and pushed a hand through his hair, glaring at Sebastian. "You know, if you'd stop self-destructing for two seconds, I could actually help you."

"Touchdown!" Sebastian leaped to his feet, his arms in the air. "Sorry, what?"

Lucian sighed and said nothing, but Theo could feel the frustration coming off of him, probably because he felt it, too. Sebastian seemed hell-bent on wrecking himself. Granted, they all had their issues. Hell, Theo was trying to manage his feelings for Lauren because he was scared of commitment, scared of repeating the mistakes he'd witnessed as a kid, mistakes he witnessed every day in his office. Bastian's issues were just so much more obvious than the others.

"Wait," said Theo, noticing Lucian's bruised knuckles. "Did you punch Bastian?"

Lucian smirked. "Not this time."

"Seriously, do you need anything?" Max asked, turning his attention to Theo, who shook his head. "Well, here. I brought you this." He shoved a paper bag into Theo's hands. He frowned and started pulling stuff out of the bag. Tea, chocolate, a bottle of whiskey, a book of crossword puzzles, some fancy jerky. He glanced up at his grumpy brother. "Is this a care package? Max, that's so sweet," he said, teasing and sincere at the same time.

"Shut up and eat your jerky."

"So you're okay?" asked Sebastian now that the football game had gone to commercial.

"I'm fine. Really, it was totally routine. Didn't burst, I only spent one night in the hospital. I'm good. I'll probably work from home for a few days."

"Does anyone want anything to drink? Water, soda? I think I'm going to make myself a cup of tea before I have to head out," said Lauren from the kitchen. "And Theo, I think it's time for your pain meds."

"You have to leave?" he asked, glancing at her over his shoulder. He was surprised at the disappointment tugging at him.

"Yeah, I have rehearsal. Fiddle of Nowhere has a gig in a few days and Aiden and I need to make sure we've gone through the new arrangements." She smiled, her eyes bright. "We've got a killer new arrangement of 'Don't You Forget About Me' that we need to work on."

"Oh. Right. Uh, maybe a bottle of water?" She met his eyes and winked, and he felt it right in the center of his chest, like someone had just poured hot water over him. She nodded and disappeared into the kitchen.

"So what's the story here?" asked Lucian quietly, tipping his head in the direction of the kitchen, the sounds of Lauren filling the kettle and rummaging through cupboards echoing through the apartment.

"What do you mean?" he asked, knowing exactly what Lucian meant but not wanting to have this conversation with Lauren in the next room. Lucian said nothing, just cut his dark eyes between Theo and the kitchen. Lauren reappeared and handed Theo a bottle of water and his pills, giving his shoulder a squeeze.

Lucian shot Theo a look as Lauren retreated back to the kitchen. Theo just shook his head. "You don't need to meddle in my life. Everything is fine."

Lucian's eyes softened. "I'm not meddling." He leaned in closer, dropping his voice even further. "But she's a good woman, Theo. I'd hate to see her get hurt."

Theo clenched his jaw as guilt seesawed through him, tugging at his insides. "I'm feeling tired. Do you mind?" All of his earlier doubts came roaring back thanks to Lucian's words.

Lucian blinked and then backed off. "Glad you're okay, little brother. Call if you need anything."

"Don't need anyone whacked right now, but I'll keep you posted."

"Please do."

Max followed Lucian to the door, then doubled back to tug Sebastian off the couch and away from the TV.

"Oh, hey!" said Sebastian, snapping his fingers and pointing at Theo as Max dragged him toward the door. "You should bring Lauren to Aerin's wedding." Lauren reappeared at the sound of her name, a mug of tea cradled between her hands. Bastian smiled grimly at Lauren. "If you come, you'll get to meet our parents. It'll be great." Theo swore he felt a chill run down his spine. He hadn't talked to either of his parents in months. He hadn't seen his father in over a year. And given how precarious everything with Lauren felt, he wasn't sure bringing her to a Prescott family event was the best idea.

But Lauren just smiled, shrugged, and took a small sip of her tea. "Sure, why not?"

His brothers said their goodbyes, and the door closed behind them, the apartment feeling much quieter in the aftermath of the Prescott brothers circus.

"I've never actually met your parents," said Lauren softly, sitting back down on the couch beside him. He looped his arm over her shoulder.

"I know. That was on purpose."

"Oh. Well. Um, I'm sure it'll be fine. Or, I could just not go, if you don't want—"

But that was just it. He did want. He wanted very much. The idea of facing his parents and their toxicity with Lauren at his side was so much more palatable than going alone. Yeah, his brothers would be there, but they'd all be engaging in their usual avoidance tactics. Lucian would find a pretty young thing to seduce, Sebastian would have way too much to drink, and Max would just glower his way through it all. They weren't exactly allies when it came to situations involving Adelaide Thorne-Prescott (although she'd gone back to just Thorne after the divorce) and Quentin Prescott.

He pulled her in for a quick kiss, already aware of just how blurry their boundaries were and not seeming to be able to do a damn thing about it. "No, I do. I definitely do."

13

*L*auren couldn't believe that her plan had worked.

That was what she kept thinking when she returned to Theo's after her rehearsal and they'd snuggled on the couch and ordered Chinese food. She kept thinking it when they fell into bed together that night, her head on his warm chest. Kept thinking it as she woke up in his arms on Monday morning, his chest warm and firm at her back, his hand heavy and possessive on her hip.

Now, as she walked the three blocks from the library back to his place, her guitar bumping against her right leg, her overnight bag jostling against her left hip, she still couldn't quite believe that it had worked. She wasn't trying to manipulate him in any insidious way—although she did feel a twinge of guilt over not telling him what he'd said while still under the effects of the anesthesia. She knew he loved her, and she knew how she felt about him. All she was doing was giving him the space he needed to process his own feelings and work through some of his baggage. Once he saw that being with her wasn't the most terrifying thing in the world, he'd realize what they could have. She'd *show* him what they could have. It was the only move she had, honestly, and she had to believe it would work. Yes, she knew he didn't have a winning track record when it came to relationships and she knew that his parents' nasty divorce had left scars, but this was different. This was founded on ten years of friendship, and she believed that that would make the difference. After all, he'd been the one to point out that Rachel and Joey's relationship had worked because it was based on friendship.

Rachel and Joey didn't end up together, her brain chimed in helpfully, and she pushed the thought away.

Because if it didn't? She'd not only lose her potential boyfriend, but she'd probably lose her best friend in the process. All she could do was hope that the reward outweighed the risk she was taking. She was doing her best to lean in to that hope, but the doubts and the anxiety were still there, under the surface.

But then when she walked into Theo's apartment at the end of the day and laid eyes on him, she felt like melted butter, all sweet and soft. He wore a pair of gray sweatpants and a black hoodie, pushing his almost never seen glasses—he was strictly a contact lens wearer—up his nose as he paced back and forth, talking on the phone. As she went to go put her stuff away, she smiled and gave him a silent wave, her heart doing a happy little flip at the wink he sent her way. He grinned at her as she reappeared in the living room, and the melty feeling trickled through her again.

"Right, so if he's not using his time in a fifty-fifty split, I'd advise you to keep a detailed calendar where you can document every single missed visitation." Theo went quiet as he strode up to her, his phone still pressed to his ear. He wrapped his arm around her waist and then tugged her down onto the couch so she landed in his lap, straddling him, and she had to press her lips together to avoid letting out an undignified squeak. "At least six months. I know. It's a long time. But the more documentation we have, the better. Then I can file a motion to modify custody to reflect the actual time split between the two of you." He went quiet again, listening to his client. "No, I get it. We need to prove that he's not using the time he's allotted as per the custody agreement. Custody is use it or lose it, so if we can prove he's not using it, it should be pretty straightforward to have the court modify the schedule." He nodded as he listened. "Hang in there. You're a rock star mom, and we'll get this sorted out. Call me if you need anything, anytime." He ended the call and wrapped his arms around her, pulling her down for a kiss.

She dissolved into him, the stress of her day fading away as his tongue traced the seam of her mouth. He tasted like Earl Gray tea and home. God, kissing him felt so good. So natural and right, and like they should've been doing this for the past several years now. She moaned softly against his mouth and he deepened the kiss, taking her mouth greedily. But his phone started ringing and he pulled away with a sigh.

He glanced at the screen. "Sorry, I have to take this. It's one of the senior partners."

She nodded and climbed off of him, heading into the kitchen only to find that Theo had already started dinner. Peering through the oven's window, she could see a casserole bubbling away. A salad was ready and waiting in the fridge, too. He was probably doing too much, given that he'd had his appendix out less than seventy-two hours ago, but she knew there was nothing she could do or say to keep him on the couch.

"Don't get too excited. It's just chicken tetrazzini made with a store-bought rotisserie chicken." She glanced at him over her shoulder, going still when she saw the expression on his face. He'd either won the lottery or someone had died, and she didn't know which it was. But his eyes were bright, his shoulders tense, his entire body practically vibrating.

"Is everything okay?"

A huge smile broke out across his face and relief trickled through her. "That was Sanford Lennox, one of the senior partners at the firm. I'm being considered for junior partner."

"Theo!" She moved forward to wrap her arms around him. "That's amazing! It's everything you've been working toward for the past five years now." Her chest felt tight with the pride suffusing her. He worked so hard, and it felt incredible to see his hard work paying off like this.

"It's far from a done deal at this point," he said with a shrug that made his hoodie pull tight across his shoulders in a very appealing way. "I'll have to meet with the senior partners and they'll put it to a vote. But if I get it, I could make senior partner by the time I'm thirty-five."

"That's amazing. I'm so proud of you." She squeezed his shoulders, her stomach fluttering at the hard muscle beneath her fingers. His gorgeous blue eyes were soft and warm, and he lifted a hand and tucked a stray strand of hair behind her ear. She couldn't help the little shiver that coursed through her. It was heady and surreal getting to experience him like this.

"We should get some cupcakes to celebrate," she said, pressing her cheek to his solid chest. His heart thumped steadily against her and she closed her eyes, soaking in the moment.

"Mmm," he said, his deep voice rumbling in his chest,

vibrating against her cheek. "I'd rather do something else." His hands dipped lower, skimming her ass. "The next three days are going to kill me." She wriggled against him, tormenting both of them as his rock hard dick frubbed against her stomach. He groaned and gripped her tighter, pinning her in place. "No more of that."

"Or else what?" she asked, biting her lip and blinking up at him through her lashes. God, it was fun pushing his buttons and causing him to lose control. It was a power she could quickly get addicted to.

He chuckled. "You do something to me, Lo, something no one else ever has. I get my hands on you and I feel like I'm about to go crazy with wanting you. Maybe I wanna make you feel some of that craziness." Then, with the sexiest, naughtiest smile—how was it that everything he did was sexier in glasses? —he stepped away from her and took her hand, shutting off the oven as they passed by. He led her straight into his bathroom, where they stopped in front of the massive mirror. He stood behind her, his hands on her hips as he kissed her neck. "Get naked."

"But, I—"

"I wasn't asking, sweetheart." The stern edge in his voice had every nerve ending in her body standing at attention.

"But you can't—"

"And I'm not going to. But that doesn't mean I can't make you feel good. Naked. Now." He dipped his head and tugged on her earlobe with his teeth. "Be crazy with me, Lo."

Did he know how powerless she was when it came to him? With any other guy, this feeling of giving herself over recklessly would've felt dangerous and wrong. But with Theo, she didn't feel anything but safe and wanted and whole in a way she'd never experienced with anyone else.

As he kissed her neck, his cock a hard pillar at her back, she started unbuttoning her blouse with shaky fingers. It hit the floor, along with her bra, her pants, and her underwear. It felt so...so *decadent* to be completely naked while Theo was fully clothed. Decadent and wicked and exciting.

His fingers dragged down her right arm, leaving a trail of goosebumps in his wake. "You have the most beautiful skin. So soft." His fingers curled around her ribs, then skimmed down over her waist and to her hip. He gripped her, holding her against him. "I've fantasized about kissing every single one of these freckles." He dropped a kiss on her shoulder. "This one. And this one." He moved to the other side of her neck. "This one, too. All of them. Over and over again until I have them memorized." Her heart melted and pooled in her stomach, her entire body coming undone for him. She swallowed around the thickness in her throat.

His hands came up to cup her breasts, and she gasped as he rolled her hard, aching nipples between his fingers. "I love how responsive you are," he rumbled into her ear. "It's so fucking hot." He pinched her nipples, just enough to make her arch her back. She let out a shuddery moan. "Now spread your legs for me, sweetheart. Let me make you crazy." She did it, wanting to go wherever he was taking them. He dropped one hand down to cup her, and then trailed his fingers over her slit. "Open your eyes. Watch. Doesn't my hand look good between your thighs?"

"Mmmhmm," she managed, fighting the urge to squirm against him.

"Whose pussy is this?" he asked, his voice raw and frayed.

"Yours. Oh, God. It's yours." He rewarded her with a slow, teasing stroke over her throbbing clit.

"That's right, sweetheart." She pressed her ass against

him, and he groaned, circling her clit with a faster, firmer stroke. The sight of his big hand working between her legs was almost too erotic to bear, but she couldn't look away. He lifted his hand to his mouth and sucked his fingers. "You taste so sweet, Lo. So fucking sweet." And then his hand was back between her legs, working her throbbing clit. Fire licked through her as she writhed on his hand, her lips parted as she stared at their debauched reflection.

"That feels so good, Theo. Oh, God. Yes! Right there. Mmm," she panted out, her legs starting to shake a little at the effort to stay upright under the onslaught of his talented fingers. His touch dipped lower and he thrust two fingers inside her, his thumb circling her clit. He bit at her neck, his eyes bright and ravenous in their reflection.

"I can't wait to get back inside you, Lo. I can't stop thinking about filling you up again."

She made a strangled sound and threw her head back against his chest. Her entire body felt like one giant throb, every single nerve ending pulsing for him. At his touch, at his words, at the fact that it was her best friend Theo saying these dirty things to her as he stroked her clit and fucked her with his fingers.

Pleasure scorched through her, tightening her pussy around his fingers and she gripped his arms, digging her fingers in. "Shit, you're gonna make me...oh, shit. Shit!" With a loud moan, she came so hard that she could feel every single pulse of her clit, as though it had a heartbeat of its own. Her legs buckled and Theo caught her, holding her against his chest as she trembled with the aftershocks of her orgasm.

After a moment, when she'd stopped shaking, she spun in his arms, met his eyes and without a word, sank to her knees.

The need to make him feel as good as he'd just made her feel was almost overwhelming. She was still tingling and pulsing between her legs, but the only thing she could think about was giving him a taste of the pleasure he'd given her.

She tucked her fingers into the waistband of his sweatpants, toying with it. She licked her lips and kissed his hard cock through the fabric. "Can I?" she asked, her voice a shaky whisper.

He stared at her, his breath coming in harsh pants. "I shouldn't, but fuck, sweetheart. Yeah. God, yeah."

She smiled and worked his pants down over his hips, finding him completely bare underneath. She nuzzled her cheek against the hot, smooth skin of his hard cock. "If I'd known you were commando, I would've been on my knees for you the second I walked in the door."

"Jesus," he murmured, pulling his hoodie off and then sliding his hand into her hair. He wound the strands around his fist, giving a playful little tug, sending zings of electricity dancing over her scalp. "Love how your red hair looks wrapped around my hand like this," he said, staring at them in the mirror. She glanced over to look at their reflection and for a second, she could've sworn her heart stopped completely. The sight of Theo's big hand clutching her hair, Lauren completely naked and on her knees in front of him, the head of his thick cock less than an inch from her mouth...She had to remind herself to breathe. He made a gruff, sexy sound as she took just the head of him into her mouth, swirling her tongue around him. She was never going to get enough of his taste, of the warm weight of him on her tongue.

She moaned as she took him deeper into her mouth, reveling in the low, growly "fuck" he let out. His hand tightened in her hair, and she glanced up at him, smiling around his cock. The heat in his gaze was scorching, blistering, and totally, completely addictive. He lowered his free hand to her face, his thumb tracing her lower lip.

"You're so beautiful, Lo. God, I've wanted you for so fucking long."

Adrenaline and giddiness rushed through her, twisting together into something so big and so bright she could hardly breathe. The knowledge that he'd wanted this—them, her— as much as she had filled her with even more hope. They'd figure this out. If she gave him some time and some space, gave him the chance to see how good it could be between the two of them, everything would work out.

She cupped his balls and squeezed gently as she worked her mouth over him, swirling her tongue around the plump, velvety head of the world's most perfect cock. Thick and long and so incredibly sexy. Hot and smooth and gorgeous. As she sucked him deeper, he let out a low groan, his hips starting to move with her. She glanced at his tiny little incisions, already healing and pulled back, stroking him leisurely.

"Do you want me to stop?" She leaned forward and trailed kisses up his shaft, seemingly unable to keep her mouth off of him.

"I think I'll die if you stop," he said gruffly, a grin pulling up the corner of his mouth.

"Well, we can't have that." She kissed the head of his cock, flicking her tongue over the slit. She could taste how turned on he was, and in that moment, all she cared about was making him feel good. Then she took him as deep as she possibly could, picking up the pace. She could feel the muscles in his legs and stomach start to tighten along with his grip in her hair. But the sting in her scalp only served as encouragement to push him over the edge. To help him release all of the tension singing through his body. She pulled back just long enough to murmur, "Can't wait to taste you, baby," before taking him back into her mouth. The only sounds in the room were the wet slide of her mouth over his hard cock, her soft exhales and Theo's increasingly anguished groans. It was a moment Lauren wanted to live in forever.

"Oh, fuck, *fuck*, sweetheart. You're gonna make me come. Oh God, Lo." The single syllable of her nickname came out almost as a growl as he thrust into her mouth and she tasted him on her tongue. She moaned, wanting to memorize the taste of him, of this man that she'd spent most of her adult life wanting. He came in several long spurts, and she swallowed down everything he gave her, feeling almost drunk on making Theo come. On tasting him. On making him lose control with only her mouth. But then he hissed and pulled back, pressing a hand to his stomach.

She looked up at him with a frown, her brows knitting together as she wiped at her lips. "Are you okay? Did I—"

He let out a pained chuckle. "No, sweetheart. Just...shit. I probably shouldn't have come."

"Oh." She pressed her fingers to her lips. "I'm sorry."

He reached for her and hauled her to her feet, pulling her against him. "Don't you dare be sorry for that. Besides, I was a goner from the second you got on your knees." He tried—and failed—to hide another grimace.

"Come on, Mr. Future Junior Partner. Let's get you dressed and back on the couch," she said, stepping away to gather up his clothes and hand them to him. "I'll go turn the oven back on. And I think you're probably due for some pain meds.

Why don't you get settled and I'll get everything ready? Sound good?"

He caught her by the wrist and pulled her to him. "Everything sounds good with you, Lo." And then he kissed her, a sweet, lingering kiss that felt like a sunrise—full of hope and promise and something new.

14

*T*heo shoved a hand through his hair and fought the urge to rip it out by the fistful. What was supposed to have been a simple preliminary mediation meeting had turned into a screaming match between his client and his soon to be ex-wife. The mediator had long given up trying to mediate anything, and frankly, Theo couldn't blame him. These two were an absolute mess; it was hard to believe that they'd ever liked each other at one point, never mind loved each other enough to promise each other forever.

"Well, I'm glad I refused to sign that prenup because otherwise I'd be walking away from this joke of a marriage with nothing!" yelled Tiffany Babcox, his client's soon to be ex-wife.

"You deserve nothing because you were a joke of a wife!"

"Please, everyone, if we could just get back to..." The mediator tried, trailing off as Tiffany and Edward continued hurling insults at each other.

He missed working from home. He missed Lauren's quiet,

comforting presence as he answered emails and read through hundreds of pages of discovery. He missed hearing her work out a chord progression on her guitar from the next room, the strings humming melodically under her talented fingers. He missed taking a break to cuddle and make out like teenagers whenever the mood struck.

Granted what they'd done this morning had been very, *very* adult. After his alarm had gone off, he'd quietly padded into the bathroom and hopped into the shower, not wanting to wake her. She'd come home late from a gig the night before and wasn't scheduled to work at the library until noon, so he'd intended to let her sleep. Lucky for him, Lauren had had other plans and had followed him into the shower. It was the first time they'd had sex—well, the kind with his body inside hers, anyway—since that first night and it had been *so damn perfect* that he couldn't stop replaying it.

She'd slipped in behind him, sliding her hands around his waist and up his chest, exploring the ridges of his muscles before working her way down to his eager dick and stroking him, slowly, almost teasing. But he hadn't been in the mood for teasing, and so he'd spun her around, pinned her against the shower wall and taken the condom she held between her teeth. After sheathing himself, he'd started working her clit with his fingers, amazed at how hot and wet she already was. Unable to hold back, he'd hooked her leg around his waist and worked his way inside her, inch by inch, giving her time to stretch around him. He'd taken her slow and deep against the shower wall, her hands in his hair, mouths melded together.

"I will never get enough of you inside me," she'd whispered, then skated a hand down his chest and between them to stroke and rub her swollen clit. The sight of her fingers working over her pussy was one of the sexiest things he'd ever seen in his entire life. Ever.

"Mr. Prescott?" Theo blinked as the sound of his name pulled him out of his memory of Lauren in the shower and back into the conference room. "Don't you agree?"

He shuffled the folders that were spread out on the table in front of him and gave a non-committal shrug because he had no idea whatsoever what Doug Kowalski, opposing counsel for this case, had just asked him.

"Oh, please," said Tiffany, waving a manicured hand through the air. "It doesn't matter what he thinks or what *he* thinks." She gestured dismissively to her ex and Theo's client, Edward Babcox. "The fact is, we were together for fifteen years. I raised your children, I kept your house, and now you're leaving me for a younger woman. Pay up or shut up."

Theo slowly turned to look at his client, shooting daggers at him with his eyes. Then he smiled at Doug and Tiffany. "Excuse me, I just need a moment alone with my client." He grabbed Edward's elbow and practically hauled him out of his chair, marching him out of the conference room and a safe distance down the hallway.

"Do you have a mistress?" he asked point blank, not pulling any punches.

Edward at least had the decency to look chagrined. "I didn't think it was relevant?"

Theo curled his hands into fists, then shoved them in his pocket. "Goddammit, Ed." He sighed, trying to get a handle on the frustration bubbling up inside him. "I'm on your side and I want to help you, but you gotta tell me this kind of stuff, man."

"Does this hurt our case?" he asked, a slightly panicked look taking over his face.

"Uh, yeah, just a little," said Theo, his voice dripping with sarcasm. "She can claim you're at fault for the divorce because you committed adultery, which increases her chances of a judge awarding her alimony." He shook his head slowly, trying to gather his scattered thoughts. "Please tell me you haven't been spending tons of money on this woman."

Ed went pale. "Well. Um. Define tons of money."

Theo's eyes scanned the hallway, looking for another garbage can to kick as frustration surged through him. "The judge could interpret spending huge sums of money on your mistress as a reckless use of marital assets, which again, would play massively in Tiffany's favor when it comes to awarding alimony."

"Shit."

Theo blew out a long breath and leaned against the wall, facing his client. "The best we can do is come clean and make a fair offer. You've lost any ground you had to stand on. If we can mediate a settlement, you'll be better off than if we end up in court, because I can't think of a single judge who isn't going to award Tiffany everything she asks for."

Ed frowned, his face going a little red. "I thought you were supposed to be some kind of whiz kid attorney."

Theo shook his head, both flattered and annoyed at Ed's description of him. "I'm good at what I do, but a chef's only as good as his ingredients—what I have to work with can make a big difference. If you'd told me about this from the beginning, I could've helped you. And I'll still try my best, but the cards being what they are, our options are limited." He squinted at Ed. "Why didn't you tell me about this weeks ago?"

Ed slumped against the wall, his hands shoved into his pockets. "I guess I was embarrassed." He sighed heavily, and even though he was a cheating jerk, Theo couldn't help but feel a little bad for him. It wasn't sympathy, exactly. Pity, maybe. "I know that Tiff deserves better."

"So then what happened?"

He shrugged and shook his head sadly. "Things started off so great. We were so in love. The sex was fantastic and everything was just so easy."

"What changed?" How did a couple go from being so in love that they were willing to pledge their commitment to each other to cheating and bitterness and resentment? He knew it happened—he saw it every damn day at work, had lived it as a kid—but he couldn't wrap his mind around how things could shift so far from where they'd been. Deep down, Theo wondered if it was because that original love was simply a delusion brought on by sex and the excitement of someone new.

Ed let out a little snort. "We got married and had kids. Life got busy. The sex dried up. I was immersed in my work and often home late, which made her clingy. She used to be so supportive of my goals, but then it changed and it seemed like our marriage became all about what she wanted, all the time. It didn't matter what I did or what I gave her—it was never enough. So I pulled away. I know I did, and it was shitty of me. But I did. It used to be so easy between us, and after a decade, I felt like I didn't even know her. I wasn't sure if I'd ever loved her in the first place." He shrugged again. "I guess I wanted to feel wanted again. So when Melissa came along...things were already so bad between me and Tiff that it...shit, it just felt good to have someone look at me like that again."

Theo nodded, taking it all in, a heaviness sitting on his chest. If he and Lauren got together for real, like an actual relationship with the possibility of a future and everything that entailed, is this how it would end up? Screaming at each other across a conference room table, full of bitterness and anger and disappointment?

No. They weren't going to end up like Ed and Tiffany, and for more than one reason. First, he couldn't imagine ever feeling anything other than warmth and tenderness toward Lauren, who was sweet and kind and open. She'd been his best friend for a decade now, and nothing was going to change that as far as he was concerned. Second, he had no plans of ever getting married, to Lauren or anyone else, because he'd seen firsthand too many times how marriage changed people, and not usually for the better. He didn't want that—for himself, or anyone else in his life. Third, he and Lauren weren't a couple. They were two friends who were testing out some sexual waters, but that was a far cry from ring shopping and house hunting.

As he and Ed headed back toward the conference room, Theo couldn't help but feel a little smug. Maybe he and Lauren had cracked the code by keeping labels and commitment out of it. He and Lauren were not Ed and Tiffany, and they never would be.

"Thank you so much for coming out tonight!" said Lauren into the microphone. She could feel a trickle of sweat making its way down between her breasts, spots from the stage lights still dancing in front of her eyes. "We're going to play one last song to end the night. You guys have been great!" She nodded to Aiden, who counted them in, and then the band launched into their newly arranged cover of "Don't You Forget About Me," complete with banjo and fiddle lines. A fresh wave of energy charged through her as they played through the rollicking song they'd spent the last couple of weeks arranging and polishing. She leaned into the mic, smiling as she sang the lyrics.

She loved being up on stage, a guitar in her hands, so much. The energy of the crowd, the idea that she was doing something that brought joy to others, the power and beauty of the music moving through her...it was her happy place, totally and completely.

Although, Theo's bed was giving the stage a run for its money when it came to her all-time favorite places. As his face flashed through her mind, her eyes scanned the crowd, but she couldn't see him. The lights were too bright to see beyond the first couple of rows of people, and they'd packed the house tonight. Even though they were just a cover band, Fiddle of Nowhere had a growing fan base and were drawing bigger and bigger crowds at their gigs. They'd evolved from a bar band with banjos to an act people bought tickets to see. She felt proud of how hard she and Aiden and the others had worked to build this, even if it was just a fun side project for her.

She had to admit, she was feeling a bit stagnant when it came to her own music. Yeah, she was still performing and still writing songs, but ever since the audition for Lynne Townsend, she'd felt as though any momentum she'd had had completely stalled out, and she couldn't fully pinpoint why. She was used to the rejection, but for some reason, this particular one had really knocked the wind out of her sails. It felt more...more final than the others. Like it was proof that she wasn't going to make it and that opportunities were drying up.

A heaviness sat in her stomach, like she'd eaten rocks for dinner instead of the takeout sushi she'd grabbed after work. Maybe it was time to accept that this was all there was. She'd work at the library and play her gigs and that would be her little life. Something that felt like grief flashed through her at the thought, and she did her best to blink it away, focusing on getting through the end of the song before she started doom-spiraling about the state of her dreams.

A couple of minutes later, the final song of the night ended, the last chord still reverberating through the speakers. Lauren took a bow with her bandmates, letting herself soak up the cheers of the crowd for a moment. Buzzing with energy, she turned and headed off stage with everyone else, where they all chatted about the show and guzzled cold bottles of water that a thoughtful bartender had set out for them. Once the house lights had come on and the crowd had started to disperse, she set her water aside and set about the ultra-glamorous work of packing up all of their gear. She glanced over at the drum kit that their drummer, Nathan, was currently taking apart and she was glad she only had to worry about a couple of microphones and guitars. They'd load most of their gear into Nathan's cargo van—a hand-me-down he'd gotten from his uncle that was still emblazoned with a bright red "Ray's Catering" logo on the side—except for her two guitars, which would come home with her.

As she worked to unplug the tangle of cords from a nearby amplifier, she heard a familiar voice from just behind her.

"Hey," said Theo, sliding his arms around her waist. "Any chance a groupie could get a little action?"

She laughed and spun in his arms, forgetting all about the cords. "Hey. Did you like the show?"

"You guys were awesome. I could hear people around me talking about how good you were. It's too bad the others couldn't come—they would've loved it, too." More than the compliment, it was the obvious pride in his voice that made her feel like she was glowing from the inside out. He dipped his head and brushed his lips over hers. "You were so sexy up there tonight," he said, his voice taking on that growly tone that always had her insides turning into liquid gold, all warm and bright and melty.

She curled her fists into the fabric of his white Henley, heat already starting to pulse between her legs. "Help me clean up so we can get out of here," she said, nuzzling her face into his neck and inhaling his scent. They'd been doing this for over a week now and she was completely addicted to him. She lived in a state of both perpetual soreness and perpetual horniness. It was the most exquisite kind of torture she'd ever experienced.

"Yes ma'am." He pulled away with a cute wink and then set about untangling the cords and winding them into perfect loops. She didn't even know how many times he'd helped her pack up after a gig. Enough times that he knew his way around an amplifier and a snarl of cords. She hummed to herself as she worked, carefully laying her acoustic guitar down into its case and then closing the lid, flipping the latches shut. The energy from the successful show still buzzed through her, and Theo's touch and words and only amplified it.

"Lauren, can you come here for a sec?" called Aiden as he poked his head out from backstage, his dark brown curls flopping into his eyes. "We've got a bit of an issue."

She frowned, rubbing her palms on her thighs. "What's wrong?"

Aiden jerked his thumb over his shoulder. "He's trying to stiff us."

The buzz she'd been feeling turned cold, leaving her a little breathless—and not in a fun way.

"You want me to come with?" asked Theo as he stepped up beside her, his hands in the back pockets of his jeans.

She nodded, gratitude chasing away some of her anxiety. She always felt better when she was with him, like everything was just easier when he was around. They headed backstage and followed Aiden to the club owner's little office, where he sat behind a dinged-up black metal desk going through that night's receipts.

"I already paid him," he said dismissively, waving a beefy hand in Aiden's direction.

"No, you paid me $1500 when we agreed that it would be $2000 plus ten percent of ticket sales."

Bob, the club owner, shrugged. "I don't remember that."

Lauren swallowed thickly and then pulled her phone out of her pocket. "Really? Because I have the email right here."

He smirked. "An email isn't a contract."

Theo took Lauren's phone, his eyes scanning across the screen. "I mean, it's not signed, but this is definitely a contract."

Bob let out an impatient huff. "Who's this guy?"

Theo grinned. "I'm their lawyer. Look, it's in writing here in the email that the flat fee is $2000 plus ten percent of ticket sales. You're Bob Haskell, right?"

"Yeah."

Theo flipped the phone around to show him the email. "And this is your email address?"

Bob scowled. "Yeah."

"So we've established that you entered into a written agreement—also known as a contract—with Fiddle of Nowhere to perform tonight for the agreed upon fee and cut of ticket sales. The name, date, location—everything's here. So you've got three options, Bob. One, you pay the band what you promised and we leave. Two, you don't and I'll file papers tomorrow morning to take you to court."

Bob's scowl deepened to the point where his jowls trembled. "And what's option three?"

Theo handed Lauren her phone back and stepped forward, bracing his hands on Bob's desk. "Do you know who Lucian Prescott is?"

Bob went completely pale, so pale that Lauren thought he might pass out. "Yeah. Yeah, okay. Hang on." He turned and opened a small safe under a table against the far wall. He counted out another wad of bills and shoved it into Aiden's hands. "I don't want trouble with Lucian, okay?"

Theo smiled. "And now you won't have any."

As they turned to leave Bob's cramped office, she grabbed Theo's hand and said softly, "I am so turned on right now. I love it when you get all lawyery."

He chuckled. "I think he was more intimidated by the mention of Lucian's name than my legal prowess. But I'm glad I was here to help all the same."

Aiden turned, counted out Lauren's share of the money and then slipped the rest into an envelope to disperse to the rest of the band. "Thanks, man."

"No problem. Happy to help."

Aiden nodded and turned, off to pay everyone else. The second they were alone, Lauren tugged Theo down for a kiss.

"Thank you," she murmured against his mouth. "For helping. For being here."

He slid his arms around her waist. "I didn't overstep, did I? I just know that you get so stressed out dealing with stuff like that I and I wanted to help."

She shook her head. "No, you didn't overstep. I'm glad you were here."

He kissed her forehead, sending warmth cascading through her. She loved these casual, affectionate gestures and how natural they felt. A part of her wanted to ask him if they felt natural to him too, but she didn't want to push it. Things were so good, and she knew he could see and feel it too. She didn't need to wreck it by making him feel like she was boxing him in.

"I'll always have your back, Lo," he said, cupping her jaw and tracing his thumb over her cheekbone. "Nothing's gonna change that."

God, she hoped he was right.

Footsteps echoed across the now nearly empty stage, the sound of heels clicking against the wooden floor. "I'm sorry, I didn't mean to interrupt," said a woman's voice.

Lauren turned, recognition flooding her and sending her heart vaulting into her throat. "Oh my God, you're—"

"Sadie Hopkins," said the woman, extending her hand with a warm smile. She had a halo of golden curls threaded with gray, an angular face, and a wide smile. Her skin had a sun-kissed look that Lauren was sure came from living in Southern California and not a Manhattan spray tan.

Trying to keep the tremble out of her voice, she turned to Theo. "She's Lynne Townsend's producer."

Theo's eyes went wide. He pointed at his chest and then in the direction of stage left, silently asking her if she wanted him to give her some privacy. She nodded, smiling at him. He gave her hand a squeeze, picked up her two guitars and carried them off for her.

Sadie smiled warmly. "A man who'll help you cart your gear around? Now that's a keeper."

Lauren's stomach twisted itself into a rock hard pretzel as she watched Theo go, knowing that Sadie was completely right—he was a keeper—and that it might not be up to her at all whether or not she kept him. Forcing herself to focus, she cleared her throat and tucked a strand of hair behind her ear, not quite knowing what to do with her hands.

"Great show tonight," said Sadie casually, rocking back on her heels. "Do you do all the arrangements yourself?"

Lauren licked her lips. "Me, and my bandmate Aiden, the one who was singing and playing piano tonight."

Sadie nodded. "And did you work together on that arrangement of 'Don't You Forget About Me?'"

Lauren shook her head. "No. That was me."

"And what about 'I Believe in a Thing Called Love?'"

"Also me."

"'Mr. Brightside?'"

She bit her lip and shook her head. "That one was Aiden's."

Sadie nodded. "I saw your audition, the one you did for Lynne. For what it's worth, they should've picked you. In my opinion."

Lauren felt as though someone had dropped hot coals into her stomach. "Seriously?"

"Seriously. You're really talented."

"Wow, I..." She trailed off, shaking her head. "Thank you. That means a lot coming from you." Sadie had not only mentored and produced Lynne Townsend but several other mega successful artists Lauren admired.

"You're welcome. Listen, I don't want to keep you," she said, nodding in the direction Theo had gone, "but I'd love to sit down with you and talk about the future."

"Seriously?" Lauren's voice came out a little squeaky and she cleared her throat again, her pulse hammering away in her temples. "Sorry, I do have a bigger vocabulary. I just can't believe you're here and you want to talk to me...this feels surreal."

Sadie smiled again and reached into her back pocket, then extended her card to Lauren. "Believe it, babe. I don't want to put you on the spot right now, so I'll just give you this. Take a look at your schedule and let me buy you a coffee. I'm in town for the next week." She pointed at the card. "That's my cell on there."

Lauren nodded, holding the card in two hands as though it were something incredibly precious. And honestly, to her it was. "Okay. I'll call you to set something up."

"Please do. Because Lauren, I think you've got something special. *Seriously* special," she added with a wink. Oh, Lauren liked her a lot already. She seemed warm and kind and genuine with a laid-back vibe.

Naturally, she gave a dorky little salute which she immediately regretted. "Wow. I can't believe...thank you. I will. I'll call you. Is five minutes from now too soon?"

"Well hey, if you know your schedule, why don't we get something on the books now?" Both women pulled out their phones. "How about next Friday, three in the afternoon?"

Lauren nodded. She'd have to leave work early, but she was sure she could get Dori to cover for her. "That's perfect."

"Great. Give me a call if anything changes." She smiled

and turned, walking off the stage and leaving Lauren alone. A rush of excitement charged through her, and as soon as she was sure no one was watching, she let out a whoop and jumped up in the air, feeling lighter than she had in a long time.

15

*L*auren swung idly from side to side in her desk chair, her eyes roving around the nearly empty library. It was a Tuesday night, which was her evening to work, and a glance at the clock told her that it was nearly eight o'clock. She was on the reference desk alone, and aside from helping someone with the photocopier, she hadn't had anything to do for the past hour. Glancing around again to make sure no one was looking in her direction, she pulled her phone out of the desk drawer and texted Theo.

Lauren: I'm borrrrrreeedddddddddd

As usual, his reply came back almost instantly, but it wasn't the speed of his reply that had her inhaling sharply, heat creeping up her neck and to her cheeks.

Theo: I just got out of the shower and I'm really wishing you were here. Showering alone is no fun.

She glanced up and looked around again, feeling as though she were doing something very, very bad right now. But there was no one around and she couldn't resist the opportunity to engage in a little flirty sexting with Theo. It was something they hadn't done before, and a thrill charged through her at the idea.

It was absolutely fascinating, getting to see this side of him. She knew him so well—how could she not, given how close they'd been for so long? —and yet she was uncovering all of these new, hidden parts of him and it only made her want more.

Lauren: I'm wearing that dress you really like.

Theo: The green one?

Lauren: Yeah. The one that ties in the front.

Theo: I do love that dress. I *was* wearing a towel...

Her stomach fluttered and her heart picked up its pace at the idea that he was naked right now, his skin damp and warm from the shower. She shifted in her seat, rubbing her thighs together.

Lauren: Unf. You're killing me.

Theo: No dying on me, Lo. I can't wait to see you in that dress later.

Lauren: I have to say, I look very put together today.

Theo: You won't when I'm done with you.

A smile broke out across her face, and she pressed a hand to her heated cheek.

Lauren: What are you going to do to me?

Theo: I'm going to peel you out of that dress as soon as you get here because as good as it looks on you, I think it'll look even better on the floor. Then I'm going to pick you up and throw you on the bed, where I plan to eat your pussy for as long as I damn well please.

Lauren: And then?

She could barely type the words out, her hands were trembling so much from how hard and fast her heart was pounding. Holy shit, this was sexy. She glanced around again, feeling like if someone saw her, they'd be able to tell what she was doing. She imagined a neon sign glowing above her head that said "sexting with her boyfriend who doesn't quite know he's her boyfriend" with a giant arrow pointing directly at her red face.

The thought was almost sobering enough to snap her back to reality, but then Theo replied.

Theo: And then I think I'd like to bend you over the desk in the living room. I love the way your ass looks when it bounces against my hips.

Lauren rubbed a hand over her neck and let out the tiniest whimper. Thankfully, there was no one around to hear it. She wracked her brain for what to write back, but he was so much better at this than she was, in a way that almost made her feel off balance, but didn't because she trusted him.

Theo: Or maybe I'll tie your hands behind your back and put you on your knees.

Lauren: I am so wet right now. My panties are soaked.

And she wasn't being creative—it was true. She could feel the slick heat from between her legs, and she shifted in her chair. It was delicious being so turned on, so achy and wet for him and not being able to do a damn thing about it because of where she was. Delicious and naughty.

Theo: I know, baby. I'm so hard for you right now it almost hurts.

Lauren: Are you touching yourself?

Theo: No. I'm saving it all for you.

Lauren: Good. Because I want it all, and it wouldn't be fair if you could touch yourself while I'm stuck here in public.

"Excuse me, can I get more time on the computer?" At the sound of the man's voice, Lauren let out a tiny shriek and almost sent her phone flying. "Sorry, didn't mean to scare you."

She shook her head, setting her phone down beside her computer. "It's okay. Which one are you on?"

He pointed, and she opened up the window with the computer management software. After she'd extended his time by another thirty minutes, she picked her phone back up again.

Theo: Not to change the subject, but I wanted to check on two things with you.

Lauren: Shoot.

Theo: First, are we still going to Willa and Kayla's Halloween party on Friday?

Friday. Just the mention of the word had her palms sweating and her stomach clenching. She'd barely been able to stop thinking about the upcoming meeting with Sadie Hopkins and she'd been in a perpetual state of nervous excitement. She was having coffee with a super successful record producer who thought she was talented. Her mind kept racing ahead, imagining things like record deals and hit singles and sold out concerts where thousands of fans sang her own lyrics back to her.

Lauren: Yep. Got my costume and everything.

For half a second, she'd been tempted to ask him how he felt about doing a coordinated costume—like Beetlejuice and Lydia, or Barbie and Ken—but she'd been too worried that it might freak him out, so she'd decided to leave it alone. Things were so good between them that she didn't want to rock the boat by making him feel pressured in any way.

Then again, she'd been censoring herself a lot lately when it came to her non-boyfriend, and it was starting to wear a little thin.

Time. She just had to give it time.

Theo: Okay, great. Second question.

Lauren: Hit me.

Theo: I'm looking at flights and stuff—you're 100% good to come with me to Aerin and Javier's wedding? It's in Dallas on the 7th, so we'd go for the weekend. But no pressure. If you don't want to come, that's cool.

Lauren: I'm in. I'm off that weekend and don't have any gigs, so we're all good.

Theo: Okay. I'll book the flights. I already booked a room a while ago.

Lauren: Oooh, hotel sex!

Theo: You read my mind. I'm going to finish up some work. Text me when you're leaving, okay?

Lauren: Will do. Don't work too hard.

His meeting with the senior partners was coming up in just a week and he'd been spending all of his free time—well, the free time leftover when he wasn't giving her toe curling orgasms—preparing.

Theo: Don't worry, I'm saving all my energy for you.

She tucked the phone back in the drawer, then swiveled idly back and forth in her chair. Everything important in her life had felt so stagnant for so long—her feelings for Theo, her music career—that now it felt like everything was moving at warp speed. She closed her eyes for a second, allowing herself to picture everything she wanted, not just for herself, but for them. Theo making junior partner. Signing a contract with a major record label. A future with Theo—one that actually included labels. One that didn't freak him out.

For the first time in a long time, these thoughts didn't feel like dreams. They felt like possibilities.

From his spot in the kitchen, Theo heard his front door open and Lauren set her bags down in the entryway. He smiled as anticipation curled through him. He'd planned a surprise for her tonight, and he couldn't wait to see her reaction. Couldn't wait for all the things he'd planned in the name of taking her mind off of her upcoming meeting with Sadie Hopkins and the stress she'd been feeling over it. The idea had taken root the other night when they'd been sexting, and he'd spent the past couple of days planning and organizing.

"Hey," she said, poking her head into the kitchen and smiling at him. His heart did its usual flippy floppy thing in his chest when he laid eyes on her. Like it was a fish out of water gasping for air. Which wasn't the most attractive image, but it felt like the most accurate because more than anything, he felt like he was flailing. The lines were so blurry that he didn't know where friend Lauren and more-than-a-friend Lauren began and ended. And while it was what he'd wanted —what he still wanted—he had to admit that the lack of any clarity made him feel restless. But not restless enough to do anything about it because that prospect was completely terrifying.

Did he have feelings for her? Yes.

Did he want to be more than friends? Yes.

Did he want to rock the boat and have everything unravel? Fuck no.

"Hey," he smiled back, leaning forward to kiss her forehead. Then he grabbed a pair of oven mitts and pulled the tray of nachos out of the oven, filling the kitchen with the scents of melted cheese and warm tortilla chips.

She inhaled and made a soft little moan that had blood

flowing straight to his dick. He'd never felt so completely insatiable with a woman before. It didn't matter how many times he had her, it only made him want her more. Want her over and over again in a way that was both addictive and petrifying.

"You made nachos?" she asked, leaning a hip against the counter. He loved how completely at home she looked in his place. Loved seeing her toothbrush on his bathroom vanity. Loved the sight of her guitar propped up in a corner of the living room.

Fuck.

"Yeah." He pulled off the oven mitts and went to the fridge, pulling out a bottle of her favorite white wine. "And we have this."

Her eyes lit up. "Ooh, fancy! Let me just go put my stuff away and I'll be right back."

"Okay."

"You know, Aspen made a joke about renting out my room," she called over her shoulder as she headed for his bedroom.

Theo laughed, not knowing what to say to that. Was it fucked up that he was totally willing to let her move in, but not willing to call her his girlfriend or make any kind of promises?

Yes. Yes, it was, and he knew it. Knew it and didn't have the slightest clue what to do about it.

So instead he focused on retrieving two wine glasses from a nearby cabinet, opening the bottle, and then taking the two glasses along with the tray of nachos into the living room where he'd set up everything else.

When Lauren emerged from his bedroom, she'd changed into her favorite comfy outfit—his Columbia Law sweatshirt and a pair of black leggings. He loved it when she wore his clothes—he liked seeing her covered in something that belonged to him. She smiled as she approached, her eyes roving over the coffee table that was covered with the nachos, wine glasses, and an assortment of her favorite candy.

"What is all this?" she asked, sitting down on the couch next to him and tucking her feet up under her.

"I thought you could use a little stress relief. I know how anxious you are about your meeting with Sadie."

She bit her lip and smiled at him. "Thanks, Theo. This is really sweet."

Warmth suffused him, along with a happiness that came from making her happy. And she didn't even know what else he had in store for the evening.

He handed her the remote along with a glass of wine. "Here. Pick whatever you want."

She put on an episode of *Arrested Development* and then took one of the plates he'd set out, helping herself to the nachos, then settled back against the couch, munching happily as the show played.

"You know," she said after several minutes of silent chewing, "from what you've told me, your family is kind of like the Bluths."

He threw back his head and laughed. "I'd never thought of it that way, but they are a bunch of rich, dysfunctional assholes. Please at least tell me that I'm Michael."

"Of course," she said, setting her plate down and grabbing a handful of gummy worms. "And Sebastian is obviously Gob. Would Aerin be Lindsay? And I'm not so sure about Lucian and Max."

"None of the Bluths are as scary as Lucian or as grumpy as Max. Aerin's got the skinny blonde thing down, but that's about where the similarities end." He pulled her against him and tucked her into his side. She laid her head on his shoulder, snuggling into him. After a few moments of easy silence, he said, "I know you're freaked about this meeting, and I get it. But you've got this." He pressed a kiss to her temple. "She saw your audition and then sought you out. Whatever she wants to talk to you about, I'm sure it's good."

"And if it's not?" she asked, her eyes still glued to the TV screen.

"Then another opportunity will come along. I know it will, because you're so talented. I believe in you, Lo."

She let out a little sigh. "That makes one of us."

He tipped her chin up, forcing her to meet his eyes. "Then I'll believe in you enough for the both of us until you get there."

She leaned forward and kissed him, her mouth warm and sweet against his. "Thanks, Theo. That means a lot to me."

He kissed her again, then stood, turned off the TV and extended his hand to her. "Come on. I have more stress relief planned."

Her cheeks flushed and she laid her hand in his, practically vaulting up off of the couch. He loved that she was just as hungry for him as he was for her. Fuck, his list of things he loved about her kept growing and growing, didn't it?

He led her into his bedroom, which was dark save for the few candles flickering around the bed. He wrapped his arms around her from behind, trailing kisses over her neck. She swayed back against him, her ass nestled against his growing erection. "Naked and facedown on the bed," he said, reluctantly letting her go. She turned to face him, holding his gaze as she pulled his hoodie off over her head, revealing her breasts. Then she hooked her fingers into her leggings and tugged them down over her legs. He was almost tempted to tell her to leave her panties on—all the better to tease her and drive her crazy—but then she slipped them off too and he wasn't about to tell her to put them back on. Glancing at him over her shoulder, she climbed onto his bed and laid face down as he'd asked.

A surge of something so powerful charged through Theo at the sight of Lauren spread out on his bed. Waiting for him. Trusting him. He sucked in a breath and then reached for the small bottle on the bedside table. Carefully sweeping her hair away from her neck and shoulders, he then squirted some of the slippery massage oil into his palm.

"This might be cold," he warned, just before he rubbed his hands together and then slicked them down her back, from her shoulders to the top of her ass. He splayed his hands over her back, reveling in how much of her he could touch at once.

She moaned into the pillow as he started working on her tense shoulders. "Oh my God, that feels *so good*."

He leaned forward and kissed her jaw. "I'm just getting started, sweetheart." She sighed, and he worked his hands over her shoulders, down her back, kneading the pale globes of her ass until her hips were shifting on the bed and his dick was throbbing eagerly against his jeans. With each stroke up and down her back and to her ass, he dipped his hands just a little bit lower, teasing the seam where her ass met her thighs, where her thighs met her pussy. Teasing and stroking and slowly, with each pass, urging her legs a little farther apart.

When he started massaging her inner thighs, the tips of his fingers brushing against her outer lips, she let out a shuddery moan and spread her legs wider, arching her hips up. Pink and glistening, he could see how turned on she was from this, and another surge of powerful lust tinged with something he couldn't quite name charged through him. Spreading her open with his thumbs, he stroked one finger down her slit.

"Oh, fuck, Theo," she moaned, writhing against the pillow. "This is so freaking hot. Don't stop. Please don't stop." She arched her hips up even higher off the bed, a silent plea for more. He groaned and circled his fingers slowly around her clit with one hand, still massaging her thigh with the other. She gasped and pressed into his hand, her thighs shaking a little. Fuck, he loved how responsive she was to him. It was beyond sexy knowing he could turn her on like this. Knowing he could make her wet, make her shake, make her beg, make her come.

He kept circling his slick fingers over her clit, feeling her swell under his touch. He spread her open with one hand, then slid two fingers into her, rubbing her clit with the palm of his hand as he stroked her from within.

"Oh, shit!" She bucked against his hand and he felt her come, spasming around his fingers, fresh wetness flooding him. She rode his hand, her hips jerking. He pulled his hand free and guided her onto her back, and he chuckled when he noticed that her legs were still shaking. She reached for him, grabbing at the front of his jeans and his impossibly hard dick, but he gently pushed her hand away.

"Tonight is about you, sweetheart. And I'm not done yet." Then he took the little bottle again and squirted more of the massage oil onto his palms. Slicking his hands over her breasts, he teased her nipples with gentle strokes and little pinches. Her back arched up off the bed, her eyes closed, a red flush coloring her from her hairline to the tops of her breasts. He teased and played, massaging her breasts, giving her time to come down from her orgasm so he could give her another. After a few minutes, her hips were once again writhing. Not able to wait anymore, he tugged her to the edge of the bed, dropped to his knees and closed his mouth over her pussy. The coconut flavor of the massage oil mingled with Lauren, and Theo was pretty sure he'd never be able to look at a macaroon again without getting hard.

He skimmed a hand up to her breast, massaging her as he swirled his tongue over her swollen clit. All of his senses were filled with Lauren—the sound of her moans, the taste of her pussy, the feel of her against his mouth, under his touch, the sight of her splayed for him, flushed with pleasure, the smell of the massage oil and her arousal. All he wanted was to make her feel good. To show her with his body what he couldn't say out loud.

He licked a path downward, fucking her with his tongue, her hips moving in time with him. Sliding his hands down her body, he pushed her thighs open and back so he could have even better access. Then he closed his mouth over her again, kissing her slowly and deeply, feeling each flutter of her pussy against his tongue. After several moments, he pulled back, kissing her inner thighs.

"You have the most beautiful pussy," he said, his voice low and rough. He stroked a finger up and down her drenched slit. "I can't get enough."

"Oh, God," she moaned as he sucked her clit into his mouth. "It's yours, Theo. It's all yours."

A possessiveness unlike anything he'd ever felt before sang through him, and he ate her with long, deep sweeps of his tongue over her swollen flesh. Her thighs started to shake even harder and he knew she was close. He could barely keep his mouth on her, she was shaking so hard. But he didn't stop, keeping up the steady rhythm of his lips and tongue working over her.

She screamed, her hands fisted in the sheets as her head thrashed back and forth. "Fuck, Theo, I'm gonna...Oh, God... Oh, God...Fuuuuuuck. Theo!"

Her hips jerked almost violently and he felt her clit start pulsing against his tongue. Gradually he gentled his licks and sucks, slowly pulling away, letting her come down gently. Her hands tugged at his shoulders, pushing at his shirt.

"You. Naked. Now," she said, her voice hoarse, her skin flushed, her eyes bright.

He grinned at her from between her legs. "Tonight was supposed to be all about you."

She sat up and started unzipping his jeans. "And I want you inside me. Now."

Like he was gonna argue with that. Like he had any choice when it came to Lauren, in so many ways.

He tugged his shirt off over his head and then shucked his jeans and boxers in record time. He was almost painfully hard, his cock leaking for her. And when she leaned back on her elbows, spread her legs and said, "Come get your pussy," he was done. Totally, completely done.

He climbed on top of her and slid inside her in one stroke. She clenched around him, welcoming him, her tight heat making him grit his teeth and fight the urge to pump his hips.

"Oh, shit," he whispered, unable to stop himself from thrusting slowly in and out.

"What?" she asked, her eyes glazed with pleasure.

"Condom," he managed to pant out as he stroked in and out of her again, fighting not to lose control at how incredible she felt around him. Even though he knew he needed to stop, he couldn't. Now that he was inside her bare, he couldn't seem to stop fucking her.

"Oh."

Using every ounce of willpower he had, he started to pull away, but she stopped him, locking her legs around his hips. "I'm on the pill, so unless you have a reason we need one..."

He shook his head, thrusting back into her, burying himself to the hilt and letting out a loud groan. "No, I'm good. Fuck, Lo. You feel incredible. Shit. Don't move. I need a second." He'd never been bare inside a woman before, and somehow it only felt right that the first time was with Lauren.

She moaned and tightened around him, somehow pulling him even deeper. Winding her arms around his neck, she pulled him down for a slow, deep kiss, the movement of her tongue matching the slow grind of his hips. Wrapping his arms around her, he rolled them onto their sides, her body, still slick with the massage oil, sliding against his in a way that had every nerve ending in his body screaming for more. Moaning and gasping, they rocked together, sliding and grinding in the slowest, most exquisite tangle of bodies. She wove her fingers into his hair, trailing kisses along his jaw and down his neck as they moved together. When she pulled back, her eyes were practically glowing in the soft light. Glowing in a way that made him feel like she was the only person who'd ever truly seen him.

I fucking love you.

The words were on the tip of his tongue, but he couldn't bring himself to say them. Couldn't bring himself to face how drastically they would change everything. This, what they had now, would have to be enough.

"Theo," she whispered, her fingers feathering over his jaw, his mouth. "This...Oh, God. You feel so good inside me."

He started to move faster, her words spurring him on. He rocked his hips harder, deeper, burying himself in her over and over again until a throbbing heat gathered in his balls and at the base of his spine. The knowledge that he was about to come inside her, to fill her up was what pushed him over the edge. With an anguished groan, he came, pulsing inside her. She cupped his face and kissed him as he emptied himself, giving her everything he had.

If only he could give her everything she wanted.

16

*L*auren strode into the little coffee shop in the East Village with her shoulders back and her head held high, trying to project an aura of confidence she was definitely not feeling. Her palms were sweaty, her stomach was in knots, her pulse pounding away in her temples. Even though she was ten minutes early for her meeting with Sadie, she spotted the other woman sitting at a table by the large front window. She looked up from her phone and waved when she saw Lauren. Subtly wiping her hands on her jeans, Lauren smiled and headed for Sadie's table.

"Hey, nice to see you again," said Sadie, exuding a laid-back SoCal vibe. She gestured at the chair across from her. "Have a seat. You want a coffee? Tea? Latte?"

Her instinct was to politely decline, but she decided that it looked better if she ordered something. She didn't want to give away how nervous she was. Sadie probably met with aspiring musicians all the time and this meeting was no big deal to her. But it wasn't like Lauren was knocking back lattes with Grammy-winning music producers on the regular.

"Yes, thank you. A chai latte, please."

Sadie smiled and rose from the table. "You got it. Be right back." She sauntered up to the counter and Lauren tried not to stare at her as she ordered their drinks. She forced herself to look around the coffee shop and people watch, to look out the window at the gray October sky. A couple of people dressed in Halloween costumes walked by—a man dressed as an alien, a woman dressed as a disco ball, a teen couple dressed as Jasmine and Aladdin. Her heart gave a little tug at the sight of the coordinated costumes, and she wished she'd had the nerve to ask Theo to do one with her. Something had shifted between them the other night, when he'd provided the most excellent stress relief in her life. He'd been more... open with her. More vulnerable and exposed, even though he hadn't said anything. A spark had flared to life inside her that night, fueled entirely by the hope that he was seeing what they could have and opening up to the idea that it wasn't that scary.

When Sadie returned to their table with a latte for Lauren and a green tea for herself, Lauren had managed to calm her racing heart, just a little. Whatever this was about, everything would be fine. Truly.

"So you're probably dying of curiosity as to what I wanted to talk to you about, huh?" she asked with a wry grin.

Lauren managed to smile back, toying with the paper sleeve on her cup. "Oh, just a little."

Sadie laughed, a warm, melodic sound that helped Lauren relax a little more. "I wanna mentor you, Lauren."

She froze, her eyes wide, her ears buzzing. "I'm sorry, what?"

"I think you have a killer talent. With the right coaching, you could be the next Maren Morris. The next Sheryl Crow.

The next Joni Mitchell. I see something in you that I don't see in many others. You've got this glimmer inside you that I want to nourish."

Lauren was so shocked that she could barely get her mouth to move. "Oh my God," she finally managed, her stomach spinning and swirling while her heart shook in her chest. "I'm...Holy shit, I'm honored. And thrilled. Is this real?"

Sadie laughed again, tucking a strand of her curls behind her ear. "It's real, babe."

Lauren blew out a breath, a tiny laugh escaping her. "So, um, what would the mentorship entail?"

Sadie leaned back in her chair, took a sip of her tea and then folded her hands in her lap. "We'd work together on a daily basis. We'd jam, write music, and I'd guide you in the right direction when it comes to songwriting, musical technique, that sort of thing. All with the end goal of putting an album of new material together, which I'd produce and record for you."

Names flashed through Lauren's brain, names of successful artists who had worked with Sadie. Names like Fiona Apple, Lana Del Rey, Miranda Lambert, Jewel, Halsey. The idea that her name might one day be as well-known as theirs—that her music might actually be out there for people to listen to—was almost impossible to wrap her head around. She'd wanted this for so long that she'd become so focused on the struggle and had lost sight of the end goal.

Lauren took a sip of her latte, her hands trembling. "That sounds incredible. I can't...I don't even know what to say."

Sadie smiled and shrugged. "Say you'll come out to LA and work with me."

The smile dropped from Lauren's face and she took another sip of her drink to try to cover her reaction. "LA?"

"Well, yeah. That's where my studio is. That's where I work." She gestured at the coffee shop around them, then pointed out the window. "Personally, I find it hard to create in New York. Everything is so gray and busy and noisy that I can't see or hear or think properly, you know? It doesn't work for me. But LA does. It's colorful and warm and peaceful in a way that New York could never be. There's a gorgeous apartment you can stay in, free of charge."

Lauren sat back in her chair, feeling completely deflated. Of course, now, when things were finally shifting in the right direction with Theo, she'd get offered the opportunity of a lifetime on the other side of the country.

"For how long?" she asked, twisting her cup in circles.

"A year, at least. Maybe longer. We'd need to spend several months working together and writing music, then recording. Then we'd be in the pre-release promo stage, and then touring."

"Right. Yeah."

Sadie sipped her tea and didn't say anything for a moment, then drummed her long fingers on the table.

"I can see that I've thrown you for a loop." Leaning forward, her elbows on the table, she cradled her tea between her hands. "Not that it's really any of my business, but is your hesitation about the boyfriend?"

"Oh, um." Lauren shook her head and blinked rapidly. "He's not...we're just..." But she couldn't bring herself to finish either sentence. *He's not my boyfriend. We're just friends.* Neither were exactly true. "This is just a lot to take in."

Sadie nodded. "I get it. You'd be uprooting yourself to do this, and that takes some consideration. Why don't you take some time to think it over? There's no rush. But for what it's worth, Lauren, I think you have something unique, and I want to be a part of that. Together, I think we could make something truly special. Oh, and I almost forgot to mention —there's a bursary, once you agree. Part of the mentorship program. It's not a lot, but it should be enough to take care of your bills."

In that moment, Lauren could see two paths stretching before her, clear as day: one where she stayed in New York and had a relationship with Theo, and one where she chased her dream and moved to LA to work with Sadie. She managed to smile at Sadie, nodding.

"Thank you so much for this opportunity. I...I need to think it over, but I'll get back to you soon, I promise."

Sadie smiled and shrugged again in that immensely appealing affable way she had. "Sure. Like I said, no rush. You've got my card; get in touch when you know what you want to do. I'm headed back to LA tomorrow, but you can always get me on my cell or send me an email."

She nodded. "Okay. Thank you, Sadie. I'll be in touch."

Sadie stood and pulled on her jacket. "I know you will. Be well, Lauren. Talk soon, I hope."

As soon as Sadie was out the door, Lauren slumped back in her chair, emotions crashing through her, each one loud and insistent as it tried to drown out the others. Elation and excitement and pure joy, shouting to be heard over the doubt, the fear, the sadness and disappointment. How could she give up her dream to stay here when she and Theo weren't even official in any capacity?

But how could she walk away from the man she'd spent the past decade loving? Especially now that things were finally happening between them?

She didn't know. She didn't have any answers. The same questions, the same emotions, the same hopes and doubts swirled through her as she sat in front of the window, watching the world go by, drinking her latte. After a while, she pulled out her phone and texted Theo.

Lauren: Good luck this afternoon! I know you'll knock 'em dead.

Theo: Thanks. Just heading into the partners meeting now. How did your meeting with Sadie go????

Lauren: It was good. I'll tell you all about it later. Break a leg!

Theo adjusted his eye patch as he walked through the door to Willa and Kayla's apartment, "Monster Mash" playing on the speakers and at least a dozen guests already mingling in their tiny living room. He quickly scanned the small space, looking for Lauren, but he didn't see her so he made his way toward the kitchen. He turned and almost ran smack into Dori, who was dressed like a giant Whoopie cushion.

"Hey, great costume," he said, setting down the twelve pack of beer and bags of chips that Willa had asked him to bring.

"Thanks," she said, pushing her too-big glasses up her nose. She gestured to the wig she was wearing, giving her a head of silver curls that would've made Dorothy Zbornak proud. "I'm an old fart."

He laughed. "Love it. Have you seen Lauren?"

She shook her head, her wig tilting perilously to the side. Damn. He had news to share—good, exciting news—and he didn't want to tell anyone until she was here.

"Haven't seen her yet," said Kayla as she entered the kitchen, holding an empty chip bowl. She was dressed as

Marilyn Monroe, which wasn't a huge stretch for her, given her curvy figure and blond hair. A skinny bald man with a scar running down his face followed close behind her, and Theo did a double take when he realized it was Willa dressed as Dr. Evil.

"Okay, everyone's costumes are officially cooler than mine," he said, gesturing to his very run of the mill pirate costume.

Willa smiled and took a small bow. "I tried to convince Brandon to come as my hairless cat, Bigglesworth, but he didn't want to for some reason."

"Willa, you know how I feel about pussy," Brandon said dramatically from behind Theo. He turned and saw Brandon wearing a black T-shirt with a graphic of a phone battery at one percent emblazoned on the front.

"Okay, now that's scary," he said, pointing at Brandon's shirt.

"Check out the back," he said, turning around and showing off the words "The Wifi is Down."

"Even more horrifying," said Kayla as she opened a fresh bag of chips and dumped them into the empty bowl.

"Hey, didn't Lauren have her meeting with the producer today? I feel so out of touch with everyone because we haven't gotten together in a while," said Willa, pouring a large bottle of ginger ale into a punch bowl.

Theo nodded. "She did, but I don't know how it went. I had a meeting right when she was finishing up and I didn't get the chance to talk to her." He felt as though his entire body were zinging with electricity, both in anticipation of sharing his news and hearing Lauren's.

Kayla thrust the bowl of chips into his hands. "Go put these in the living room, please."

"Yes, ma'am." He turned and headed back into the thick of the party, weaving his way in between people laughing and talking and eating. He had to turn sideways and raise the bowl above his head to squeeze past a guy in an eggplant emoji costume. Just as he was setting the bowl down, he saw Lauren poke her head through the front door. Her hair was swept up into a high ponytail, and she wore a purple leotard, shiny pink leggings, and baby blue leg warmers that matched the sweatband on her head and the ones on her wrists.

He watched her for a second, and he felt so...so alive. Like every single piece of his adult life was finally coming together. Like he was finally...maybe...changing. Because staring at Lauren, he felt like he was staring at his future.

She turned and her eyes met his. A small smile pulled up the corner of her mouth and for a moment, their eyes locked from across the room, something big and bright and unspoken passing between them. With all that big brightness inside him, Theo couldn't stay still any longer, and he wove his way through the costumed guests, meeting her at the front door.

"Hey, I—" she started, but he didn't give her the chance to say anything because his mouth was on hers, kissing her hungrily. She let out the tiniest little moan and swayed into him, her fingers curling into the billowing fabric of his pirate shirt. After a moment, she pulled back, her breathing a little ragged.

"If I promise to give you my booty, will you let me walk your plank?" she asked, a playful glint shining in her pretty green eyes.

He laughed and tucked her against his side, looking up to see all of their friends staring at them with comically shocked expressions on their faces.

"Um, *excuse me*," said Willa, letting out an incredulous laugh. "But since when do you two kiss like that?"

"That wasn't kissing," said Kayla, shaking her blonde curls. "That was a full-on make out. They're having sex!"

At that, several heads turned in their direction and conversations died.

"No one's having sex, people," said Dori, waving her jiggly pink arms. "Mind your business."

Theo felt his cheeks go hot, and he rubbed a hand over his mouth. A familiar panic started to rise in his chest.

"How long have you been dating?" asked Brandon, his arms crossed over his chest, clearly pissed at being left out of grade A friend group gossip.

Lauren shook her head. "Oh, no. We're not dating. We're just..." She glanced up at him, both the tone of her voice and her expression totally unreadable. But there was something there, a hesitation, a doubt, that made Theo hold her a bit tighter. "We're still just Theo and Lauren. But now with orgasms." Her tone was light, and she'd probably fooled everyone but Theo with it.

Willa, Kayla, Brandon and Dori all exchanged glances. "And we think this is a *good* idea?" asked Brandon, his arms still crossed, a frown on his face as his eyes bounced back and forth between them. "Like, this absolutely is not going to fuck up our friend group or end up with someone in tears, right?"

Theo swore he felt Lauren shiver, and she stood up a little straighter. "No, definitely not. This isn't a romantic thing. We're just friends. Only now we have sex sometimes."

A heaviness sat on Theo's chest, oppressive and painful. Right. They weren't dating, and that was the way he'd wanted it, right? The way he still wanted it. The way it had to be.

So then why did he feel like she'd just kicked him?

"Right, yeah," he said, clearing his throat when he realized everyone was staring at him and waiting for some kind of response. "Nothing to worry about. We've got everything under control." Both sentences felt like a lie, but they'd have to do because he didn't know what the truth was anymore. Clearing his throat again, he turned to Lauren. "So how did your meeting go?"

"Oh, um." She hesitated, biting her lip. "It was good. Really good. She wants to work together." Again, there was something in her voice that had him on edge.

"That's amazing!" he said, giving her squeeze as everyone chimed in their excitement. She smiled, but it didn't quite reach her eyes.

"So does this mean you're getting a record deal?" asked Willa, practically bouncing on her toes with enthusiasm.

Lauren's smile grew. "I mean, maybe, yeah. She wants to mentor me, write songs with me and eventually put together an album."

Kayla let out a whoop and rushed forward to give Lauren a hug. "That's such incredible news! I always knew it would happen for you."

"We can tell everyone about how we knew her when," said Dori, beaming with pride.

Seemingly uncomfortable with the attention on her, Lauren turned to Theo. "And you? How did your big meeting go?"

He grinned. "You're looking at the newest junior partner at Kingston, Lennox and Finley." He wasn't sure what kind of reaction he'd been expecting from Lauren, but her pulling slightly away with a sad smile on her face was definitely not it. Everyone else chimed in their congratulations, and she just stood there with that half smile on her face, almost as if she were frozen in place. Then she shook her head and threw her arms around his neck, pulling him in for a hug.

"Congratulations," she whispered in his ear as their friends started to disperse. "I'm so happy for you." But when she pulled away, she didn't look happy. She looked like someone trying to put on a brave face. He lifted a hand, tracing a thumb over her lower lip.

"Hey. Are you okay?"

Her eyebrows knit together, but she nodded. "Yeah. Yeah, of course. It's just a lot of big news to take in in one day, you know?"

He dipped his head, brushing her nose with his. "We can celebrate later."

She nodded again, but that wariness was still there. "Yeah. Sure. C'mon. Let's go find some snacks." She took his hand and pulled him into the living room, and Theo told himself to stop being stupid and just enjoy the party. He was probably just projecting his own muddled feelings onto her.

So why had it felt so shitty when she'd said that they were just friends?

Oh, right. Because that wasn't true anymore. At least, not for him.

17

"And here are your room keys. I hope you enjoy your stay at the Ritz-Carlton Dallas. Please don't hesitate to reach out if there's anything y'all need." The suited woman behind the heavy mahogany desk slid an envelope across to Theo. Lauren had paced a few steps away to admire a piece of art on the wall, leaning forward and squinting her eyes slightly. He tapped her arm with the envelope and she spun to face him.

"I can't decide if this is people having sex or a woman floating above a bed."

He tilted his head, studying the abstract art, not seeing anything besides slashes of white, pink, blue and gray. "Maybe it's supposed to be that scene from *Ghostbusters*." He put on a growly voice. "There is no Dana, only Zuul."

She grinned and pointed at him. "That's a really good Sigourney Weaver impression, if I do say so myself."

He laughed. "Let's go find our room so we can change. The rehearsal dinner's starting in..." He quickly checked his phone. "Twenty minutes."

She pretended to pout. "Twenty minutes is not enough time for freaky hotel sex."

He grinned and wove his fingers through hers, leading her toward the elevator. "I promise there'll be plenty of that later. I have a whole list."

Her cheeks went pink as she bit her lip. "Oh, me too."

The flight to Dallas had been completely uneventful, thankfully, and now that they were checked in, his sister's wedding weekend was officially underway. He still didn't know how to feel about the fact that she was getting remarried. Her first marriage and subsequent divorce had nearly wrecked her, and he knew better than most how bad it had been because he'd been the one to pick up the pieces. And now she was signing up for round two. Granted, he was pretty sure Javier Flores was a much better human being than Aerin's first husband, but still. How she could stomach taking the risk again was beyond him.

He tapped one of the keys against the lock and pushed open the door to their room. As Lauren followed him inside, she let out a small gasp and rushed forward.

"Oh my God, Theo! Is this a suite? This is huge!"

He smiled as the door fell closed behind them with a quiet click. He loved watching her enjoy things—her enthusiasm was contagious, and warmth trickled through him knowing he'd put that enormous smile on her face.

"Yeah, I upgraded the room. Thought we could use this weekend trip as an excuse to celebrate you working with Sadie and my promotion."

Her smile flickered just the tiniest bit. "Right. Good idea."

Leaving their bags by the door, he closed the distance between them and laid his hands on her shoulders. Things had been mostly back to normal between them since the night of the Halloween party, although she hadn't been over as much this week. Then again, he'd been so busy in his new role that maybe she'd just been giving him space and not pressuring him for time he didn't have.

"Are you okay?" he asked, rubbing his thumbs along her collarbone.

"Yeah, I'm good. I'm still taking everything in, you know? Lots of changes."

He nodded, relief making him feel a bit lighter. "But they're good changes, right?"

"Yeah. We're both getting to follow our dreams." And yet there was a flatness to her tone that didn't make it sound like following their dreams was a good thing. "I know how hard you've worked to get where you are, and I know what your job means to you. I'm happy for you."

He cupped her cheek and kissed her. "And I'm so fucking proud of you, Lo. You never gave up."

She circled her arms around his waist and tucked her face against his chest, sighing and relaxing into him. "How do you always smell so good?" she asked, a hint of anguish in her voice. His cock perked up at the neediness in her tone and he wondered how mad Aerin would be if they were late to dinner. With a low growl, he picked her up and tossed her over his shoulder, marching them into the adjoining bedroom. She giggled and pretended to struggle, then laughed even harder when he tossed her down on the bed.

His heart dropped into his stomach at the sight of her spread beneath him, her red hair flaming against the soft white duvet, her nose wrinkled and eyes shut in laughter. She was so beautiful that for a second, he could've sworn that time stopped, maybe even moved backward a second or two.

He dropped down over her, rocking his hips against her.

"So what's on your hotel sex list?" he asked, his voice coming out low and gravely.

"Mmm," she said, letting out a little moan as he buried his face in her neck, inhaling deeply before kissing a path between her jaw and her shoulder. "Sex in the tub. Sex in the shower. Maybe we could role play…"

His head jerked up, a smile spreading across his face. "Oh yeah? What kind of fantasies do you have?"

She met his gaze, her eyes bright with arousal. He loved how comfortable she was with him now—any initial shyness was gone. "Maybe I'm the maid and you forgot to leave a tip, so you'll have to make it up to me some other way."

He ground against her again. "That's really hot. What else?"

"We could be two strangers who just met in the hotel bar."

"Also hot." He bent down and kissed her, exploring her mouth with slow sweeps of his tongue.

"And what's on your list?" she asked when she broke the kiss. She let out a small hiss as he tweaked her nipple through her blouse.

"I want you naked whenever we're in this room. I'm going to fuck you on every single surface in here, and I don't want clothes in my way."

"Mmm, yes please, baby. Please," she whispered, her eyes hazy.

"I want to tie your hands behind your back, put you on your knees, and fuck your gorgeous mouth in front of that big window."

"Oh, God." She writhed against him, her skin flushing the prettiest shade of pink. Her hands skimmed down his chest and to his jeans, and she palmed his throbbing cock through the fabric.

Just then, his phone buzzed from his pocket, pulling them both out of the moment. She shot him a rueful grin. "I guess we should get changed and head down, huh?"

He sat up and pushed a hand through his hair, glancing at Lucian's text message wondering where he was. "Yeah. Shit. I should've booked an earlier flight." He stood and extended his hand to her, helping her up off of the bed. She ducked into the bathroom with her bag, emerging a few minutes later with her hair wound into a messy braid with a few loose tendrils framing her face. She'd changed into a black lace cocktail dress with long sleeves, a pair of strappy silver sandals, and large hoop earrings. She'd also touched up her makeup. Her eyes roved over Theo, taking in his light gray dress shirt, navy blue tie, and navy blue dress pants.

"You look beautiful, Lo," he said, his throat tight. He couldn't stop staring at her. Something inside him almost hurt as he looked at her, and he didn't know what it was. Regret? Longing? He didn't know. He'd never been good at giving voice to his emotions.

She blushed and smoothed her hands down over the dress. "Thank you. You look nice, too." She gathered up her purse and they headed for the door. "I'm excited to meet your family," she said, tucking her hand in his as they waited for the elevator. The rehearsal dinner was taking place in a restaurant inside the hotel, just as the wedding reception would be tomorrow night, making everything nice and convenient. Aerin was nothing if not efficient.

Dread settled in the pit of his stomach as they stepped into the elevator. "You've met my brothers lots of times," he said, deflecting. The numbers on the elevator ticked downward and the pit in his stomach yawned and stretched. Anxiety pulled at him, and for a second he thought about suggesting they say forget it and head back up to the hotel room instead. But he knew she'd never go for that.

"I don't mean your brothers. I mean your parents. And I haven't seen Aerin in a long time."

He turned to her, taking both of her hands in his. "Listen, no matter what happens tonight, please know that I'm not like them, okay?" He'd spent his entire adult life making sure of it. He just hated the idea that she'd meet them, see how awful they were, and run screaming in the other direction. And no, thank you, he didn't want to unpack what that fear said about how he was thinking of the two of them.

She hesitated, her eyes wide, but she nodded. "Okay. I promise I won't judge you by your family."

The elevator dinged and the doors slid open smoothly. Following the signs along with the noise, they made their way to the restaurant. The inside was dimly but warmly lit, with glowing sconces on the wall illuminating the decorative white brick. Windows gave a view of the hotel's courtyard with its fountains and lush green trees. About three dozen people were mingling around the restaurant, some standing at the marble topped bar on the other side of the room, others clustered together in small groups laughing and chatting. Servers circulated with appetizers – smoked salmon on little toasts, shot glasses full of what Theo was pretty sure was gazpacho, and prosciutto wrapped melon with goat cheese. His stomach gave an appreciative rumble—he hadn't eaten since the sandwiches they'd grabbed at JFK.

His eyes landed on Javi and Aerin in the far corner with Lucian, Bastian, and Max, and he had to admit, his sister looked absolutely radiant. She was wearing a red, strapless cocktail dress, the crimson hue the exact same shade as her fiancé's tie. Javi was wearing a simple navy blue suit and white shirt, his arm wound around Aerin's waist. Someone said something and they both laughed, then looked at each other. Theo swallowed around the thickness in his throat at the obvious tenderness passing between them. God, she looked so happy. So serene and content and glowing.

He gave Lauren's hand a gentle tug. "Come on, let's go say hi." She nodded and he led her through the restaurant, waving at a few other people he knew as they passed. When Aerin spotted him, she practically shoved her glass of champagne into Javi's hands.

"Theo!" She grinned from ear to ear, and he let go of Lauren's hand just in time to catch his sister as she launched herself at him.

"AerBear!" He wrapped her in a hug, her feet dangling off the ground. He squeezed her tight, realizing in that moment how much he'd missed her. She was ten years older than him, and when they were growing up, she'd been the one—sometimes the only one—to look after him in any kind of nurturing way. She'd protected him and comforted him and helped him with his homework. She'd done everything she could to shelter him from their parents' nastiness. It was because of her that he was only slightly messed up and not Lucian or Bastian levels of messed up. She'd saved him, in a way.

He set her down and she took a step back, smoothing her dress. "You remember Lauren," he said, gesturing to her.

Aerin smiled again, cutting her eyes between Theo and Lauren. "Yes, of course! I'm so glad to see you. Thank you for coming." She turned to Theo, smacking his arm, hard. "I knew you had a plus one, but you didn't tell me you were

bringing *Lauren*. I'm so glad you finally figured out that she
—" But Aerin cut herself off at the look on Theo's face. "That
she'd make a great wedding date," she finished smoothly,
then plucked her champagne glass out of Javi's hands. "This
is my fiancé, Javier Flores." Lauren and Javi shook hands and
Lauren offered her congratulations.

"Okay, now that everyone's here, Javi and I have some
news to share," she said, her eyes suddenly bright. Javi took
her hand, giving it a squeeze, and Theo's heart picked up its
pace because of how badly he was hoping he knew what she
was going to say. She reached into her little clutch and pulled
out a black and white ultrasound picture. "Our surrogate is
pregnant with twins!"

"What?" said Bastian, pulling the picture out of her hands
and squinting at it.

"Yep. There's Baby A," said Javi, pointing at the grainy
picture, "And there's Baby B."

Words failed him, so Theo pulled Aerin in for another
hug. She'd wanted so badly to have a baby with her previous
husband, but the fertility treatments they'd tried hadn't been
successful. Now, thanks to a surrogate, she was finally getting
her wish of becoming a mom, and in that moment, Theo's
heart could've burst for her.

Lucian and Max both offered their congratulations as
well, everyone sharing hugs and handshakes. Aerin carefully
wiped away a stray tear, her overwhelming joy palpable.

"When are the twins due?" asked Lucian, sipping his
scotch.

"Mid-June." Aerin's eyes were bright, excitement radiating
off of her.

Theo glanced over at Lauren, who was watching
everything unfold with a warm smile on her face. He reached

out and took her hand, lacing her fingers with his. Aerin noticed, cocked an eyebrow at him and then took a sip of her champagne.

Max raised his glass. "Welcome to the family Javi, and welcome Prescott-Flores babies."

Javi raised his glass too. "Thank you. We can't wait to meet them."

"Uncle Bastian has a nice ring to it, don't you think?" said Sebastian, tossing back the rest of his drink. "Oh, man. All the things I'm gonna teach these little squirts."

"We'll have to see about that," said Aerin dryly. "I don't think my babies will need to know how to pick the winning pony or survive a bar fight anytime soon."

"Hey! I meant things like snowboarding and how to cook the perfect steak, but if you're gonna be rude about it, fine. Ugh, watch them grow up to be *skiers*. Gross."

"They're going to be spending most of their time in Texas and Southern California, so I think your fears are unfounded," said Javi, shaking his head a little.

With Lauren's hand in his, seeing Aerin so deliriously happy with her fiancé and impending motherhood, Theo couldn't help but wonder if he could be that happy, too. If he could have what Aerin had—love, support, happiness, a future filled with the promise of even more love, especially with not one but two babies on the way. And while that kind of future was still a giant *if*, he knew that the only person it was even remotely possible with was Lauren.

"Hey, look who it is," said Bastian, holding out his hand and pulling their cousin Noah into a man hug. Noah's brothers Hudson and Levi trailed close behind. Noah, Hud, and Levi were the sons of Caleb Prescott, their father Quentin's only brother. Quentin and Caleb couldn't have been more different—where Quentin was driven by wealth and power and used people the way a painter used a brush, Caleb had been selfless and dedicated to his community. He'd walked away from the family business and the wealth that came with it in order to join the NYFD. Sadly, he'd died while rescuing others on September 11, 2001, leaving behind his wife and three young sons.

"This is my cousin Noah," he said introducing Lauren. "And my cousins Hudson," he said, gesturing to the fair-haired guy with colorful tattoos poking out from beneath the collar of his shirt and the cuffs of his sleeves. "And Levi." Levi, as usual didn't smile, just nodded. His grumpiness was probably why he and Max got along so well.

As they shook hands, Theo added, "Noah's a firefighter, Hudson's a tattoo artist, and Levi's a paramedic."

"We're the normal Prescotts," said Noah, flashing a grin at Lauren.

"Yeah, the ones who don't have sticks up their asses," agreed Hudson, pushing a hand through his hair. "Well, two out of three of us, anyway."

"Hey, I told you I'd let you tattoo me, but you wouldn't do it," said Bastian, frowning.

"Because I wasn't going to tattoo 'YOLO' across your hand." Hudson shook his head. "I only do quality tattoos, not dumbass tattoos people will regret in a year. Or less."

"But YOLO will always be true," said Bastian, rolling his eyes and making Noah laugh.

Aerin pointed at him. "Fun fact: Noah was on the cover of the NYFD charity calendar last year," she said, grinning mischievously.

Noah rubbed a hand over the back of his neck. "I will

forever regret sharing that with everyone. Next time I do anything for charity, I'm keeping it a secret."

"One, you suck at secrets," said Levi, grinning into his beer. "And two, you do everything for everyone all the time, so good luck there. You are a walking, talking charity."

"Look, someone's gotta look after Gramps and it's not like you have the money to invest in Hud's shop, so..."

"There you all are! I've been looking for you. The lighting in here is so dim, I can hardly see my own hand in front of my face." Even though he hadn't talked to her in a long time, Theo instantly knew the sound of his mother's voice. His shoulders tensed and Lauren gave his fingers a squeeze. He plastered a neutral expression on his face as he turned to her. Her blond hair was perfectly styled in artful waves around her freshly nipped and tucked face, but her blue eyes—the same blue as Theo, Max and Bastian's—were as icy and cutting as ever.

"Hi, Mom," he said, not moving in for a hug or a kiss, which she didn't seem to notice. She sipped her glass of wine and then moved forward to give Aerin a peck on the cheek.

"And you must be Javier," she said, eyeing Javi, judgement coming off of her in waves.

To the man's credit, he simply smiled and met her eyes. "I am. It's nice to meet you."

"Hogging all the attention, as usual, Adelaide," said Theo's dad from the other side of the group, sidling up and sipping at his drink. A woman at least a few years younger than Lauren had her hands draped around his arm. His dark brown hair had faded over the years to a salt and pepper shade, but aside from a few more lines on his face, he still looked like the same man who was incapable of loving anyone other than himself.

"Where did you find this one, Quentin? The playground?" Adelaide's voice dripped with disdain and Theo swore he felt his blood pressure go up.

"Better the playground than the graveyard where they keep ghouls like you."

"He only hates me because I took half his money and ruined his life," said his mother sweetly, her laugh a little too loud and brittle.

Quentin turned to the men, his back to Lucian, freezing him out as usual. "Let that be a lesson: never get married to a heartless—"

Aerin held up her hands. "Okay, great! *So nice* to have the whole family back together. Why doesn't everyone take their seats for dinner? It should be served shortly." She took her mom's elbow and started guiding her in one direction. "Your seat is over there, Mom, and Dad, you and your date are sitting over there." She pointed to the far side of the restaurant.

As soon as their parents were out of ear shot, Theo turned to Aerin. "I don't understand why you invited them."

She gave a little shrug. "Because inviting them was easier than dealing with the drama if I didn't. I'd have been hearing about it for years. Not worth it."

The dinner itself was uneventful, and Theo was happy to sit and chat with Lauren and his brothers, although he was a little concerned about the amount of scotch Bastian was putting away. The food was delicious—a green salad with dried fruit, nuts and crumbled blue cheese, stuffed chicken breast served with a creamy, buttery sauce, cinnamon-infused baked sweet potatoes, and sauteed vegetables, and an assortment of cookies and pastries for dessert. Once everyone had eaten their fill, they all stood to mingle and refresh their drinks. While Lauren chatted with Aerin on one side of the room, Theo made his way to the bar to order another drink. He'd successfully avoided his parents for the remainder of the evening; if he could steer clear them until he was safely back in New York where he had avoiding them down to an art form, he'd be golden. Staying away from them wasn't optional; he'd only been around them for a few minutes and he already felt tense and angry and completely uncomfortable. It was as though with every single second he spent around them, he lost sight of the best parts of himself, little by little.

As he waited for his order, he checked the time on his phone, wondering how much longer he'd have to stay to be polite and not disappoint Aerin. All he wanted to do was to drag Lauren back to their room and bury himself inside her. He needed the anchor of her body under his, her mouth, her hands, her moans, her laughter...

"You know, you always were the smart one," said his mother from beside him, a hint of a slur to her words. Everything inside him tensed up, but he forced himself to stay perfectly still. She was like a predator, and if she smelled fear, she went in for the kill. It was the only way she knew how to communicate.

He fought the urge to roll his eyes. "We're all smart, Mom. Well, maybe not Bastian, but the rest of us..." He shrugged, trying to inject a little humor into the situation.

She laughed, but it was a mirthless sound. "Ha. Well, I'm not so sure about Aerin. I thought she was smart for leaving Eric. Smart for starting her own agency. But getting remarried? Maybe she's not as smart as I gave her credit for."

Something inside Theo went cold as he remembered having nearly identical—although less meanspirited—

thoughts about Aerin getting remarried. He could feel his mother's influence wriggling around inside him, like worms eating a rotten piece of meat. He wanted so badly to excise whatever of her was in him. If he could find a way to do that, maybe then he could be the man that Lauren deserved. But she was a part of him and he didn't know how to change that. He couldn't alter his DNA any more than he could rearrange the planets. So he simply picked up his drink and took a sip. His mother did the same and he suddenly didn't want his drink anymore.

She sighed, leaning her slender arms on the bar. "Well, at least this Javier fellow's rich. I'll give her that much."

Something inside him snapped and he turned to face her. "That's a shitty attitude to have about your only daughter's wedding."

She laughed, but she wasn't laughing *with* him—he'd have to actually be laughing for her to do that. No, she was definitely laughing at him, the peal of her laughter almost mocking. "Oh, please. Take off your white hat and get off your high horse. I'd have thought by now that you know how the world works. You're a divorce lawyer, for Christ's sake. Money matters, and women like money. Women crave money—trust me, we all think that way."

Theo glanced across the room to where Lauren stood with Aerin and shook his head. "No, *you* think that way. I doubt very much that womankind has authorized you to speak on their behalf."

"You're so naïve, my baby boy." She shook her head sadly. "It's all a game. All of it. Women want money, or power, or whatever. We want something, and we know that men want sex with pretty women. To get what we want, we play the game. We scheme. We manipulate. It's past time you grew up and realized that." She nodded in Lauren's direction. "You think your sweet little redhead isn't playing games with you to get what she wants?"

Theo frowned, and he knew he should just walk away from the conversation, but he couldn't. He felt compelled to defend Lauren, even though he knew his mother's opinion wasn't worth a damn. "Lauren's not like that. I've known her for ten years, and she's not anything like the type of woman you're describing."

His mother laughed again and patted his arm. "She's obviously very good at the game if she's got you fooled."

"She's not playing games with me. She's always been honest with me, and she'd never manipulate me. She's not like that." He opened his mouth to say more, but then decided it wasn't worth the time or energy. "Good night, Mom. I'll see you at the wedding tomorrow."

"Keep your eyes open, Theo. The innocent-seeming ones are always able to cut the deepest."

He scowled at her and shoved away from the bar, making a beeline for Lauren.

18

"Get on the bed, now." Theo's voice was low and rough as they stepped into the hotel room. Lauren could feel the tension radiating off of him, and she knew it had everything to do with seeing his parents tonight. She'd only witnessed snippets of their dynamic, but if that was what Theo had grown up with...she couldn't even imagine. Her heart ached for him, and even though his commitment issues sucked, she felt like she maybe understood them just a little bit better. It made her so angry to know that he'd grown up with those two self-centered jerks raising him, angry to the point of wanting to scream at them. How could they have done that to him? How dare they make this amazing person feel like less than?

Apparently she'd hesitated too long, because he snaked an arm around her waist and started walking her backwards through the room towards the bed. He dipped his head and tugged on her ear with his teeth. "Get on the bed now before I fucking make you."

She melted at his rough tone and she scrambled

backwards to get on the bed, wanting to be whatever he needed right now. She couldn't change his crappy childhood or his toxic parents, but she could give him this. She could give him the oblivion he was so clearly needing. He needed to work through whatever it was that he was feeling, and if a little rough sex was his way of dealing, she was more than game.

As she moved up on the bed, she watched him undress, shedding his shoes, his pants, his shirt, his boxer briefs with quick, precise movements until he was completely naked, his cock already hard and thick. He picked up his discarded tie, tilting his head as he considered her. Then, he cocked an eyebrow, sliding the tie through his fingers. Butterflies erupted in her stomach as he slowly climbed onto the bed.

"Undress for me."

It was a simple but thrilling command, and one she hurried to obey, shrugging out of her dress, her bra, her panties, until she was completely naked, her nipples hard, her pussy wet and throbbing. There was an intensity about him right now that promised all kinds deliciousness.

He took one of her hands, dragging the silk of his tie over her wrist. "The idea of you bound for me, completely mine...I can't stop thinking about it. I almost can't handle it, it turns me on so much."

She held her other hand out. "I'm yours, Theo. Do whatever you want with me. Use me. Take me."

"Fuck," he ground out, but he took her wrists and started binding them together with the tie. He sat back for a moment, admiring her, and she could only imagine how completely debauched she looked right now, naked and bound for him. Then he leaned down, his breath feathering against her ear. "If you want to stop, say 'Ross Gellar.'"

She bit her lip, hiding her smile. "A mood killer, for sure."

His kiss was surprisingly gentle when his mouth found hers, and she whimpered, lust pounding through her as he teased her with little licks into her mouth. He moved down her body, kissing her throat, her collarbones, her breasts. He tormented her nipples with little bites and hard sucks, making her moan and arch into his touch, begging for more. More than anything, she wanted to soothe him with her body. Wanted everything he was about to give her.

He licked a path from her breasts up to her neck and finally took her mouth again in a hot, deep kiss. "You're so goddamn beautiful, Lo. So fucking sweet. I wish—" He cut himself off and kissed her again, stopping himself from saying whatever he'd been about to. Guilt pulsed through her, twisting and tangling with her lust.

She hadn't told him about potentially moving to California. She wasn't ready to face whatever that conversation would bring yet. After the wedding, she'd tell him and they'd talk about it, but she already had a sinking feeling she knew how it would go.

He'd tell her to go to LA. And she would. And that would be it. He wouldn't beg her to stay. He wouldn't give up his hard won promotion to come with her. And so she'd be left with a choice—a maybe-relationship with Theo, or her dreams. And it felt massively unfair that she'd be the only one with a choice to make, because she was pretty sure he'd never actually choose her. He'd never made her any promises, and she'd told him she was okay with that.

She'd lied. Because she wanted it all—the commitment, the promises, the security of a future.

"Spread your legs for me, gorgeous," he said, his voice husky. When she did, he let out a low chuckle. "Good girl."

Then he traced his fingers over her lips, exerting just enough pressure that she knew he wanted her to open. She did, and he slid two fingers into her mouth, groaning when she sucked him eagerly, savoring the salt of his skin on her tongue. He withdrew his fingers and then circled her clit with steady, firm strokes. Her hips arched up to meet him, his touch setting her on fire, just like it always did. He slid one finger inside her, stroking her and stretching her, and then he pulled it out, raising it to her mouth and tracing her lips with it. "See how fucking good you taste?" She moaned and sucked his finger into back her mouth, reveling in tasting herself on him. He pulled his finger free and kissed her again, a hard, deep, claiming kiss that only stoked the flames of her arousal higher.

He slipped his hand between her legs again, stroking and massaging her aching, throbbing clit. "I love how wet you get for me, Lo. Fuck, I need to taste you." He moved down the bed and settled himself between her legs, inhaling deeply. "I'm going to make you scream my name, sweetheart." He nipped at one of her outer lips, the sharpness of his teeth balancing right on the edge between pleasure and pain. "I'm going to make you come so hard you forget how to breathe." He licked her then, one slow sweep of his tongue from her entrance to her clit, making her hips jerk. "Whose pussy is this?" His voice was practically a growl, the sound of it rippling through her, making her spine arch.

"It's yours, Theo. It's all yours." He could claim her heart, too, if he wanted it. It was his for the taking.

He moaned against her as he started to eat her in earnest. "Such a good fucking girl, my Lo." His tongue swirled over and around her clit in a way that had her insides clenching and her breath coming harder and faster. He pushed her legs up and back, spreading her even wider for him. "Keep your legs there, baby. Don't move." He closed his lips over her clit and slid two fingers into her, sending pleasure spiraling through her, making her feel like she was floating a few inches off of the mattress. Her legs started to shake and she tightened around his fingers as the first sparks of her orgasm flared to life.

But then he slid his fingers free and lifted his head. "No coming yet, sweetheart. I'm going to make you beg for it." She bit her lip, loving this dirty, controlling side of him. It was such a sharp contrast to the sweet, funny goofball she'd fallen in love with. He sat up and moved up on the bed. "I want your mouth on my cock."

The tingling agony of her denied orgasm still pulsing through her, she rose to her knees—a little awkwardly thanks to her bound wrists—and straddled one of his legs, grinding herself on him. He gave her ass a smack, the grin on his face so wickedly sexy she felt her pussy spasm in response. "If your lips aren't around my cock in the next three seconds, you're going to be sorry."

Deciding she wanted to play with fire, she reached out and stroked his cock with just the tips of her fingers, teasing him. She ran her fingers through the bead of moisture at the head of his cock, playing. Provoking. He shivered under her touch, his muscles taut. But then he let out a growl and suddenly she was on her back with her head hanging over the edge of the bed. He stood in front of her—or was it behind her? With her head upside down, she wasn't sure—his cock in his fist. Then he bent and whispered in her ear, "Squeeze my hand three times if this gets too intense for you, okay?" She nodded and took his hand between her bound ones while he used his other to feed her his cock, sliding it between her lips and pushing deep into her mouth. She moaned around him, swallowing his thick length as best she could. She pulsed between her legs as he slowly fucked her mouth.

"I'm so fucking hard for you, Lo. That's it, sweetheart. Fuck, take it all." He moved his hips a little faster, making her eyes water. She felt like she was both falling and floating with her head hanging over the edge of the bed, Theo's cock filling her mouth. He let out an anguished moan and moved his hips even faster.

He slid free of her mouth and helped her sit up, kissing her with a surprising softness given that she could practically feel him hanging on to the edge of whatever cliff he was dangling from by his fingertips. He eased her back onto the bed, then lifted one of her legs and rested it on his muscled shoulder. Just the tip of his cock nudged at her entrance and she writhed, the need to have him inside her obliterating everything else. With agonizing slowness, he pushed inside, the fit almost excruciatingly snug with her leg raised. He held her leg in place with one hand, the other splayed across her stomach, his thumb stroking her clit in maddeningly slow circles.

But then all of the gentleness seemed to vanish, and he withdrew and slammed back into her, making everything inside her pulse and tighten. With his cock filling and stretching her, stroking the spot deep inside her that always sent her over the edge, his thumb on her clit, she was so, so close to exploding.

And then the bastard took his thumb away, a wicked grin on his face.

"No!" she cried, arching her hips up, seeking out his magic touch again.

He chuckled. "I told you I'd make you beg." He worked his cock in and out of her, taking his time, seemingly in no hurry. But she'd been dangling on the edge for far too long and she couldn't take it anymore.

"Please, Theo. Make me come. Touch me, please," she moaned.

He returned his thumb to her clit, massaging and circling as he fucked her harder. "Come for me, Lo," he ground out, unrelenting in his movements. "I want to feel you come on my cock as I fuck you."

"Oh, shit, Theo!" She lifted her arms above her head, her fingertips brushing against one of the pillows, hanging on for life as he rode her hard and deep, sending her over the edge. Everything inside her tightened to the point of pain and then it all exploded in one massive wave of pulsing, throbbing pleasure, all of the tension ebbing out of her as she shook, her hips writhing against Theo's. He stiffened and she felt his cock pulse inside her.

God, the sight of him above her, his face a mask of pleasure and release, his muscles straining, sweat slicking his chest, was heady and surreal, even all these weeks later. He turned his face and placed a gentle kiss on her ankle, then carefully slid out of her and lowered her leg down. She lay there in a puddle of melted nerve endings as he disappeared into the bathroom, returning a moment later with a warm washcloth. She gasped when she felt the cloth between her legs as he gently, tenderly cleaned her up.

A moment later, he helped her up, untied her wrists, pulled the duvet back, and tugged her into bed with him, settling her on his chest. His heart thumped steadily against her check and she traced an idle circle on his ribs with her fingers.

"Thank you," he whispered, pressing a kiss to the top of her head. "For letting me...I really needed that." His big hand moved up and down her spine, a warm, gentle caress.

She kissed his chest. "You're welcome. Always happy to be of service." She tried to make her tone light and fun, but she knew she missed the mark by quite a bit. A few beats of silence passed, and then she asked, "So, do you want to talk about it?"

"No." His tone was firm, his answer clearly final.

"Okay."

"I'm sorry. I'm being an asshole."

She lifted her head and met his eyes. "You're not. It's okay. If you change your mind, I'm right here."

But after a few more minutes, his breathing became deep and even, and she knew he'd fallen asleep.

19

*L*auren smoothed her hands down the front of her icy blue cocktail dress, weaving her way between tables and wedding guests and toward the bar at the back of the room. Around her, the reception was in full swing, Beyoncé playing through the speakers as guests danced and drank and mingled. But Lauren wasn't really in a dancing or a mingling mood, and she was hoping that a glass of wine might help.

The ceremony had taken place several hours earlier and she'd been moved to see how happy Theo—and all his brothers—were for Aerin, who'd looked absolutely stunning in her form-fitting lace dress that was the prettiest shade of pale gold. Lauren's throat had tightened at the way Javi only had eyes for his bride, happiness practically radiating off of him.

Would Theo ever look at her that way?

She didn't know. Things had shifted between them and they'd explored new levels of trust and intimacy. And yet... she didn't feel any closer to him, or to the future she wanted with him. They were in a holding pattern and she didn't know how to break them out of it without breaking them altogether.

Shaking her head, she focused on making it to the bar, smiling when she spotted Javi on the dance floor, an enormous grin on his face as he and Aerin danced with his two daughters from his first marriage. They'd been the only bridesmaids during the ceremony and both looked adorable in their pretty burgundy-hued dresses.

"Whoa, easy there. We almost had a head on collision," said Theo's cousin Hudson, grinning and flashing a set of killer dimples at her. God, this wedding was basically hot guy central. Between all of the Prescotts and their perfect DNA and all the cute baseball players from Javi's team, she had her pick of eye candy. But there was only one Prescott she wanted —the one who was deep in conversation with his cousin Noah somewhere.

"Sorry," Lauren said, flashing him a rueful smile. He winked at her and moved aside for her to pass and she hurried the rest of the way to the bar. That glass of wine was feeling more and more important with every single second that ticked by. The room was gorgeously decorated, with crystal chandeliers glowing softly, burgundy and gold fabric swags hanging from the ceiling, and floor to ceiling windows offering a beautiful view of the courtyard and the trees strung with fairy lights. As she watched everyone dancing and laughing and talking, she felt more and more like she didn't belong here.

Weddings were about family. About promises of the future. About romance and happily ever after. And every single one of those ideas made Lauren feel like an outsider who didn't belong. She wasn't part of Theo's family. They weren't together.

She was in love with him, but after the way he'd shut her out last night—after the intimacy and vulnerability they'd shared—she was pretty sure romance and happily ever after weren't where they were headed. Especially with the idea of moving to California looming. She knew she had to make a decision soon—she couldn't ask Sadie to wait on her forever.

She stepped up to the bar, leaning her arms on the cool surface of the wood, waiting her turn for the bartender to come take her order.

"Hello, Lauren." She glanced over to find Lucian standing beside her, looking handsome in his sleek dark gray suit and black shirt. To be honest, she wasn't sure that she'd ever been alone with Lucian, and he was even more intimidating up close. Tall and broad and dark. Dangerous, according to what she'd heard second-hand from Theo and Bastian.

"Lucian," she said, nodding.

"What are you having?" he asked, his deep voice smooth, almost like velvet.

"A glass of white wine."

All he did was reach forward, his hand extended. The bartender saw him and hurried over immediately, took his order, which included her glass of wine, and then thanked him profusely when he tipped her generously.

She took a healthy sip of her wine and then leveled her gaze at him. "Is it true that you're in the mafia?"

He laughed, and it was almost magical to see the way laughter transformed his face. When he laughed like that, she could see the resemblance to his brothers. "No." He nudged her with his elbow in a shockingly playful gesture. "I'm more...mafia-adjacent." He gestured over his shoulder. "They exaggerate."

She nodded and took another sip of her wine, and she could feel Lucian's gaze on her as he studied her. There was nothing sexual or flirty about it, though. He leaned his arms on the bar, taking a sip of his whiskey.

"Are you having a good time?"

"Oh, yes," she said, toying with the stem of her wine glass. "Everything's been lovely."

He turned to her, a little smirk on his face. "Now, Lauren, you're a talented musician and a total sweetheart but you're a terrible liar."

She felt her cheeks heat. "Well, it's always a little awkward going to a wedding when you're not really connected to the bride or groom."

He narrowed his eyes at her. "Terrible. Liar." Then he glanced around. "Where's your date?"

She gestured to the far side of the room. "Talking with Noah. He mentioned that he has a friend going through a divorce and Theo offered to give him some advice." She glanced around, not seeing them. "Maybe they went to talk somewhere quieter."

Lucian chewed on his bottom lip, and she could tell he was wrestling with whether or not to say what was on his mind. After an agonizing moment, he finally said, "He does care about you, you know. He may not be able to show it in the way you want, but he does."

Her eyebrows rose in surprise and then she nodded. "I...I know."

She could tell from the expression on his face that he wanted to say more, but instead he shook his head. "Regardless of what ends up happening between you and my idiot brother, I want you to know that you can always come to me if you need help or you have a problem. Anything you need."

"Is that a consolation prize because you think he's going to break my heart?"

He smiled sadly and shrugged. "I hope I'm wrong."

She trailed her finger through a drop of condensation on the bar. "That makes two of us." She picked up her wine glass and clinked it against Lucian's. "Thanks. You're like the scary big brother I never had."

"Am I really that scary?" he asked, holding his arms out at his sides as she started to back away through the crowd.

"Only when you want to be." This evening, he'd been nothing but kind, even if he was "mafia-adjacent." She had a feeling she didn't want to know what that meant.

The wine was doing its job to perk her up a little, and she wanted to find Theo and get him out on the dance floor. She headed in the direction where she'd last seen him with Noah and then spotted a small hallway. Walking down it, she picked up her pace when she heard the sound of male voices in conversation, recognizing one of them as Theo's. They were coming from a small, windowed alcove that looked out onto the beautifully illuminated pool. But then she heard her name and before she could change her mind, she ducked into the alcove just ahead of the one containing Theo and Noah. She pressed a hand to her mouth, embarrassed that she'd stooped to eavesdropping.

"...Lauren seem pretty serious," said Noah. "Maybe we'll be toasting and dancing at your wedding next."

Her heart thundered in her chest as she waited for Theo's response. It sank when he laughed.

"Oh, God no. Lauren and I aren't a couple. She's one of my closest friends, but I'm single."

Lauren felt like she'd been punched in the chest. Everything inside her hurt and she couldn't seem to catch her breath.

"Oh, I didn't realize." Noah sounded surprised, which was cold comfort in that moment.

"Lauren's great, but what we have is just a friend thing."

She pressed her fingers to her lips and hurried down the hallway and away from Theo and Noah before they spotted her. Her lungs felt like they were going to burst when she stumbled back into the wedding reception. Despite the loud Bruno Mars song pumping through the sound system, she couldn't get Theo's words out of her brain.

I'm single. What we have is just a friend thing.

She forced herself to keep her head up and to keep walking forward even as her body felt like it was collapsing in on itself. Her legs felt weak, and all she could think about was how stupid she was. How stupid she'd been to think he'd ever change. How stupid she'd been to let herself fall in love with someone who'd never let himself love her back, even if he did love her, somewhere deep down inside.

Finding an empty table, she sank down into one of the chairs, her head heavy. Her heart already felt smaller than it had ten minutes ago, shrinking until it was nearly invisible. She felt like a complete and utter fool. How could she have let herself get into this situation, knowing Theo the way she did?

Because she'd let herself hope that they could be more, and now in the space of only a few moments, those hopes were completely dashed. She sighed and slumped back in the chair, sadness and disappointment and humiliation all pulling at her, making it feel as though gravity had somehow intensified. Her eyes felt scratchy, irritated with tears she refused to let herself shed right now. She glanced around, looking for Theo. She wasn't sure if she wanted him to appear or not.

"Okay, now you are far too beautiful to be sitting here alone, looking so sad," came a deep male voice with an appealing drawl. She looked up, her eyes slamming into one of the most gorgeous men she'd ever seen in person—not including Theo, but she wasn't including him right now because he was an ass. Perfectly styled golden brown curls, piercing blue eyes, just the right amount of stubble framing full lips on top of a tall, broad, athletic frame. Whoa.

She sat up a little straighter and managed to let out a small laugh. "Nice line."

He grinned. "Thanks. Did it work?" He gestured at the empty seat beside her. She smiled despite herself.

"Sure. Knock yourself out."

He sat down with an easy, casual grace. "I'm Beau. Beau Beckett. I play for the Longhorns."

"Lauren MacKinnon."

"It's nice to meet you, Lauren." He said her name like it was the most beautiful name he'd ever heard.

"So, you're a baseball player? Does that mean Javi is your manager?"

"That's right. How do you know Javi and Aerin?"

"Oh. Um. My..." She trailed off as fresh humiliation slammed into her. "My date—my *friend*—is her brother." She couldn't seem to stop herself from putting emphasis on the word.

Beau's eyebrows rose. "Your friend? Not your boyfriend?"

She let out a bitter little laugh. "Apparently not."

He pointed at her, all cocky confidence and charm. "Nope. Not buying it. Not for a second."

"You're not buying what?"

"That a woman like you is single. How is that even possible?"

She laughed, slightly less bitter this time. Even though she wasn't remotely interested in doing anything that involved leaving this table with Beau, she had to admit that it felt nice to be flirted with. "Oh, trust me. It is."

He shook his head sadly. "You wanna know a secret?"

"Um. Okay. Sure."

He leaned in closer and she couldn't help but notice that he smelled really nice. "You are the most gorgeous woman in this room. Hands down. If you tell Aerin I said that, I'll deny it with my dying breath—because she'd probably skin me alive—but it's the truth."

She blushed despite herself. "Well, thank you. That's very sweet, I think. Even though you're clearly trying to get in my pants."

He arched an eyebrow at her. "Would that be such a bad thing?" He sat back, giving her the opportunity to check him out. And she did, a little, but then she rested her chin in her hand, blowing out a long breath.

"You're barking up the wrong tree tonight, slugger."

He licked his lips and nodded slowly. "You got some complicated stuff going on with this 'friend' of yours?" he asked, making air quotes around Lauren's most hated word.

She snorted out a laugh. "Yeah. You could say that."

"Okay. Fair enough." He leaned in again, this time raising his hand and tucking a strand of hair behind her ear. "But if things don't work out with him, you come find me. Because you're too damn gorgeous to be this sad. Promise I can take your mind off your problems."

"What the hell's going on here?" Theo's voice was

surprisingly close. Lauren whirled, blood rushing to her cheeks. One look at Theo and her heart leapt into her throat, hammering away. Yes, Beau was very good looking and charming, but Theo was...well, he was Theo. He was the guy who made her laugh and who helped her solve her problems and who always had her back, no matter what. Who brought her a chai latte on a stressful day and came to her shows and held her hair back when she puked. Theo, with his thick blond hair and gentle blue eyes and tall, muscled frame that she knew felt like heaven as he moved above her, or behind her, or underneath her.

Theo, who looked like he was ready to murder Beau.

Jealousy unlike anything he'd ever felt before pounded through Theo's system as he watched the guy sitting beside Lauren tuck a strand of hair behind her ear. The sight of another man's hands touching her was enough to tinge his vision red.

"What the hell's going on here?" he ground out, acid churning in his stomach. Lauren blushed, her eyes fixed on him. Good. At least she wasn't looking at the asshole hitting on her anymore. Fuck, he felt like a possessive caveman, ready to throw Lauren over his shoulder and drag her back to their room.

"I take it this is your *friend*?" asked the man, leaning back in his chair, seemingly completely at ease, which, as far as Theo was concerned, meant his survival instincts were shit. He stared him down, his jaw clenched so tight he was probably in danger of cracking a molar.

Theo's lip curled and he barely recognized his own voice

when he spoke. "Why don't you go find someone else's date to hit on?"

The other man stood, but his movements were relaxed, unhurried. Apparently, he had a death wish. "Y'all have a nice night." He winked at Lauren and then turned and disappeared back into the crowd.

"What the fuck, Lo?" he growled out before he could stop himself.

"Are you jealous?" she asked, her voice flat in a way that had his brain been working properly, would've been a warning signal.

He shoved a hand through his hair, trying to get a handle on the possessive anger still churning through him. "That guy was all over you."

She arched an eyebrow. "So?"

"So? What do you mean, so? You're here with me." *Because you're mine, Lo. Fuck.*

She stood, meeting his gaze, her eyes flashing with something dangerous. "As a friend. Which means that I'm single and free to flirt with whoever the hell I want. God knows you certainly think of yourself that way."

"What are you talking about?" he asked, some of the anger ebbing out of him as panic and worry started to flow in.

"You know, it's really unfair, Theo, that you don't want me, but you don't want anyone else to have me either."

He opened and closed his mouth. Is that what he was doing here? Treating her like a toy he didn't want to play with, but didn't want any of the other boys playing with either? He scrubbed a hand over his face, his stomach twisting in knots. Fuck, he was the world's biggest asshole, wasn't he? He wanted her in his life and in his bed, but on terms he could never expect her to agree to long term, even if the terms had been her suggestion.

When he didn't say anything, she sighed and then worried her lip between her teeth, her arms crossed over her chest. When she met his eyes again, he was rocked by the sadness in hers. "I think we need to talk," she said softly. "Let's go find somewhere quiet."

His heart beat sluggishly in his chest as he nodded. "Sure. Yeah." He reached out to take her hand, but she curled her fingers away from him and he felt his thoughts start to scatter.

Wordlessly, he followed her out to the hallway where he'd just been talking with his cousin and then through a set of French doors that led out into the courtyard. It was deserted, the only sounds coming from the burbling fountain and the traffic on the other side of the trees. She sat down on the ledge of the stone fountain, her hair moving around her shoulders in the gentle breeze. Moonlight hit her pale skin, making her look like she was glowing from within. She was the most beautiful woman he'd ever seen.

"I don't even know where to start," she said, twisting her fingers together in her lap. "Just give me a second to organize my thoughts. I...I have a lot I need to say."

He nodded and sat down next to her, a few inches further away than he normally would've. He rubbed the back of his neck, feeling both too hot and too cold.

"I heard what you said to Noah," she said after a moment. "I heard you laugh at the idea of ever being in a serious relationship with me. I heard you say that we were just friends, and that you're single." She looked up and met his eyes, her own bright, the hurt he'd caused etched on her face. "It felt really, really shitty to hear you say that, Theo."

God, he was such a fucking asshole. Not because he'd said those things to Noah, but because of the way he'd let the lines get so blurry between them that he'd wound up hurting her. Before he could figure out what to say, she started talking again.

"It sucked because you and I both know that we've been living in more than friends territory for weeks now. Maybe even longer, if we're honest. At least, that's how it's felt for me. Hearing you laugh at the idea of a future ripped me to shreds, Theo, because I'm in love with you, and I have been for a long time."

He sucked in a shaky breath as adrenaline shot through him. But it wasn't a good kind of adrenaline rush. No, it was the kind that had dread settling in the pit of his stomach, fear clawing at him. Lauren was in love with him. And that was terrifying because being friends with benefits was one thing, but love...no. He didn't do love. Love would only end up with everything crashing and burning in a way that was ten times worse.

He cleared his throat, trying to figure out what to say. It was hard, with the panic and the fear and the overwhelming sense of dread engulfing him, but he finally managed to make his mouth form words. "You're the one who suggested we not label things. That was your idea, not mine."

"Because I didn't want you to freak the fuck out! Which is exactly what you're doing right now." She moved closer and took his hands in hers, his skin tingling at her touch. God, he wanted so badly to be what she needed, but he couldn't change who he was. He couldn't just ignore what he'd experienced and what he believed. Those things were hardwired in. "I know this is scary for you. I know. But I don't understand why you can't at least try. Why we can't try."

When he didn't say anything, she shook her head and then searched his eyes. "Am I worth trying for? Because I would do anything for you, Theo."

His throat constricted and he swallowed, refusing to give in to the emotion threatening to pull him under. "I wish things were different, Lo."

She closed her eyes for a moment but left her hands twined with his. "This is so frustrating because if you would just let yourself trust what you feel..."

"And what do I feel?" he asked, his voice coming out a little snappier than he'd intended it.

"After you had your appendix out, you were still groggy from the anesthetic, and..." She shook her head and took a breath. "You said that you were in love with me, but that you could never love me the way I deserved. Knowing how you felt, I suggested that we not label things to give you time to get used to the idea of us being together, being more than friends, but I can see now that until you let go of all the stuff you're clinging to, you're never going to let yourself actually be in love with me. And I just don't think that's ever going to happen. I did, but..." She didn't finish her thought, just sucked in a shaky breath.

His back stiffened and he hated that his first reaction to her confession was a sense of betrayal. "Why didn't you tell me this sooner? You kept this to yourself for weeks, and I can't help but feel that you're manipulating me." His mother's words from the night before came back, bouncing around his skull and for a sickening second, he wondered if she'd been completely right about Lauren, and then immediately felt like the world's biggest asshole for even thinking it.

Her eyes widened. "I'm not manipulating you! I was trying to give you space without you freaking out. But I can see now that your freak out was pretty much inevitable because you've convinced yourself that all of these limiting beliefs you have about love and relationships and happiness are carved in stone and completely unchangeable, and that's bullshit, Theo. Total bullshit." She stood and paced away from him, her skirt whirling around her legs. "What would happen if you let yourself actually love me?" she asked, holding her arms out at her sides, her exasperation and frustration with him palpable. "Would the sky fall? Would the world end?"

"No, but we would. Loving leads to hating. It's the same coin, just a different side, and eventually it flips. It always does. I saw it growing up, and I see it every single day at work. If I let myself love you, eventually we'll end up hating each other. And I don't want to feel that way about you. I don't want to lose you, Lo."

"You don't want to lose me, but you refuse to admit that you love me, or entertain the possibility of a real relationship between the two of us. You think I'm manipulating you because—" She cut herself off, her lips pressed together in a thin line. "Whether you know it or not, you've already been loving me. No one else takes care of me and makes me laugh and supports me and makes me come the way you do. That's love, Theo. You're in it, whether you like it or not."

He pushed to his feet, restless energy surging through him. "I'm broken, Lauren! What do you want me to say? I'm broken, and I know it. You know it too, and you tried to pull my strings to get what you wanted, and now look at us."

Tears shone in her eyes and her lip trembled as his words reverberated around the courtyard.

"Where did you ever see this going? I need to know." She

crossed her arms over her chest. "Because maybe I'm feeling a little manipulated, too."

He rubbed the back of his neck, trying to figure out what the hell to say. Where *had* he seen this going? Had he just been leading her on this entire time? He didn't know what to think anymore.

When he didn't say anything for a long moment, she took a step closer to him, the look on her face one of sheer longing tinged with a deep heartache. "Was it true? When you said that you were in love with me?"

He flinched, unable to stop himself. "Everything I said was true. That I'm in love with you, and that I can't love you the way you deserve. Like I said, I'm broken. I didn't have healthy relationship role models growing up. All I see every day is how it all crumbles apart. Anytime I've ever tried to make it work with someone, I've only ever caused her pain. And hurting you was the last thing I ever wanted to do, Lo, but I can see it's too late for that now."

Tears slipped down her cheeks as she nodded slowly. His entire body felt like a block of ice, pain slicing through his chest at what he'd done. At what he'd allowed to happen.

"I can't do this with you anymore," she said, her voice barely above a whisper. "I...Sadie wants me to move to Los Angeles to work with her, and I'm going to do it. I'm leaving."

He took a step back, completely blindsided by yet another piece of information she hadn't shared with him, and once again he couldn't help but feel like a puppet on a string. "You never mentioned the part about moving to LA," he said, his voice low and gravely. He swallowed around the lump in his throat. She was slipping through his fingers, and he had no choice but to let her go. Emotions all converged—guilt, anger, sadness, regret—so tightly wound together that he couldn't tell one from the others.

"I needed some time to think it through on my own." She clenched her fingers into the fabric of her skirt.

"You should've told me."

"Why? So you could ask me to stay and keep following you around like a sad little puppy dog, hoping you'd one day decide I was worth taking a chance on? No thanks. You're not my boyfriend—you've made that clear—so you don't get a vote here."

"But I'm your friend, and doesn't that count for something?"

Fresh tears slipped down her cheeks and she wiped them hastily away. "I don't know what we are anymore." She shook her head and then glanced over her shoulder. "I'm...I'm gonna go."

"Back to the room?"

"Back to New York."

He opened and closed his mouth, but for once in his life, arguments were failing him.

She moved closer, her chin trembling as she let out a shuddery breath. "I love you, Theo.

And I'm sorry that such a beautiful thing ruined our friendship."

She turned and disappeared through the French doors back into the hotel. He sank down onto the stone fountain and dropped his head into his hands, wave after wave of grief slamming into him, along with a healthy helping of guilt.

He'd just lost his best friend. She was gone.

20

*L*auren's plane was in the air before the sun rose the next morning, and as far as she was concerned, it wasn't a moment too soon. She knew she couldn't run away from the pain in her chest, from the splintered shards where her heart used to be, but she could try. She could put as much distance as possible between herself and Theo—a whole country's worth—in the hopes that his rejection would hurt less.

After she'd walked away from him the night before, she'd gone back up to their hotel room, refusing to let her gaze linger on the bed where they'd had such passionate sex just twenty-four hours ago. Refusing to let herself replay the entire conversation that had unraveled their relationship. Instead, she'd focused on changing out of her dress and gathering up her things as quickly as possible. She didn't know if Theo would come up to find her, but she doubted it. They'd said everything there was to say. A part of her had hoped he would come looking for her because it would mean that maybe there was a still a chance...but he hadn't, and she'd been equal parts disappointed and relieved. Once she'd packed her bag, she'd headed down to the lobby, where the concierge had called her a cab. She'd checked herself into the Best Western a few miles from the airport and then booked a flight for first thing the next morning. It had felt childish and impulsive, leaving like that, but she'd known that she couldn't bear seeing Theo again when everything was still so fresh and raw.

She'd spent a restless night tossing and turning, sleeping in fits as Theo's voice echoed through her dreams. Thankfully the night ended when she got up at 4 AM to get ready for her flight. She'd showered, dressed and taken the hotel shuttle to the airport. By six AM, she'd been airborne.

As she sat on the plane, drinking a burnt-tasting cup of coffee, she swung back and forth between complete numbness and wild, almost uncontrollable emotion. There was bitterness and anger, foolishness and humiliation, grief and sadness, and pain. So much pain she didn't know what to do with it.

She thought she'd had her heart broken before, more than once, but now she wasn't so sure. She'd never experienced this kind of bone deep sorrow, this kind of all-consuming loss. And she knew it was because she hadn't just lost the guy she was dating; she'd lost Theo. Her best friend for the past ten years. She'd lost them and everything they were to each other in one fell swoop.

She pressed a hand to her chest, trying to soothe the ache there. But there was nothing she could do about the gaping wound Theo had left behind. Not unless someone invented time travel and she went back to the night of the double date and kept her mouth shut. Or maybe she could go back to the morning Theo had come home from the hospital and she'd convinced him to see where things might go between them. Again, if only she'd kept her mouth shut.

But no, that wasn't entirely fair. She'd wanted a relationship with him. Hell, she'd been in love with him for longer than she was willing to admit. She'd followed her heart and let herself hope, and that wasn't something she was willing to regret, even if she did regret the loss of the friendship. Regret. Right. It felt more like mourning.

She closed her eyes, pleading with herself to fall asleep. To drop out of the world for just a couple of hours so she could stop hurting. But it wouldn't come, because every time she closed her eyes, all she could hear was Theo's laugh at the idea of ever being in a committed relationship with her. The stony look on his face as he'd accused her of manipulating him.

She opened her eyes and rubbed at them, trying to dispel some of the grittiness. Had she manipulated him? She hadn't set out to, but maybe she had, in an unintentional way. Because she'd known how he'd freak out and she'd been trying to avoid it. Maybe she should've seen the way she'd had to ease him into the idea of being together as a red flag instead of an obstacle to overcome. Her chest felt tight as doubt ate at her. Maybe she'd been chasing something that was never, ever going to happen. Maybe, maybe, maybe. But the truth was, all of those maybes didn't matter anymore, because Theo was no longer part of her life. She honestly didn't know if she'd ever see him again. She didn't know if she could.

And yet she couldn't stop coming back to the fact that he'd admitted he was in love with her. He'd admitted it and then he'd told her that he couldn't love her the way she deserved because he was broken. She wasn't sure if she believed him, but she was done chasing him. That much she knew for sure.

She slumped down in her seat, her throat thick and raw, and she blinked furiously, trying to stem the tears threatening to fall. Her eyes burned with the effort, and her chest ached. Her entire body ached, loneliness settling over her like a scratchy, heavy blanket.

Needing something to do so she didn't start sobbing in front of a plane full of strangers, she pulled her phone out of her purse and opened her email, drafting one to be sent as soon as she landed.

Hi Sadie,

Thanks for giving me so much time to think everything over. I'm in! I'm beyond thrilled to be working with you and so excited to get started. I'll be in LA before the end of this week. If the offer of the apartment still stands, I'll take it.

Talk soon,

Lauren

"Prescott, that brief was supposed to be on my desk thirty minutes ago," said Sanford Lennox, one of the firm's founding partners. Sanford was in his early sixties, with salt and pepper hair, glasses always perched halfway down his nose, and a penchant for cardigans and loudly-printed ties.

Theo looked up from his computer and saw Sanford take in his desk with a frown. It was littered with files, Post-It notes, empty Starbucks cups and the remains of more than one take out meal. He'd spent the past week trying to bury himself in work so he wouldn't think about Lauren, but his focus and concentration had been utter shit because all he could think about was Lauren. He was coasting on caffeine and the sheer will to stay awake because he couldn't sleep. He was living off of protein bars and salads because he couldn't eat. He was a disorganized mess at work because he couldn't think. All he could do was miss her and hurt and try to convince himself that letting her go was the right thing to do, even if it had meant hurting her.

Because now she was free. Free to be with the kind of man she deserved, to receive the kind of love she deserved. Letting her go had felt like severing a limb, but it had been the right thing to do. He had to believe that because otherwise, he might start punching things.

"Shit, yeah, it's here. Sorry," he said, shoving through a few folders on his desk and sending an empty salad container tumbling to the floor.

"You're not usually this messy, or this disorganized," said Sanford casually, paging through the folder Theo had just handed him. "Although this is nicely done. Good work." He surveyed Theo's desk again and sighed, tapping the spine of the folder against his palm. "You're better than this, Theodore. You're a talented attorney with a keen mind and a sharp instinct." He leaned a hip against Theo's desk, surveying the mess again before leveling his assessing gaze at him. "What's her name?"

"What?" He rubbed a hand over his mouth, his too-long stubble bristling against his palm. He'd crossed the line from groomed to unkempt at least two days ago but he couldn't seem to bring himself to care.

"Kid, I've been a divorce attorney for over thirty years. I know heartbreak when I see it."

Theo sighed, his shoulders slumping. "I'll be fine."

"I know you will be. We all are, eventually. But the getting there can be damn hard sometimes."

For a moment, they just sat in silence, and then Theo said, "Lauren. She was one of my closest friends and...it didn't work out, mostly because I'm an asshole." He glanced up, expecting to see pity or annoyance in Sanford's expression, but he only saw kindness.

"Is it fixable?"

He shook his head slowly, not really wanting to talk about this with anyone. "No. I can't change who I am, and she has this amazing opportunity out in Los Angeles, so..." He shrugged, trying to act more nonchalant than he felt.

"Who you are isn't set in stone, Prescott. That's the beauty of life. You make mistakes, you fuck things up, and you get to wake up tomorrow and try again. The only real tragedy is if you let those mistakes define you and paralyze you instead of being your greatest teachers. Growth is a choice. Mistakes will always happen. Your past will always be there. But what you do tomorrow...that's up to you." He rose from his spot against the desk. "Go home. Eat something. Take a shower. Get some sleep. Start fresh tomorrow. Work from home for a day or two if you want." He tapped the folder against the edge of Theo's desk. "And tidy up, kid." With that, he turned and walked out of Theo's office.

He sat very still, turning Sanford's words over and over in his mind, examining them and weighing them to decide if he believed them or not. He wasn't sure. Yes, tomorrow was a new day and a chance to start fresh, but it wasn't that simple. He wished it were, but it wasn't.

He swiveled in his chair and gazed out the window, taking in the light snowflakes fluttering down from the sky, and as usual, his thoughts went immediately to Lauren. She loved the snow, especially the first snow. Was she still in New York? Was she seeing this right now? Or had she already left for LA? It felt so completely foreign that he didn't even know where she was that it intensified the ache deep in his chest.

What was she doing right now? Was she thinking about him as much as he was thinking about her? He hoped she wasn't hurting the way he was. He hoped she was leaving him in her dust and moving on to bigger and brighter things. Happier things with the kind of love and commitment she deserved. And even though the idea of Lauren with someone else made him feel like he might puke, he couldn't hold her back. He saw now that he'd been doing that for far too long. Her words about following him around like a puppy dog came back to him, stinging and sharp, slicing him like tiny knives.

Slowly, he gathered up his things, put on his coat, and slung his messenger bag over his shoulder. When he stepped out of the lobby and onto the sidewalk, snowflakes swirling around him, he flipped up his collar, bracing himself against the chilly wind. As he walked the half a mile to the Chambers Street subway station, he replayed everything in his mind, over and over again. Sleeping with Lauren the first time, letting his pent-up lust for her get the better of him. Her idea that they could stay friends and have sex and that nothing would change, which he'd latched onto like an idiot. How amazing the past several weeks with her had been. How he'd felt like maybe, just maybe there was hope. But then when she'd said she was in love with him...there'd been nothing but fear. He'd known then that he was going to hurt her and it was too late to stop the damage.

But better to hurt her now when the damage would be minimal than to pretend he was someone he wasn't and hurt her ten times worse down the road. And deep down, there were still embers of anger and doubt at the way he felt like she'd manipulated the situation. He didn't know if that was fair, but there it was all the same.

His phone buzzed from inside his bag, and he pulled it out. Every single time his phone had gone off over the past week, his heart had gone into overdrive, hoping against hope that it might be Lauren. But it never was, and he knew it wouldn't ever be. What she'd said by that fountain in Dallas had been a goodbye. And he knew her well enough to know that once she'd made up her mind about something, that was it. End of conversation.

End of friendship.

Brandon: Dude, everyone's mad at you.

Theo sighed. He hadn't seen or heard from his friends since returning from Dallas. He had a feeling Lauren had been in touch to say goodbye and she'd probably told them what an enormous asshole he was. He couldn't blame her. He *was* an enormous asshole.

Theo: I know. I'm sorry. I wish things were different.

Brandon: So why aren't they? You broke her heart, bro. Not cool.

The knowledge that he'd hurt Lauren opened up a fresh wound deep inside him. He'd known it, but to hear it from someone else made it fresh again.

Theo: It's not that simple, okay? Things got complicated.

Brandon: Did they? Or did you just turn chickenshit like you always do in relationships? I never thought you'd do that to her. Not to get all parental on you, but I'm disappointed in you, Theodore. Very disappointed.

Anger and impatience flared through him, but they

weren't directed at Brandon. No, they were directed entirely at himself and the mess he'd made.

Theo: I know, and I'm sorry. I wish things could've worked out between us, but it's for the best. She deserves better than me.

Brandon: I don't know. Maybe you should let Lauren decide what she deserves.

Theo walked in silence for a moment, not sure what to say to that.

Theo: I'm sure she told you what an asshole I am. She doesn't deserve an asshole.

Brandon: She didn't tell me anything except that you're the love of her life. She could've thrown you under the bus and she didn't because even though you hurt her, she still cares about you. Just so you know.

All of the air went out of Theo's lungs and he had to stop walking just to catch his breath, earning him a few jostles and annoyed comments from others on the sidewalk. The love of her life? No. He couldn't be the love of anyone's life. Not even Lauren's.

He loaded up a podcast on his phone, jammed his earbuds in, and headed down to the subway, forcing himself to keep moving. By the time he got home, he'd managed to not think about Lauren for almost fifteen whole minutes, which had to be a new record for the week. But then he stepped inside his apartment and all he could think about was how empty and quiet it felt without her there. He dropped his keys onto the console table beside the front door with a loud clatter and shrugged out of his coat, the shoulders damp with melted snowflakes.

Everywhere he looked, he saw Lauren. Making herself a cup of tea in the kitchen, humming to herself. Sitting on the couch with her guitar in her lap, a notebook open in front of her. Laughing with him at the table over Indian food and wine. Naked in his bed, curled up next to him, her body warm and soft and perfect.

He walked into the bedroom and started changing out of his suit, tossing the clothes haphazardly onto the unmade bed. He hadn't changed the sheets yet because her scent still lingered on them and he couldn't bring himself to let that small reminder of her go. His hands shook a little as he pulled on a pair of sweatpants and his Columbia Law sweatshirt, a feeling of numbness sweeping over him with the knowledge that these little bits of Lauren would slowly fade out of his apartment, and then she'd be gone. Really, truly gone.

He sank down on the bed and flopped back, staring at the ceiling, wondering what the hell he was supposed to do.

21

*L*auren was quickly discovering that Los Angeles had a very different vibe from New York. Where New York was often gray and cloudy this time of year, LA was bright and sunny, warm and laid back. The pace felt slower somehow, probably because the sidewalks weren't always crowded with pedestrians rushing everywhere. She missed the New York skyline, but had to admit it was nice looking out her window and seeing palm trees lining the road. LA felt cleaner, but she missed using the subway and was still getting used to having to Uber everywhere. She missed her favorite restaurants, but was finding new places to enjoy. And she had to agree with Sadie's assessment—LA had a warm, easygoing vibe that wasn't there in New York.

She missed her friends. She missed Theo. She missed New York. But she was trying her hardest not to dwell on all of that. Trying and failing, but the effort was what counted, right?

Thankfully, she had the novelty of living in a new city and the excitement of working with Sadie to distract her from the fact that her heart was a tiny, shriveled up black thing taking up as little space as possible in her chest. She hadn't heard from Theo in the week since she'd arrived, and as each day passed, her hope that she might shrank just a little more.

Sadie's studio was actually a converted guest house on her property, and she spent her days with Sadie working on songs, ideas, and concepts, playing around with things. They'd take breaks to swim in her massive pool or nap in the hammocks just outside. If she hadn't been so heartbroken, she would've been living some of the most exciting, rewarding days of her life. But it was all tinged with a sadness she couldn't shake. She wondered if she ever would.

"You said you were working on something last night?" asked Sadie, taking a sip of her green tea and then setting it down carefully on the little table beside the glossy grand piano.

She nodded, picking up her acoustic guitar. "It's got a hint of a country twang to it in my head." She strummed slowly, playing the G, E minor 7, C add 9, D, C chord progression in three-quarter time she'd come up with.

Sadie pointed at her and sat down at the piano. "I like that. Keep that going." As Lauren played, Sadie started picking out a complementary tune on the piano, one that highlighted the dissonance of the C add 9, giving it a bittersweet, melancholy feel. After a moment, she lifted her hands from the keys. "What are you thinking, lyrically?"

A tiny bit of heat rose to Lauren's cheeks. She'd been working with Sadie for a week now, but this was the first song she was sharing with her that was so intensely personal. "Um, I've got some scribbles." She flipped open her notebook, refusing to let herself turn back to the page where Theo had doodled a picture of the Loch Ness monster saying "I believe in me!".

She swallowed, her throat painfully tight. Then, refocusing herself, she strummed through the chords again, this time adding the lyrics she'd been working on.

"Never forget the way you looked at me

When I told you I loved you, and you set me free

Told me you couldn't, told me to go

Could've let me down gently, could've let me down slow

Out by that fountain, the air smelled like rain

Said our goodbyes and got on a plane

Left you behind, but forgot my heart

Left it with you, never said I was smart..."

She took a shuddering breath, feeling the weight of Sadie's eyes on her as she moved into the chorus.

"Wish I was still wearing your sweatshirt

Wish I was with you, still unhurt

Wondering how I can miss what I never had

You were never mine

Thought you were my last first kiss

Never thought you'd break my heart like this

I wanted forever, you wanted out

You were never mine"

She sucked in a shuddery breath, her eyes stinging, her chest feeling hollow.

"Oh, honey," said Sadie, rising from the piano and rushing to Lauren's side. She looped an arm around her shoulders and pulled her in for a side hug. "Are you okay?"

Her guitar slid from her hands, dropping between her

legs and she let out a sob, her shoulders shaking. "No. I'm really not. Sorry."

Sadie slipped her fingers under Lauren's quivering chin and tilted her face up, forcing her to meet her gaze. "You never need to apologize for your emotions, okay? Never." She gave her another squeeze and Lauren leaned into her, soaking up the warmth and comfort Sadie was offering. "You wanna talk about it? Let me make you some tea and we can talk about it."

Lauren nodded, wiping at her eyes as Sadie stood and busied herself in the studio's kitchenette. Outside, the sun shone, birds sang, the pool gurgled softly. It was a beautiful day in paradise and Lauren was completely miserable.

After a few minutes, Sadie returned, handing Lauren a steaming mug of tea. She took a tentative sip and then sputtered and coughed, the sharp whiskey flavor catching her off guard. "Is there booze in this?"

Sadie smiled and shrugged. "Felt like you could use a little liquid comfort."

Lauren shot her a half smile and took another small sip, bracing herself this time. She blew out a breath and shook her head. "He broke my heart, Sadie. My best friend in the whole world broke my heart."

"What happened?"

She bit her lip, wondering when this would all start to hurt less. "We first met in college. I was dating his roommate. Didn't work out with the roommate, but Theo and I became friends and stayed friends over the past decade. I'm not sure when exactly I fell in love with him. I think it happened slowly, you know? Bit by bit. And it was always little things that would push me a little deeper. The sound of his laugh. The smell of his sweatshirt when I'd wear it. The way the skin around his eyes would crinkle when he smiled. Just being with him, around him. He made me feel happy and safe and like I could do anything."

"And he's gorgeous," added Sadie with a wry smile.

Despite herself, Lauren let out a little laugh. "And he's gorgeous," she agreed. "Everything came to a head and we slept together. I thought it could be the start of a new phase in our relationship, but he's pretty jaded. His parents had a really bad divorce and he's never trusted himself to be in a relationship. That, and he's a divorce lawyer, so he sees the ugly side of love and relationships all the time. He thinks he's broken, but I don't know if I agree with that. But I do know he's terrified of being with someone and having it all go to shit."

"As opposed to how things went with you?" Sadie asked with an arched eyebrow.

"Self-fulfilling prophecy, I guess." She let out a shaky breath. "I don't want to love him anymore. Not when he won't let himself love me back. I want to stop missing him, stop needing him. I don't want to hurt like this anymore. I lost one of the most important people in my life, and I don't know how to move past it."

Sadie frowned sympathetically and looked down into her tea. "All you can do is take it one day at a time, babe. Work through it with your music. Process it and give it as much time as it takes. This isn't a small thing to bounce back from. And love isn't a faucet you can turn off and on. It's more like the sun. It's either there, or it isn't, and it's not within your control." She picked up Lauren's guitar and gently put it back in her hands, exchanging it for the boozy tea. "When you're ready, let's work on this song some more. I think you've got a gem here."

Taking a deep breath and trying to push all of the hurt and the disappointment and the loneliness aside, she strummed her guitar. "Okay, let's do it."

It was the Sunday following Thanksgiving when Theo stepped through the elevator doors and into Lucian's sprawling loft-style penthouse. Weak sunlight streamed in through the massive floor-to-ceiling windows lining the far wall. They offered an impressive view of the city, with Central Park to the east and the Hudson River to the northwest. The expansive space opened before him, showcasing a living area with luxurious furniture arranged to prioritize the view and the massive stone fireplace built into the wall, along with a grand piano. They'd all taken lessons but Theo had left all the piano playing in his life to Lauren; Lucian was the only one of them who'd kept up the hobby. To Theo's right stood the kitchen, and a hallway off of the kitchen led to Lucian's master suite, which included a small, high-tech safe built into the wall.

Lucian sat at the glass and chrome table off of the kitchen, a glass of scotch in his hand. Bastian lounged on the couch, scrolling on his phone, looking like pounded dog shit. Theo shrugged out of his coat, tossing it onto the piano bench.

"I have a closet, you know," said Lucian dryly, eyeing Theo's discarded coat with exaggerated irritation. Rolling his eyes, Theo picked it up and made a show of carefully hanging it up in the closet by the front door.

"You summoned me?" he asked, sitting down onto the

couch Bastian wasn't occupying. He kicked his leg out, jostling Bastian's foot. "What are you doing here?"

"He's staying here temporarily because he got himself kicked out of his apartment." Lucian's voice was flat, his irritation much less exaggerated this time.

"What? How?" asked Theo, pushing a hand through his hair. He couldn't keep up with Bastian's antics anymore.

"You run one tiny and only slightly illegal gambling ring and everyone has a fit." Bastian shook his head, as though the entire world was crazy and not him. Theo made a mental note to start compiling a list of good defense attorneys because the odds of Sebastian needing one felt worse and worse.

Moving on from Bastian and his inability to stop self-destructing, Theo returned his attention to Lucian. "What did you want to talk to me about?"

Without a word, Lucian stood from the table and headed for the kitchen, where he poured a generous glass of scotch. Then he turned and came into the living area, where he handed Theo the glass and sat down next to him on the couch, leaning back into the corner.

"Am I going to need this?" Theo asked warily, eyeing the glass in his hand.

"You might."

"Okay," he said warily, taking a small sip.

Lucian narrowed his eyes and shook his head slowly. "What the fuck are you still doing here?"

Theo's eyebrows shot up. "Excuse me?"

"Why are you here and not in Los Angeles?"

Even just the words *Los Angeles* were like a punch in the gut. Immediately, Lauren's face swam across his field of vision, and he blinked rapidly and took a healthy swallow of his drink to force it away.

"Because it's too late, Lucian. I fucked it all up. Just like I was always going to." His voice came out rough and raw, like his vocal cords had been rubbed with sandpaper.

Lucian said nothing, simply stared at him with an arched eyebrow. "That's it? That's your excuse for letting Lauren go?"

He raised his eyebrows, impatience flaring through him. "It's not an excuse. It's a fact," he said sharply. His lungs suddenly felt tight and he had to force himself to breathe.

"Did you not tell Aerin that some risks are worth taking when she was unsure about her future with Javier?"

Theo snorted. "Yeah, I told her that. But Aerin and I are different people, and this is a very, very different situation."

"Why do you think you were always going to fuck it up?" Lucian's calm was almost maddening, heating Theo's blood as his impatience started to morph into anger.

"How could I not? Look at how we grew up. Look at what I do for a living. I have no role models, no positive examples. I have a horrible track record when it comes to dating. I don't..." His voice cracked and he took another sip of his drink, refusing to give in to the intense emotions swamping him in front of his brothers. "I don't know how to be what she wants. I can't be."

Lucian took another small sip of his drink and crossed one leg over the other. "You realize that if you let our parents and their fucked up behavior define who you are, they've won, right? Why on earth would you want to let those assholes win?"

"I don't..." Theo started to speak, but he trailed off as all of the fight went out of him. "It's too late. I'm already fucked up."

"That's bullshit. You can't change what happened in the past, but you sure as fuck get to write your own story, brother." Lucian leaned forward, his arms braced on his thighs, his dark eyes bright and intense. "You get to write it. Not them. Not if you don't let them." He sighed. "What are you so goddamn afraid of?"

He pushed up off of the couch, restless energy making his legs itch. "That I'll be a complete and utter disaster as a boyfriend, a husband, a father! That I'll break innocent people just like Mom and Dad fucking broke me. I can either break the cycle or perpetuate it and I refuse to do that."

"But what if you choose to break the cycle by making different choices? Instead of seeing everything we went through as a burden, what if you looked at it like a masterclass in what *not* to do? You're not a product of your circumstances. You're a product of your decisions, and once you accept that, I think you'll see the magnitude of the mistake you've made."

Theo dropped his chin to his chest and slowly sank back down onto the couch as the weight of what Lucian had just said rocked him to his core. His stomach bottomed out as the truth sank in, deeper and deeper. He'd been letting his past dictate his future, letting his parents rob him of happiness because he was so afraid of ending up like them. He was letting fear overrule everything, including the chance at something better than he'd ever imagined for himself.

He dropped his head into his hands, the realization of what he'd thrown away crashing into him with the force of a hurricane, making it hard to breathe. Lucian was right. He couldn't let his circumstances rule his life—he had the power to choose differently, to live differently, to not let fear cripple him.

"Oh my God," he whispered. He forced himself to look up and meet Lucian's gaze. "It's too late. I wrecked it. It's too late. She doesn't want anything to do with me. I love her so fucking much and I wrecked it."

Lucian shook his head. "If you want Lauren to forgive you—and I think she will because *that* is a woman in love—you have to forgive yourself first. You fucked up. We all do. But that doesn't mean you don't deserve to be happy. The only real tragedy is if you don't learn from this. So learn. Grow. Forgive. Stop living in fear and letting Mom and Dad mess with your head. And go get your woman back, you goddamned idiot."

Theo stood from the couch, flush with renewed hope and determination that went out of him like air escaping from a quickly deflating balloon. "She's in Los Angeles."

Lucian blinked slowly, taking a sip of his drink. "And?"

Theo spread his arms wide. "And I live here. In Manhattan. And I just made junior partner."

Lucian looked at him as if he were slow. "So?" When Theo didn't say anything, he sighed. "How many family law firms do you think there are in Los Angeles? Ballpark."

"I don't know. Probably at least a dozen, if not more."

"And how many Laurens are there?"

For the first time since she'd left him by that fountain, he actually smiled. "Just the one." He shook his head, shoving his hands through his hair. "I'm a moron."

Lucian smiled at him. "You're a moron."

"Hey," said Bastian, sitting up and pointing at Theo. "Didn't you take the California Bar a couple of years ago on a bet?"

Theo actually laughed. "Yeah, I did."

Lucian stood and headed back toward the kitchen. He

glanced over his shoulder as he went. "So we come back to my original question. What the fuck are you still doing here?"

Theo grinned and headed for the door, almost forgetting his coat in his rush to start putting a plan into action. But then something occurred to him and he paused, his coat draped over his arm. "You had it even worse than I did growing up," he said to Lucian, who was calmly pouring himself another drink. "How are you okay?"

Lucian turned and smiled but it didn't reach his eyes. "Oh, I have demons. I just know how to keep them fed so they leave me the fuck alone." He waved his hand. "Go. Figure out a way to get her back. You deserve to be happy, little brother."

For the first time in a very long time, Theo believed he did, too. He just hoped it wasn't too late.

22

*T*wo weeks in, and Los Angeles was starting to feel just the tiniest bit like home for Lauren. The sounds and smells were slowly becoming more familiar, and her daily routine of working with Sadie had her in a creative flow that she hadn't experienced in a long time. It was freeing and immensely satisfying not having to worry about anything at all except the music. No library, no paying her rent, no hustling for gigs.

No Theo.

Her heart still hurt whenever she thought of him, each memory like pressing on a bruise that wouldn't heal. It might always hurt. She hadn't been dramatic when she'd told Brandon that Theo was the love of her life. Even now, after the hurt he'd caused and the way he'd rejected her, she knew it was still true. It would always be true.

With a sigh, she stirred her tea, turning her gaze to the windows that looked out onto Wilshire Boulevard. The apartment Sadie owned and let musicians stay in free of charge was bright and airy, and fully furnished with comfortable mid-century modern style furniture. Hardwood floors, pale yellow walls and large windows made the one-bedroom apartment feel bigger than it was. The building itself was on the small side, with five floors and only four apartments per floor. She'd gotten to know a couple of her neighbors—Bodie, who owned a surf apparel brand, Heather, who was a yoga teacher, and Fabian, a European transplant trying to act and model. She missed her friends back in New York desperately, but she texted and Skyped with them regularly, and was trying to make some new friends here. Besides, she knew that the pervasive loneliness that followed her around like a shadow had everything to do with missing Theo. And that wasn't fixable.

She took her tea into the L-shaped living room and settled down on the couch, watching the light gradually fade as dusk fell over LA. She pulled her phone out of her pocket to text Willa when it buzzed in her hand. When she saw the message on the screen, she nearly dropped it.

Theo: Hey.

Her heart started going a million miles an hour before plummeting into her stomach. Should she respond? What should she say? What did this mean? She hadn't changed her number, hoping that maybe, just maybe she'd hear from him, and now that she had, she was caught completely off guard. She set her tea aside and typed out her response.

Lauren: Hey.

Brilliant. But she couldn't think of anything else. There was too much bouncing around in her brain to settle on anything.

Theo: Are you home?

She frowned at her phone. What kind of question was

that? And yet she found herself answering it all the same. Sliding back into talking to him like butter melting on a hot pan.

Lauren: Yeah, I just got back from the studio a little while ago.

Theo: Perfect. Come up to the roof.

She went very, very still and read his last message back at least half a dozen times. It could only mean one thing.

He was here.

She didn't know how he knew where she lived, or what the hell was going on, but she was already up off the couch and heading for the door, the knowledge that Theo was here pulsing through her with crackling electricity. Emotions warred with each other as she took the stairs up to the rooftop terrace. She was still hurt, still angry, but beside those emotions, there was also hope. So much hope she was nearly shaking with it.

When she stepped out onto the rooftop terrace, she gasped. She'd only been up here once before, and it certainly hadn't looked like this, with every square foot of the space covered in flowers. Roses in shades of deep red, delicate pink, pure white, cheery yellow. Bright pink lilies and bunches of daisies. Lush pink peonies and peach-hued dahlias. Daffodils and tulips and carnations. Irises and gardenias. Sunflowers, even. Hundreds of flowers, and right there, in the middle of all of the floral craziness, was Theo.

Her heart stopped completely before restarting at double time and she had to stop herself from launching herself at him. He was here. Theo was here.

He took a step forward, his brow furrowed. "Hey, Lo."

Her throat tightened at the sound of his voice, the sound of her nickname. "Hey," she managed, her mouth dry. "What...what are you doing here? How did you find me?"

"Don't be mad—Willa gave me your address."

"I'm not mad. Not at her," she added, some of the shock at seeing him again wearing off. "You, on the other hand..."

He held up his hands in a placating gesture. "I know. I know. I deserve every ounce of your anger because I fucked up. I fucked up huge." He swallowed hard and she could see the anguish on his gorgeous face. It was unfair how good he looked in his white T-shirt and beat up jeans. Unfair.

"You did," she agreed, crossing her arms in front of her.

He took another step closer, and then another, and then another until he was right there, close enough that she could feel the warmth coming off of his body, that she could smell the achingly familiar scent of his aftershave.

"I never should've let you walk away like that, and I never should've accused you of manipulating me. I get it now. You were just trying to let me figure stuff out. I know now that letting you go was the biggest mistake of my life."

"Then why did you?" she asked softly, hope vibrating inside her like a living thing.

"Because I was scared that I wasn't good enough for you. That I'd hurt you and make the same mistakes I see other people make every day. I thought that if I couldn't be perfect, I didn't deserve to be happy. I didn't deserve your love."

"And how do you feel now?"

"I'm still scared, Lo. But I'm more afraid of facing a future without you than of screwing everything up. Because as scared as I am, I love you so much that I don't know how to breathe without you."

"Theo," she whispered, the two syllables carrying love and forgiveness and hope. So much hope.

"I'm so sorry, Lauren. I'm so sorry for hurting you and for not believing in what we could have. I don't know if I'll ever forgive myself for hurting you and letting you walk away, but I hope you can somehow forgive me." He took her hands in his, and she felt a tremble in his touch that mirrored her own. "I love you. I've loved you for a long time. And if you can somehow forgive me for being a stupid ass, I'm going to keep loving you for as long as you'll let me." He traced his thumbs over her knuckles. "It's always been you, Lo."

Something broke open inside her, something warm and sweet and she felt like she was out in the sun for the first time after a long, dark winter. She wrapped her arms around him and pulled him close, burying her face in his neck. "I love you, you stupid idiot."

"I am most definitely the world's biggest idiot for letting you go," he said, his voice thick with emotion. His hand cradled the back of her head, holding her tight. "I love you." He pulled back and brushed his lips over hers, a question of a kiss. "Will you give me another chance to make it right? To love you the way you deserve?"

She bit her lip, smiling up at him. "I don't know, are you sure you're the man for the job?"

"I'd very much like to be. If you'll let me. If you'll give me another chance." He kissed her again, lingering this time, his mouth slow and sweet against hers. "I don't want to be that guy anymore. The guy who lives in fear."

"Who do you want to be?"

"I want to be the guy who brings you more flowers than you know what to do with. I want to be the guy who wakes up beside you and falls asleep next to you, every single day. I want to be the guy who loves you day in and day out, always."

He reached up and traced his thumb over her cheek. "I want to be your lobster."

Tears pricked her eyes, but for the first time in weeks, they weren't tears of sadness and loss, but tears of happiness. Tears of sheer joy.

"I forgive you," she said, and then arched up on her toes and kissed him, feeling as though she were floating. Feeling Theo's arms around her, his mouth against hers, the scent of him filling her lungs was a joy she thought she'd lost forever. When they broke apart, she curled her fingers into the fabric of his T-shirt. "What about your job?"

"I quit."

She pulled back a little, looking up at him. "You *what*? But you just made junior partner, and—" He cut her off with a kiss.

"I want to be where you are. Do you think there's any demand for divorce lawyers in LA?" he asked, grinning at her.

She laughed and kissed him again. "Oh, there just might be."

"Good. Because I'm here to stay. Wherever you are is where I belong. I love you so much, Lo."

"Are you sure about this? You give me so much, and now to give up your job and move out here, all to be with me, it's... it feels like too much to ask."

"First of all, you're not asking me to do anything—I'm doing this because I want to. And second, you put up with my neurotic bullshit, so I think we're pretty much even."

She held him tight, her stomach fluttering wildly. "I used to think I was stupid for loving you," she said.

He kissed her, his hands running up and down her back. "And now?"

"Now I think I'd be stupid not to."

He laughed and picked her up, his body wide and strong against hers. "How about you show me your apartment?" he asked, one eyebrow cocked.

She nodded, giddy with happiness. "Let's go home."

The End

Did you enjoy
this book?

*Please leave
a review!*

Reviews help
authors more
than you know!

FREE DOWNLOAD

Download Tara's story Reload for free!

Get started here: https://www.tara-wyatt.com/newsletter

THANK YOU!

Thank you so much for reading Theo and Lauren's story! I hope you enjoyed it. To get access to their extended epilogue, be sure to sign up for my newsletter at www.tara-wyatt.com/newsletter. And keep reading for an exclusive sneak peek at what's next for the Prescott brothers...

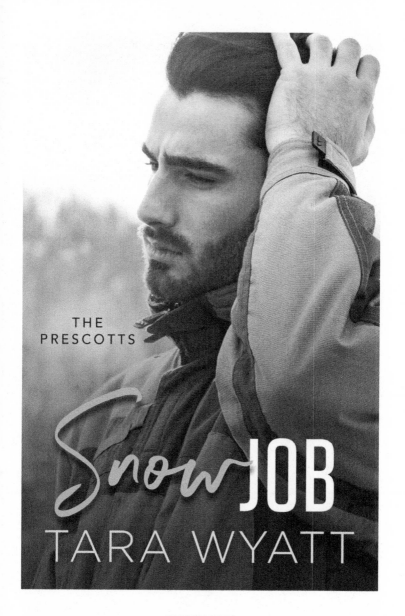

THE
PRESCOTTS

Snow JOB

TARA WYATT

SNOW JOB
The second book in the Prescotts series, coming in 2021!

Turn the page for a sneak peek.

1

"*P*rescott, I need to see you in my office. Now."
Sebastian looked up from his desk, his head
pounding dully, the remnants of his hangover refusing to let
go. He closed his email and stacked the proposals he'd been
working on into a neat pile, stood and adjusted his tie and
then followed his boss, Robert Stammler, down to his office
at the end of the hall. As he walked, he glanced out the
window at the Manhattan skyline, sunlight glinting off of the
windows of the buildings below, some of them buildings he
was directly involved with as the VP of Marketing and Project
Management for one of Manhattan's biggest real estate
development firms. The rest of his life might be in shambles,
but at least he still had his career. It was the only thing
keeping him anchored. The only thing keeping him from
completely going off the deep end.

He stepped inside Stammler's office and before he could
take even two steps, Stammler pointed and said, "Shut the
door." A creeping sense of dread worked its way down

Sebastian's spine, but he kept his expression neutral. Without waiting to be invited, he took a seat across from his boss.

Stammler tossed a file across the sleek glass desk at him. "Tell me about this."

Sebastian frowned and picked it up, leafing through it. "This is the Ashbar project." The development was a massive undertaking, nearly fifty stories tall with over six hundred apartments and ground floor luxury retail. Sebastian and his team had been in charge of marketing the high end condos as well as attracting the right retailers.

"And what did you contribute to this project?"

Sebastian frowned. He'd contributed...well, he'd been at some of the meetings, and...He shook his head. "Why do you ask?"

Stammler said nothing and pulled out another folder, tossing it at him. "Tell me about this one."

Again, Sebastian paged through the folder, his skin suddenly feeling tight and itchy. "This is Barnett Tower," he said. It was a low-rise office building in Harlem with ground floor retail as well as over 40,000 square feet of community space for after school programs. He'd been responsible for developing relationships with potential businesses looking for space as well as some of the non-profit organizations who might be interested in using the space. As he skimmed through the folder, he saw that many of the spaces were already leased and several organizations had signed on, which was news to him.

"This one," said Stammler, sliding another folder to him. A private school they were building in Queens. Another for a hospital in Harlem. Another for a massive residential project in Washington Heights. All projects on which he'd been the lead. All projects on which he'd apparently dropped the ball, and yet...the work was done. And done well.

All signed off on by Kayla Bristowe, his manager of marketing and communications.

"Miss Bristowe brought all of this to my attention this morning," said Stammler, leaning back in his chair, his thick, stubby fingers tented. "Apparently she's tired of doing your job for you."

"She doesn't do my job for me. She works under me." His mind spun, scrambling to think of an excuse to explain away the obvious fact that he'd been fucking up his job along with everything else in his life.

"Not anymore. You're fired. I'm promoting Kayla into your role since she's already doing it and doing it better than you ever did. You're a mess, Prescott," Stammler said with a sneer. "It's a shame because you're one of the smartest guys here, but you drink too much, you're never here, and you've embarrassed this company one too many times. You're done."

Sebastian felt as though the floor was dropping out from underneath him, his stomach in freefall mode. A week ago, he'd been kicked out of his apartment after a misunderstanding with his landlord—you run one tiny gambling ring and everyone freaks out—and now he was unemployed. His life was unraveling before his eyes and he knew it was entirely his own fault. His breathing became faster and shallower, panic swamping him. What was he going to do now? He was unemployed and homeless, crashing with his brother.

It was terrifying enough to make him want to go do something stupid. Something reckless and risky and thrilling so that just for a little while, he could forget about the total clusterfuck his life had become.

No. No! That was what had landed him here in the first place. He knew it and knew he needed to figure his shit out and get his act together if he didn't want to crash and burn to a point beyond salvaging.

And yet all he could think about was drinking until he was numb. Or taking what little money he had left and betting it all on something wild and crazy. Or heading to his "boxing gym" that was really an underground fighting ring where he'd let someone pummel him until he couldn't think or feel anymore.

"Collect your things," said Stammler with a dismissive wave of his hand, as though Sebastian was no one and not a guy who'd worked as a senior executive there for the past six years. "I want you out of the building within the next ten minutes."

Pulling together the ragged scraps of his dignity, Sebastian stood and headed back to his office, where two security guards were waiting for him. "Seriously?" he snarled as he strode into his office, his anger becoming sharper and more explosive by the minute. "I can walk myself out. I'm not going to steal a photocopier or something."

"Company policy," said one in a monotone voice. Jaw tight to the point of aching, Sebastian closed his eyes and blew out a breath. Then he retrieved a Banker's Box from one of the shelves, dumped the papers out of it and onto the floor and started cramming his personal effects into it. Less than five minutes later, he was practically being frog marched down the hall, sandwiched between the two security guards, the box clutched in his hands. He kept his eyes down, refusing to look at all the people who'd come out of their offices to see him escorted off of the premises.

Until he saw *her*. Kayla. The woman who, once upon a

time, he'd had a raging crush on, with her blond curls and ample curves and mouth made for sin. She was smart and confident and had never put up with his bullshit, and he'd always liked that about her. He'd never made a move because she was technically his subordinate and he was a lot of things, but he wasn't a douche to women. Never. Especially not Kayla.

And then she'd gotten him fired. She'd cost him his job, the only thing keeping him afloat in the quagmire of his life.

He locked eyes with her and she had the balls to wave at him, a little smirk on her face. "Good luck, Sebastian," she said in that breathy come-fuck-me voice of hers. It was a voice that had once filled his fantasies, but now would haunt him. "You're going to need it."

I hope you're as excited for Kayla and Sebastian's story as I am! Get your copy of *Snow Job* here:
www.tara-wyatt.com/snow-job

(PS – If you're curious about Javi and Aerin's story, take a look at *Moon Shot*, a steamy enemies to lovers standalone:
www.tara-wyatt.com/moon-shot)

* * *

THE BLOOD AND GLORY SERIES

co-written with Harper St. George

Dirty Boxing

Take Down

No Contest

* * *

THE BODYGUARD SERIES

Necessary Risk

Primal Instinct

Chain Reaction

* * *

STANDALONE TITLES

Royal Treatment

Nailed

Stripped

Little Blue Lines

* * *

For complete information on all of Tara's books, visit www.tara-wyatt.com/books.

ABOUT THE AUTHOR

Tara Wyatt is a contemporary romance and romantic suspense author. Known for her humor and steamy love scenes, Tara's writing has won several awards, including the Golden Quill Award and the Booksellers' Best Award. In 2018, she was a RITA® Finalist for her novella, *Until the Sun Sets*.

When she's not hanging out with your next book boyfriend, she can be found reading, bingeing something on Netflix, and drinking wine. Tara lives in Hamilton, Ontario, Canada with her husband, daughter, and the world's cutest dachshund.

Don't miss out on a sale or new release!
Join Tara's newsletter:
www.tara-wyatt.com/newsletter

For regular updates and to stay in the loop, follow Tara on Facebook:
www.faceboook.com/tarawyattauthor

Follow Tara on BookBub:
www.bookbub.com/authors/tara-wyatt

Made in the USA
Monee, IL
31 December 2020